BIG YELLOW DOG

A Novel

BIG YELLOW DOG

A Novel

J. A. Jones

SUNSTONE PRESS

SANTA FE

Sunstone books may be purchased for educational, business, or sales promotional use. For information please write: Special Markets Department, Sunstone Press, P.O. Box 2321, Santa Fe, New Mexico 87504-2321.

Book and Cover design › Vicki Ahl
Body typeface › Basketville
Printed on acid-free paper

——

Library of Congress Cataloging-in-Publication Data

Jones, J. A. (John Alan), 1923-
 Big yellow dog : a novel / by J. A. Jones.
  p. cm.
 ISBN 978-0-86534-907-0 (softcover : alk. paper)
 1. Vietnam War, 1961-1975–Veterans–Fiction. 2. Indians of North America–Fiction.
I. Title.
 PS3610.O625516B54 2012
 813'.6–dc23

                                    2012033144

——

WWW.SUNSTONEPRESS.COM
SUNSTONE PRESS / POST OFFICE BOX 2321 / SANTA FE, NM 87504-2321 /USA
(505) 988-4418 / ORDERS ONLY (800) 243-5644 / FAX (505) 988-1025

For Lily, 64 years
and still counting . . .

Cast of Characters

Army Buddies:

Jack Kilroy, Protagonist
Jackson, Black man from Chicago
LeRoy, Hispanic

Poker Players:

Hendley, Retired Oil Man
Joe Lima, Hispanic Mafia
Ginwright, Black law professor
    at the University of New Mexico
Simpson, Local sheriff
Ted Phillips, BIA director
(Jack Kilroy)

Santa Cala Indians:

Tino Casaquito, Religious leader
Roy, Teno's grandson
Jerry Bisbee, Stanford University student
Virgil, War captain
Governor, Head of scalp society

Federal Government:

M. J. Kilroy, Congressman
Thatcher, Judge
Wilson, Pub. Health nurse
O'Brian, District attorney
Padilla, FBI agent
Barr, FBI agent
(Ted Phillips)

Gallery Owners:

Jo Kilroy, Jack's mother
Ajax Phillips, Greek

Students:

Lou Ellwood, Anthropology
Keith, Anthropology
Kevin, Law

1

"*M*an, this dump is too much like a south Chicago used car lot," Jackson said.

I glanced at Jackson over on the other double bunk in the alcove. He was lying on his back, arms crossed under his head, one leg balanced on the raised knee of the other.

"You feeling used, Homey?" LeRoy asked from the lower bunk under Jackson's. He was the only Hispanic I knew named LeRoy, Jackson's invention. "You going to hang around with us brothers you got to have a real name. Ain't no blacks named Carlos," was the way he'd put it in the Vietcong prison camp we lived in. So, Carlos became LeRoy. After a couple of years with Jackson, LeRoy even talked black.

My name is Jack Kilroy. Jackson had named me Bad Hand, because of poker. I tended to win a lot, but that wasn't the way he explained it, not now. "Don't none of us dare shake his hand," he'd announced one day, knee raised. "Don't know where it's been." That posture just meant Jackson was bored and up to no good.

"Used?" Jackson asked with disdain. "Man, I own the lot."

"Where's the chop shop then?" LeRoy asked, mock aggrieved. "Can't be a south Chicago used car lot without a chop shop. I been there. Where you get the spare parts?"

"You sign a donor's card when they checked you in?" Jackson asked coldly.

"Sure. Wasn't given no choice."

"You saying you didn't volunteer to give spare parts? You die, you give spare parts. People die in hospitals. That's how you get spare parts out of a chop shop, too."

"Chop shops get parts from stolen cars," LeRoy said. "Everybody knows that. Nobody going to steal my parts. Only crazy people like Bad Hand here volunteers."

I had, too. I'd asked my father if he could use his influence as a Congressman to get me a deferment, and he damn near disowned me. I should have known better. He thought President Nixon walked on water, hand-in-hand with Jesus. After he chewed me out for twenty minutes and left with a threat on his lips, I packed my clothes and books in cardboard boxes and left them stacked in my dorm room. Without taking my final exams in my last semester of law school I walked down to the nearest army recruiting center and volunteered. Three months later I wrote my mother about it, just before I left for Vietnam. She and my father were divorced and I left it for her to tell him, if she wanted to. Smart, huh?

"So, what about this place is like a south Chicago used car lot?" LeRoy wanted to know.

"Well, you and me are out front," Jackson told him. "We're like foreign sports cars, all shined up and beautiful, to bring the customers in."

"Makes sense," LeRoy said. "What about old Bad Hand?"

"He's something domestic, a three porthole Buick with a sign, saying 'solid family car' on the windshield."

"I can see that," LeRoy said in agreement. "And the rest of the brothers?" he asked, waving a hand at the row of beds on the other side of the ward, filled with men in casts and slings, some suspended in traction.

"Junkers. Buy as is, no guarantees. They give the spare parts," Jackson said.

"That's harsh," LeRoy said.

"Southside Chicago ain't no Sunday school," Jackson said.

At the end of the first week a fat-assed major in dress uniform, without a Vietnam campaign ribbon on his chest, came to our alcove. "Sergeant James J. Kilroy, attention!" the young second lieutenant flunky yelled, walking a half pace behind him.

I made a show of painfully moving from my top bunk to the floor and came to attention, wincing. Jackson and LeRoy did the same. The major turned red, either from embarrassment or rage at the thought that he might be being mocked, but read off a citation awarding me a Purple Heart and a Bronze Star for service in Vietnam. He just handed me the boxes and saluted, me answering, and left with no further comment than, "Get a shave and a haircut, soldier. That's an order. You're still in the army," before marching out of the ward.

"I've been thinking about that," I said, after they'd gone. "Just changed my mind."

"No, do it," Jackson advised. "That's the kind of asshole that will check back. You don't want six months in the brig."

He was right. I walked to the barbershop with my two friends and we all got cleaned up. We'd left Vietnam in something of a rush.

"I'm getting out of here," I told them. "I see that bastard again and I'm likely to say something rash." I did not like the army. My tour in Vietnam left me with partial hearing in one ear and none in the other, chronic bronchitis, march fracture in both feet, the condition of being permanently scared and culminated in over a year in a Vietcong prison camp. I also had picked up an abiding mistrust of authority in uniform: prison guards, MPs, and commissioned officers of any army, not necessarily in that order of significance.

"What's the Purple Heart for?" LeRoy asked.

Thinking back, I must have earned the Purple Heart when mortar shrapnel tore skin off my back. The guy at the aid station, who smeared something on the raw spots, said, "Lucky."

"Lucky enough for a ticket home?" I remember asking. "'Not hardly.' Lucky to be alive?" He'd said, shaking his head, "'This just missed doing serious carnage.'"

"Shrapnel," I said to LeRoy.

"Ours or theirs?"

"Hard to say. At the time I had to sign a form to get a new shirt and have the cost deducted from my pay. I guess some clerk somewhere must have spotted it. Records are records."

"How about the Bronze Star?"

"He mumbled, didn't he? I kind of heard him say something, but I have no idea what he was talking about," I said honestly. "I know officers get them instead of Good Conduct Medals, which are reserved for enlisted men. I don't know why enlisted men get them."

Following up on my decision, I went to see the hospital social worker, a deceptively motherly-looking middle-aged woman, who had substituted efficiency for compassion.

"Can you get me discharged?" I asked. "Nothing's wrong with me that's going to get better lying on my back in the hospital. And I'd appreciate it if you could recommend a place where I can buy a good used truck, something I can live out of for a while."

"Well, Sergeant Kilroy, there is a hold on your discharge placed by Congressman Michael J. Kilroy. Any relation?"

"My father. Can he do that?"

"It says in the memo I got that he is on the armed services committee in the House of Representatives. That means he can do pretty much anything around here that he has in mind. Sorry."

I figured that my father wanted to congratulate me on my army service and have me admit he was right about Vietnam. That wasn't going to happen. My father arrived the next day, blowing into the ward like a pit bull on steroids. We'd been warned he was coming up by the receptionist at the front desk. Jackson and LeRoy fled.

"Chickens," I muttered.

LeRoy just waved his hand in acknowledgment but Jackson stopped by the alcove doorway long enough to say, "I ain't even told my old man I'm back. I'll let him know just after I get discharged and can find a place to hide. I don't need to share your ordeal; I got troubles of my own," and he scooted over to talk to some of our prison buddies stuck with casts in beds against the ward's far wall.

I must have looked worse than I felt; I'd lost a pound a month in the prison camp, and was thin and worn down when I got there. My father took one look at me as I stood in the alcove doorway and it sobered him up enough to make him clumsy in his approach. "You look terrible," he said, awkwardly reaching out to hug me. "Should you be out of bed?"

"I'm gaining weight in the hospital much faster than I lost it in the prison camp," I said. "There's nothing seriously wrong with me. I'm asking the social worker here to get me discharged."

"Fine, fine. You can fly home with me. I have a government plane waiting for me at Kirkland Field," my father said.

"Actually, I want to get away and be by myself for a little," I said. "For three years I've been living in a crowd with no privacy and a quiet time is what I need."

"We still have the fishing cabin in the Adirondacks up on North Lake," he said. "You always liked that place. Nobody would bother you there."

"Good idea," I said. "I'll keep it in mind."

"I can get you out of here this afternoon," he persisted.

"No, I have to say goodbye to friends from the camp," I said. "There are a lot of them here. It'll take me a few days to do that and I need to find some place close by to just think. I have to get my head straight."

"I called your school and they'll take you back. You just need that last semester. There's a place waiting for you in my firm," he said. "I can see you in politics with your service record."

I couldn't, but said nothing. He soon left, probably satisfied in his own mind that I'd come around. Except for the last time, he'd been right. This would be the second time he was wrong.

I went back to see the social worker and she had me fitted for a hearing aid which made my deafness no handicap at all; found a foot doctor to x-ray my feet and prescribe metatarsal pads for my broken arches, which I threw away, and another, who x-rayed my chest and advised me to stop smoking for my bronchial condition, which I ignored. She said my medical record entitled me to a thirty percent disability pension. It amounted about to what my army pay had been, not much. I told her I'd get a post office box so she could mail my checks.

"I found you an army surplus carryall, like you said you wanted, that you can have for the cost it would take to junk it. There's nothing seriously wrong with it except that it's noisy. You can take out your hearing aid when you drive it," she said.

Jackson had come with me, and asked her, "How do you know there's nothing wrong with it? It's an army vehicle. Army truck maintenance is crap."

"People don't lie to me," she said, looking him straight in the eye. It shut him up. "I got you a free driver's license," she added, seeing that Jackson had no more to say. "Your discharge entitles you to that, too."

"No driving test?" I asked.

"No," she said shortly.

I thought that was funny, but learned from Jackson's experience to keep my thoughts to myself. I gave her a list of other stuff I thought I needed: a tarp, a sleeping bag, a hammock, a full sized single-bitted ax, a file to keep an edge on it, a long handled shovel, a hundred feet of half-inch rope, a Coleman stove and lantern, a cast-iron Dutch oven, a blue graniteware coffee pot and a folding camp chair. I'd had plenty of time to make out the list in my head lying on my back on the hard hospital bed.

She called in her secretary and handed it over. "Have it here by tomorrow with receipts," she told the woman.

I gathered her secretary was used to orders of that sort for she took it without comment, merely nodding. I also wanted a rifle, a knife and a fly rod, but wanted to pick them out myself.

At my next appointment three days later I found everything I'd ordered waiting for me in her office. "I added a couple of red and blue flannel shirts and a pair of blue jeans," she told me. "You could get in trouble going around dressed in army clothes, even get in fights if you hung around the wrong places," and gave me an itemized authorization to sign to deduct the cost from my accrued pay, just like with the shirt that earned me the Purple Heart. I don't know why she thought I'd get in trouble.

She also had my discharge papers, a warrant for eight thousand dollars in back pay and over nine hundred dollars in cash which she counted out for me, saying, "You're free to go."

"You're the best thing I've run into in this whole damned army," I told her, and gave her a hug. It must have surprised her. It surprised me.

Jackson helped me carry my stuff back to the ward to get my personal gear and to say goodbye to my prison buddies. That was harder than I thought it would be.

"You got to talk to our ward boy," one of them said. "He's an Indian. He knows where you can hide out for a while," and called him over. "Hey, Kilroy, come talk to this guy."

I shook hands with the man and found his hand just brushed mine, not gripping it. I figured maybe he didn't like white men too much.

"I'm from Santa Cala Pueblo," he said, "just north of here. You can find it just following the river. Our own river empties into the Rio Grande up at San Ysabel. You can camp along our river and fish, if you want to. Nobody will bother you. We don't eat fish."

It was that easy. On the way north, I stopped at a pawn shop in Albuquerque long enough to buy a model 94 Savage 30-30 lever-action rifle and some fishing gear.

"This gun spent forty years under the front seat of a series of pickup trucks," the pawn shop owner said. "Look . . . one side of the barrel is all shiny where it must have rubbed along the floor boards." He ran a patch through the barrel and swore it had never been fired . . . said it probably had been touched only to move it from one pickup to another over the years. Maybe. I picked up two boxes of ammunition, a cleaning rod and patches. I'd fire it.

For a knife I chose a stag-handled Schrade Old Timer with two high carbon steel blades in a leather case I could attach to my belt. I never saw a stainless steel blade worth a damn, and I tended to lose knives out of my pocket. He had some fiberglass fishing poles but I chose an old marked-down Heddon spilt-bamboo that had been top-of-the-line before they invented fiberglass. Part of the fun of fishing is the gear. At one time I only used dry flies I'd tied myself, but until I got around to that again I bought a box of assorted bait hooks and chose a few number ten readymade brown and gray hackle files just to get started. "There ain't no decent fishing in the state until you get up into the Chama country next to the Colorado border," he said.

"Someone told me there were fish in the Santa Cala River," I said.

"Yeah, but you got to have permission from the pueblo governor to fish on the reservation," he said. "The reservation don't go all the way down to San Ysabel if you want to try. Or you could go through the pueblo and on up north. Fish and Game don't stock the Santa Cala so anything you catch would be cutthroat trout. They're native fish, not very big."

Sounded fine to me. Small fish are better eating than big ones and fish hatchery fish are tasteless no matter what the size. I needed food supplies: coffee, flour, bacon, but I figured I could pick that up on the way.

The carryall rode the way all army trucks ride: rough. It had overload springs and the seat was as hard as a park bench. It was a gas hog, too, but had a nineteen-gallon tank and an auxiliary one that held ten gallons, both full. Its appearance gave evidence of hard use, but the social worker had assured me it was in good mechanical condition. She would know. It would do fine.

I left the highway at the Bernalillo turnoff. I could see the green along the Rio Grande and I sure wasn't going to find any place to camp next to water up on the mesa. I stopped at a small general store in Bernalillo and asked questions while picking up a sack of yellow corn meal, a can of coffee and a slab of bacon. "They have a gas station up at San Ysabel?

"Yeah."

This store had sliced bacon, too, but that doesn't keep well without refrigeration. I added a box of sugar and several cans of milk as an afterthought, along with a blue agate ware cup I'd forgotten to order earlier. "How do I get to Santa Cala Pueblo?" I asked.

The storekeeper said, "This road runs north to state highway forty-four and that takes you to San Ysabel. That's the turn-off to Santa Cala."

I found San Ysabel was a scaly looking place, with a dirty, two-pump filling station blighted by several half-dismantled cars strewn around that the storekeeper in Bernalillo had been dismissive about, a rundown general store and several nondescript buildings I guessed to be houses. I bypassed it and drove up a dirt road toward the river like the Indian ward boy, Joe, had told me to do. Even if it wasn't the right one, dirt roads all lead someplace. This one led to a one-track bare turn off to the right and finally to a deserted one room adobe house within a hundred feet of two old cottonwoods shading the Santa Cala River. I parked and got out to look at the water. A fish jumped and something atavistic stirred inside of me. It was the first time I'd felt any emotion but fear since I could remember.

I broke out the fishing gear and caught a grasshopper for bait. Okay, so dry flies were more sporting; I wanted to catch something. Fish ate what was available, and there were grasshoppers everywhere here. I got a bite before the bait floated ten feet; a small fish hooked itself before I could react. On the four-ounce rod, I could feel every move the fish made and I'd almost forgotten to breathe as I hauled it in. Before I could detach it from the hook and throw it back, a creature sprang at the fish from a clump of willows next to the river's edge and pounced on it. My God! It was the biggest cat I'd ever seen! Except for its pink collar, it looked like a bobcat. It was a brown tabby with a short, thick tail, tapering toward the end. Its eyes were a fierce gold green in color. What in the hell was it doing here?

The cat pinned the fish against a rock with a huge paw and glared at me challengingly.

"Go ahead, Mac, eat it," I invited. I wasn't going to argue with anything that looked like that.

The cat ripped the flesh from the bones and swallowed it as if it were starving. I'd been that hungry a time or two in Nam, and nodded sympathetically. When it released what was left of the fish, I hauled it over, detached the head and ragged skeleton of the poor creature from the hook before catching another hopper and throwing the line back into the water. This time, the cat waited until I could remove the catch. "Here it is," I offered and it snatched it deftly from my outstretched hand. He could have taken a finger. The third was big enough for me to eat and I'd have kept it anyway, but when I laid it in the cool grass at my feet, the cat ignored it, engaged in the absorbing task of washing its paws and face. I cleaned it and the next one, tossing the guts back into the water after the two stripped carcasses the cat had devoured, and brought them back to the truck.

The cat followed and watched as I set up the Coleman on a handy stump over two feet high, smoothed like a table top by whoever had lived here before. I made a fire in a ring of stones near the stump and put on coffee water. After rolling the two fish in yellow corn meal, I cooked them on the turned-up lid of the Dutch oven along with two strips of bacon I'd cut off the slab with my Old Timer knife; I ate from the lid with it. The lids of Dutch ovens are slightly concave and when I finished I set it on the ground, pouring some canned milk in it for the cat, in case he was thirsty as well as hungry. I usually think of all cats as she, but this one was outrageously male from the rugged look of his head, to the tight fuzzy balls under his tail.

When the coffee was ready and I'd poured myself a cup, the cat padded over and drank from the lid. We sat companionably in silence for a bit. Then the cat came over to me to rub against my leg and I stooped to scratch him under his chin, pulling his collar around in the process. On impulse, I asked him, "You want this thing?" unhitched it and let it fall at the cat's feet. He bent and sniffed it, picked it up daintily with his teeth and carried it over to bare ground before dropping it and scratching sandy soil over it, half covering it. Uh huh. He thought it was dopey looking, too.

The cat came back and settled down a few feet from the fire, closed his eyes and purred. Fine. He talked to himself like I did. I tossed out the dregs of coffee and took out the hammock, tying it to hang between the truck and one of the trees, and stretched out for a nap. The cat sat up and watched me until I lay still before retreating back into the willows. I dozed off thinking it was the biggest damned cat I'd ever seen.

The first night on my own I slept badly. I'd taken off my hearing aid and realized that with my hearing in the shape it was in someone or something could sneak up on me. Being by myself had some drawbacks. So, I lay on my back, cradling my rifle and looking at the stars, barely dozing most of the night. I used to do that in Nam, too.

On the second night, the cat joined me, jumping up on my hammock and pushing against me until I moved enough for him to settle down comfortably. I bet he weighed close to twenty pounds. I'd seen him coming or I'd have kicked him twenty feet, but I let him stay. He could do my listening for me. He was as spooky about strange noises as I was. He was gone by morning.

Over the next few days, I fished and slept, sharing my catch with the cat, who appeared from the willows as soon as a fish flapped in the shallow water, struggling against the hook. Taking the fish seemed as important to the cat as to me and I had a fellow feeling for the beast. I talked to him, offering observations, and he'd snuggle down for a few minutes after eating to purr, morning and evening. He allowed me to pet him briefly after each meal; I did not over-extend the liberty. I figured that he was about as prickly as I was; it was hard for me to let people touch me.

On the fourth day, I heard a truck turn into my dirt road. The cat, who had been sitting companionably on the table, jumped down and streaked into the willows. Without thinking, I rolled out of my hammock, picked up my rifle and ran to hide behind the adobe hut. The truck sounded in a hurry and folks in a hurry are not restful to be around. It was a light olive-colored VW van and it squealed to a stop just short of my camp. A pony-tailed young woman slammed the door as she got out, looked around and stamped over to where the cat had discarded its collar, picking it up and inspecting it carefully.

I came up behind her, the rifle pointing over my shoulder, and said, "You looking for something?"

When I emerged, the cat did too, walking up to rub against the girl's legs. After a quick glance the girl ignored me. "Oh, Mr. Meph! Where have you been?" She scooped up the cat and hugged him. She looked like the kind of girl I used to dream about until I stopped dreaming. She wore only a sloppy t-shirt, khaki shorts and low cut sneakers.

The cat glanced at me, as if slightly embarrassed, before rubbing his head under her chin.

"What have you done with your pretty new collar, you bad beast?" she cooed.

"I don't think he liked it," I said, putting the rifle up against the stump. I didn't think I'd need it.

The woman turned to me, "Did you take it off him?" she asked accusingly. "He's been missing for a week. I'd almost given up hope of finding him."

"He suggested it," I replied defensively. "He's the one that buried it. I've been feeding him," I added, hoping to gain approval.

She shifted the cat so that her arm had its hind legs trapped while her hand cradled the cat's chest. She glanced around the camp. "Raw fish? I'll probably have to worm him. Raw food is not good for cats."

"He seemed to like it that way," I answered. Dumb bitch. She was pretty, though.

"You live here?"

"Nope."

"Well, thanks for looking after Mr. Meph. I really appreciate it," and she flashed me a smile that might have been sincere if it hadn't come so easy.

I nodded and asked, "Like some coffee?" I filled my one cup from the pot resting in the coals.

"No thanks," she said quickly; too quickly.

I shrugged.

The cup was clean and the coffee not bad. I added canned milk and sugar, sat in my chair and sipped it. I'd learned to drink it with canned milk and sugar in the army as the only way it could be drunk at all. Army coffee in an aluminum cup is terrible stuff, turning black in hot swirls as the liquid ate into the surface of the container. I planned to wean myself from the milk and sugar, going back to the black coffee I'd always drunk before I enlisted, but not yet.

The woman hesitated a moment before turning back to the pickup, posing Mac, as I called him, on the hood of the vehicle and refastening his pink collar before getting into the truck. She started off down the road and I heard her turn onto the highway and then the squeal of brakes.

A moment later the cat dashed by, diving into the willows and out of sight, followed shortly after by the truck.

"Where did he go?" the woman demanded, as if I'd conspired to hide her cat. I guessed Mac had used her lap as a launching pad to go through the window, because both of her legs were scratched and bleeding.

I nodded toward the willows. "He's in there. He spends most of his time in there," I answered.

She strode off determinedly only to backtrack when she found the thicket impenetrable. "I'll never find him in that brush," she said, close to tears. I think she was more mad than hurt.

"Probably not," I agreed.

"You don't understand. He's not just any cat. He's a Maine Coon cat, a rather rare breed. I have papers on him. He's worth four hundred dollars!"

Did I look like that should impress me? I set the cup down and stood up, reaching for my wallet. I had hundred dollar bills. I counted out four, which still left me with more money than I was used to carrying. The eight thousand dollar warrant was locked in the glove compartment along with my discharge papers.

"Here," I said, holding out the money.

"What's that?"

"Four hundred dollars," I responded. "Drop the papers by when you can and I'll burn them. No one should own a free spirit like that cat."

"What's wrong with you? I wouldn't sell my pet!"

"If he was your pet, or your anything, he wouldn't have run away. Twice. He belongs to himself," I said firmly.

"You're not going to help me?"

"Not with this, no," I told her.

She glared at me for a moment, then turned and stomped off again, slamming the van door and spinning her wheels as she left. She seemed to anger easily. Too bad. She should smile more.

An hour later the girl came back with two guys in tow. I recognized the sound of her vehicle and resisted the fight or flight urge that had become second nature in Nam. I was resting in my hammock, sharpening my knife on a flat stone I'd picked up and listening to the river. Mac was still back in the willows. I saw him peek out briefly as the van rolled up.

"Where is he?" she demanded. She'd put iodine on her scratches and combed her hair out. Looked good. I was glad I'd had mine cut. Now that there was no one to tell me to spruce up, I'd keep it short. I waved one hand toward the willows and saw a small quiver as Mac slipped further back into concealment.

"See here, you can get into trouble if you don't give that cat back," one of the blond youths with her threatened.

"I don't have the cat," I objected, squinting up at him, drawing my knife blade slowly across the sharpening stone. He was younger than me, by the look of him. Bigger, too. So was his friend. They looked like twins.

"Taking anything worth more than a hundred dollars is a third class felony," the other one said. "If we lay a charge on you with the sheriff's office, you'll go to jail."

Law student, I decided. I got out of the hammock, folded up my knife and put it carefully in its case. "No," I said. "I just got released from a Vietnamese prison camp, and no one had better ever try to put me behind bars again. I won't go."

"Hey, he didn't steal the cat," the girl said, pushing between us.

"Baby killer," one sneered while the other pulled the girl away. "Don't get in the way, Lou," he ordered. "We'll handle this."

The lawyer type pushed me and said, "How tough are you without a flame-thrower in your hand?"

"That's battery," I said mildly, using a term I was sure he understood. Catching his wrist with my left hand as he reached for me again, I twisted it and hit him in the belly with my right, a solar plexus punch that dropped him to his knees, stunned. His buddy jumped toward me, so I hit him in the nose with a left jab, hard enough to draw blood. It's wonderful how the sight of one's own blood will take the fight out of a man.

"Take your punk friends out of here before I have to hurt them," I told the girl. "They're too big to fool with. Come back by yourself this evening while I'm fishing and maybe your cat will be willing to talk to you again."

"Why can't you do it now?" she asked.

"Because the fish aren't biting now," I told her and stretched back out in the hammock. Lying down, I didn't represent a threat to the two muscle men and she succeeded in bullying them into following her back to the van. I didn't watch them leave. College boys!

I started fishing as soon as I heard the van returning, just as dusk was falling. I continued until I had a fish on the line and splashing in the river shallows. Mac couldn't resist it and came to capture it, batting it in the air several times, showing off for the girl, I suspected. He watched me catch three more, glancing over toward the stump from time to time. I didn't look around, but guessed the girl was there. Even deaf as I am, I would have heard her leave. I was showing off, too, a little bit.

I nodded to her as I brought the three cleaned fish back to camp. She nodded back, but her eyes were on Mac, who seemed not sure of what he wanted. The cat settled on sitting some distance from either of us with his feet tucked up under him and his eyes at half-slit.

I'd made some cornbread for breakfast in the Dutch oven and before I cooked the fish, cut what was left in three pieces, one little one for the cat, laying them all out on a clean rock. "You'll have to eat with your fingers," I said. "I only have the one knife."

"I have a knife of my own," she said gravely, rising and taking a red Swiss army model from her pocket. I never could see the use in a tool like that, too many fussy little bits of things with too specialized features. She took one of the small fish when I offered it. I turn big ones loose when I catch them if I can get to them before the cat does. The little ones are the best eating. Before cooking them, I'd stuffed them with slices of apple from the overgrown orchard near the abandoned house, a trick I'd learned as a Boy Scout.

I put a bite of my trout on the rock next to Mac's slice of cornbread, tapping on the rock with the blade of my knife to get his attention. He padded over and inspected the offering, eating it daintily before wolfing down the cornbread. I saved a piece of the bacon for him for desert, and he ate it from my hand.

"All that fat and salt is terrible for him," the woman murmured as she set out a tidbit for the cat. He considered it briefly but decided to refuse it, crouching down beside me warily instead.

"He doesn't like me anymore," she said shakily.

"Nah," I disagreed. "He's just being a cat. Pour a little canned milk into the Dutch oven lid pan and put it down where he can get it."

She did as I suggested and Mac followed her to drink the greasy milk, allowing her to pet him with the ends of her fingers. She didn't try to pick him up again.

"You might undo that collar," I said. "He hates that."

"How do you knows so much about it?" she muttered, but she did as I suggested.

Mac stopped his greedy licking of the lid and rubbed his head across her knee briefly.

I carefully didn't make eye contact with the woman, but I knew she glared at me. "Would you like me to make coffee?" she asked, finally.

"If you want to. You take the cup. I cut the top from a milk can yesterday I can use," I said and went to get it from the truck. I'd twisted a loop of rusty wire around it to make a handle. It wasn't great, but it worked.

"I want to apologize for what happened this morning," she said hesitantly.

"No harm done," I said.

"Neither Keith nor Kevin would agree with you," she retorted grinning. "They wanted to get the sheriff. They would have, too, if I hadn't told them I'd testify they'd attacked you."

"Thank you," I said.

"I'm sorry about the 'baby-killer' thing, too."

"I didn't understand that," I admitted.

"It's what they called anyone who fought in Vietnam. They were protesters."

"Protestors? What were they protesting, being drafted? I don't remember meeting anyone over there who was happy about it," I said.

"Oh. Well, lots of people think that we shouldn't be there, particularly doing what we were doing. Stories came out about villages being destroyed by napalm and women and babies burning."

"Napalm? Jesus! Where the hell would I have gotten napalm? I was a grunt. And I didn't kill any women and babies. I fired into the brush maybe a hundred times, but I never saw anyone die, certainly not any women and children. In fact, until we were surrounded and captured, we never saw anyone out there. We heard them, though," I added, the fear a remembered sourness in my stomach.

We sat in silence for a bit. I was thinking about Nam. I don't know what she was thinking about.

"I'm an anthropology graduate student," she volunteered as she gestured upstream. "I'm doing a study of the role of women at Santa Cala Pueblo, working with the public health nurse."

"Hmmm," I said noncommittally, sipping my coffee and watching Mac.

"I'm trying to explain about the collar. The Indians think a cat as big as Mr. Meph has to be a wild cat of some kind. I put a collar on him to show that he wasn't, to keep him from being shot. I can see it was a mistake, but I was trying to protect him."

I nodded. It made sense. Silly looking collar though. Pink! A red one with studs on it would have been better.

"Look, you going to be around here for a while? The cat likes you and is safer with you than me as long as I'm living in Santa Cala."

"The owner may come and tell me to leave just about any time," I said. "I can't promise anything."

"I'll look into that," she offered. "If it's okay, will you stay?"

I looked at her then. "I'll promise not to go and run off with your cat," I said. "You come by from time to time, and I'll tell you if I decide to leave. Here is as good as anyplace else right now for me, if I don't get bothered too much."

"I won't bother you," she assured me. "I'll just come by to check on Meph. My name is Lou Elwood," and she stuck out her hand to shake. Good sized. Good grip.

"Jack Kilroy," I said and nodded, vaguely dissatisfied.

After a last pat for Mac, she left.

I had one more visitor that afternoon, one who woke me even before Mac launched himself from my belly, where he'd elected to snooze, and scurried into the clump of red willow. This vehicle had a bad valve and was making a lot of racket. I rolled from my hammock, picked up the rifle and hid behind the corner of the adobe before it came into sight. The driver honked and I stepped out to meet him, an old Indian with a bandana tied around his head.

His eyebrows raised and he asked, "You fixing to shoot somebody?"

"Probably not," I assured him.

"You staying around here?"

"For a while, at least, unless somebody runs me off. You own this place?"

"No. Some Mexican used to own it. He died a long time ago. You want some firewood? I'll let you have the truckload for ten dollars." He indicated the load in the back of his pickup by jerking his head and pointing with his lips. I glanced at it. The load was twisted juniper logs, some dry, some green. It'd take a lot of ax work to turn it into firewood, but the price was fair enough, I thought. I had no real idea what firewood was worth.

"Sure," I said. "I probably won't use it all, but I was getting tired of scrounging little bits of scrap for my fire."

"Where you want it?"

"Over there where there's room to swing an axe," I said, pointing.

He drove another twenty feet and stopped, so I leaned my rifle back against the stump and climbed over the side of the pickup to pitch the crooked logs over the pickup railing onto the ground. He watched.

"Have some coffee," I invited him as I worked.

He grunted and served himself, watching me as I took off my shirt and went on unloading the truck.

"You been in the war?" he asked.

"Yeah."

He'd seen the shrapnel scars along my right side. It looks worse than the wound had been. When I'd finished I pulled my shirt back on, climbed over the side of the truck and reached for my wallet. I pulled out a ten and gave it to the old man, who was sitting comfortably on my only chair, drinking my coffee.

"My grandson was in the war," the old man said. He looked as solid as a brown rock. I wondered if the chair was strong enough to hold him.

"That right?" I asked, sitting on the ground up against the stump with the milk can full of coffee. I decided I needed at least one more real cup if I was going to keep having visitors all the time.

"My grandson drinks too much beer," the old man said. "Maybe you hear him walking back at night with his friends. Sometimes there's fights." He shook his head in dismay.

"No, I've not heard anything. Where does he get beer around here?"

"There's a bar down by the general store. They'll trade for anything of value. Some of the young fellows have been stealing stuff to swap for beer. Folks are upset about it."

"I didn't see the bar."

"It don't look like much. At night there's a sign in the window."

"Tell the cops."

"We don't have cops. And the sheriff don't have no say on pueblo land. Only the FBI can arrest anyone there, and they don't care about Indians unless they do something real bad."

"You talk to the bartender about your son?"

"Yeah. He threw me out," the old man said flatly.

"Sounds like a hard case. Maybe you ought to burn it down with flaming arrows like in the old cowboy and Indian movies."

"The Indians never win in the movies," he said. "You carry that rifle inside the bar and he'll call the sheriff on you. There's a law in this state about bringing a gun into a place that sells drinks."

"The sheriff drink there?"

"Lots of big shots drink in the back room. They play poker."

"I like poker. Could I get in the game?"

"Maybe, if you got money. Don't drink though. You pass out, you'll wake up outside, broke."

I'd thought about it after the old man left. Might be fun to check out that game. I was already getting bored just fishing, eating and sleeping.

2

*T*hat afternoon I drove down to San Ysabel and bought two more cups and two plates, along with cheap metal knives, forks and spoons and a razor. I had enough company dropping by to warrant the expenditure. Besides, I'd found the milk can I'd converted to an extra cup was hard to wash. I asked about the bar.

"You can buy beer to take out, all right," the storekeeper said, indicating the building next door by a jerk of his thumb. "It don't open till sundown, though."

I figured I could keep a few long necks cooling in the creek for special occasions, but I wasn't in any hurry. Back in camp I shaved before putting on one of my new flannel shirts. If this was a big money game, I had to look as if I could afford to play. That evening about nine I drove back down. There was a red neon Coors sign in the window of the adobe building next to the general store like the old Indian had said. I figured the poker game would be started by then, if the old Indian was right about that, too.

"That Coors a local beer?" I asked the unsmiling bartender.

He looked like he'd shaved early that morning and had a fast-growing beard.

"Brewed in Denver. You from back east someplace?"

"Philadelphia."

"The company says it don't travel well. Won't ship it east of the Mississippi."

"Is it any good?"

"Yeah, it's pretty good beer. We got it on draft."

"Give me one," I ordered and watched while he drew a glass. It didn't have much foam, so he must have been serving customers, though I was the only one in the bar.

"Not much business," I remarked, after taking a sip. Hmmm . . . lousy beer.

"There's guys in the back room," he said.

"Really? Maybe I'll join them," I said, sliding off the barstool.

"They're having a meeting," he said.

"I heard something about a poker game," I said. "I play poker."

"It's private. Only veterans are allowed to join."

"I served in Nam," I said.

"These are WW II and Korean war guys," he said doubtfully.

"I got my papers out in my truck. Why don't you ask while I pick them up," I suggested, leaving my glass on the bar. I hadn't paid him yet, so he shrugged and walked to the door at the corner of the bar while I went for my discharge certificate in the glove compartment.

The bartender was waiting for me when I came back. "Let me have it," he requested, holding out his hand.

I placed the folded paper on the bar where he could pick it up and sat back on the stool to sip at the beer. "It's pretty good, all right," I lied, though any beer tasted better than the river water I'd been drinking for a couple of days.

He grunted and carried my discharge into the back room. It was the original and I didn't much like it being out of my sight, but I could always go after it.

The bartender came back out without the paper and said, "It takes five hundred dollars to buy into the game."

"Fine," I said.

"Okay, go on back," and he gestured without looking at me.

As I started to leave, he added, "Pay for the beer first."

I gave him a dollar bill and waited for the change. He gave it grudgingly, but I didn't like him either.

There were five men sitting around a round oak table that must have been five feet wide.

"Thanks for letting me sit in," I said, as I walked up to it.

"You're welcome, son," the gray-haired man said. "We're sort of a non-com club; your sergeant rank entitles you to a seat. We were all sergeants in other wars."

"Thanks," I said again, moving to the vacant chair. I'm Jack Kilroy from Philadelphia."

"Seems you're quite a hero. You won a Silver Star? What did you do? Wipe out an entire village?" The gray-haired man waved my discharge paper at me.

"It was a Bronze Star," I said, "and that's the second time since I've been back that I've heard about wiping out villages. Where I was near the

Cambodian border we didn't even see any villages. I think anyone who spent time in a prison camp probably got a Bronze Star. They're not all that much."

"Don't want to talk about it?"

"Vietnam? Nope," I retorted, reaching over the table and taking the discharge paper gently from his hand, folding it and sticking it in my shirt pocket. "Nope," I said again. I didn't even want to think about it.

"My name is Hendley," the man said, standing to shake my hand. "This here's Bill Simpson, our local sheriff," he added, looking at the small, red-haired, tidy-looking man next to him.

Simpson nodded without smiling.

Next to Simpson sat a short, round-faced Spanish man who introduced himself without rising. "I'm Joe Lima." He was in his late forties or early fifties like the others.

"Phillips, Ted Phillips," the man next to him said, reaching over and shaking hands. Except for the bump on his nose and the lack of the twinkle in his eye, he could have passed for an ugly Cary Grant.

"Ginwright, I'm from Philadelphia, too," the last man introduced himself, as I sat down next to him. "We need some new blood in this game." He was a slim black man with a mustache and full head of hair, slightly balding at the temples. The vacant chair was between him and Phillips. I wondered why. A friend had once told me that there were about two hundred black families in Philadelphia that comprised the city's black elite. They all knew one another and would attend each other's daughter's piano and ballet recitals, even those who didn't have children of their own. Many of them could pass for white; none of them did. Maybe Phillips just didn't like blacks. He offered what appeared to be a limp hand. Surprised me: damned near popped blood from the end of my fingers, grinning when I didn't respond. Never show surprise to poker players. Maybe he was a real cowboy, with a grip like that. I was the one in the room who wasn't wearing a cowboy hat.

"James J. Kilroy," Hendley said, looking at my discharge paper. "That a real name?"

"Yeah."

"Kilroy; I wouldn't believe it if I hadn't seen it. Never thought Kilroy would show up at my poker table, though he seemed to be everywhere else in WW II."

"In Philadelphia, it's like Kennedy in Boston. And like the Kennedys, Kilroys have been ward-level politicians since before the Civil war."

"Democrats?"

"Bred in the bone," I said.

"You related to the congressman from Philly?" Ginwright asked. "I still got kin there."

"All Kilroys are related. We're Celts. But yes, he's my father."

"How come a congressman's son wasn't an officer?" Hendley wanted to know.

"Just lucky, I guess," I said. I hadn't always felt that way, but I did now.

"Joe here is a politician too," Hendley said. "Serves in the legislature. Ginwright teaches constitutional law down at the university."

I wondered if that meant he was also in politics.

"Are we going to play or just talk?" Simpson complained. From the short stack of chips in front of him, he was losing. Losing makes some guys surly.

"Easy, Bill, I gotta find out," Hendley said. "I ain't playing poker with no Republicans. You got five hundred dollars to buy in?" he asked me, coming to business.

"Sure," I said, pulling out my wallet and laying five hundred dollar bills on the table. There were chips stacked on the narrow table behind Hendley. I pushed my money over to him and he took it, putting it loose in the table's single drawer.

"Gotta keep the money out of sight," he explained. "Poker ain't legal here and some of these boys would be embarrassed if the state troopers busted in on us."

I glanced at the sheriff and he shrugged.

Hendley passed over twelve blue chips, fifteen reds and ten whites. "Blues are worth twenty-five dollars, reds ten and whites five. Every hand has a ten dollar ante. We play draw and five and seven card stud, all high-low, dealer's choice. No wild cards. Bets are five or ten dollars until there's a pair showing or until the last card. There's a three raise limit per round. In draw you can open with twenty-five if you want. We allow sandbagging, checking and raising. I tell you that in advance so you won't get mad if it happens. Since it's my turn, I buy the beer."

"Sandbagging? Not exactly a friendly game," I said.

"It ain't unfriendly, just serious. We started playing straight poker until a few minutes ago when Ginwright got here. We don't go to high-low until we got five players. You play high-low?"

"Sure. Seven card high-low is my favorite game."

"We'll break out a new deck in your honor," Hendley said and opened a new pack of red Bicycles. He fast shuffled a half dozen times and slid them over to Ted Phillips to cut. "Playing seven card high-low," Hendley announced. "Ante ten."

At the end of two hours I'd won about three hundred dollars, playing conservatively as I always do with people I don't know well. Both Hendley and Ginwright had also won. Joe Lima, Simpson, the sheriff, and Ted Phillips ad lost. Phillips had bought a second stack of chips and lost half of that, along with his original stake. He was in a temper, for I caught him cheating and let him know it. He'd dealt me two hands, which should have been winners only to top me with slightly better hands. The third time he dealt I had three sevens, an ace and a deuce. Instead of discarding the ace and deuce and going for high, I discarded two of the sevens and went for low. When I was dealt a three and a four, I had a seven-four low, good enough for most wins at low. I bet into him, and reraised when he raised up to the limit three times. I could only call his third raise, and when he declared high, I went low, surprising him.

Hendley stayed with us and also went for high. If I'd gone high, betting before Hendley, he'd have gone low as the only low better, guaranteeing himself half the pot. As it played out, he went with his strength and Phillips was caught with three queens against Hendley's low straight. Phillips had figured on winning at least half the pot. Instead, he'd lost several hundred dollars. He couldn't say anything about it, because he wasn't supposed to know what I'd done. But, he did know and he knew why I'd done it.

I figured the only person playing at my level was Hendley, though both Lima and Ginwright were competent. Simpson and Phillips weren't.

"We always finish up with a hand of show-down, high-low," Hendley said. "Ante ten."

That would likely cut forty dollars from my winnings if I stayed for all five cards, which I was expected to do as a winner. I hate show-down. All the cards are dealt face up and there's no room for skill.

"You play a pretty sound game," Hendley said, dealing once again.

"I played a lot in the army," I answered.

"That's what the paper said. Said you owned the whole prison camp and tore up all the IOUs the day before your escape. That's where I read about the Silver Star."

I was stunned, reaching up to touch the discharge certificate in my shirt pocket. "What paper?"

"Why, the *Albuquerque Journal*. They flew some general in from Washington with your medal and found you'd been discharged. The guys you brought out told the reporters all about it. Everybody's looking for you."

"When I cash in, I'm on my way," I said. "I don't care who's looking for me."

"Easy, son," Hendley said, continuing his role as spokesman for the group. "Nobody's going to tell any reporters where you're holed up. You're at the old Romero place east of here, aren't you? Up next to the Santa Cala reservation?"

"Well, I'm east of here, anyway. There's an old adobe without a roof and a bridge over the river not far off up the road."

"Yeah, that's the place. It's been deserted. You could probably pick it up for the back taxes. Just be a few hundred dollars, likely. Joe could find out for you."

"I don't figure on staying long in any case."

"Why not? If you owned it, you could put a gate on that road and be as private as you liked. This is good country. I hear you're fishing. There's also deer and elk hunting in the fall. Electricity runs right up the road and it wouldn't cost you anything to have a service line run in. You could fix up the adobe, put in a roof for winter, and be as snug as anywhere else."

"It's good of you to take an interest."

"To tell the truth, it's hard to get even four guys together for poker every week. Me and the fellas here are rich. I was an oilman in Oklahoma. When I came to New Mexico to retire, I found there were too many damned Texans in Taos; so I came here and bought one of Simpson's ranches. He became sheriff when he couldn't get anyone else to take rustlers seriously. His sons run his other spreads."

"No money in cattle anymore," Simpson complained. "If I could find other buyers as dumb as Hendley here, I'd sell everything and move to Florida."

Hendley grinned and went on with his recital. "Ginwright' s grandfather owned undertaking parlors allover the Midwest. Great business, undertaking. Raw material's free, so to speak. Phillips runs the Bureau of Indian Affairs (BIA) in Albuquerque. His family is in import-export. Lima, here, has a finger in everything tied to liquor up in the northern part of the state, like this bar."

"I just own the licenses," Lima said. "I lease the businesses."

"I don't fit in with you guys. I'm not rich," I said quietly.

"No, but you're not afraid to play poker for our kind of stakes," Hendley said. "The way you play you're not going to lose much. Now, we don't mind losing so much as mind not having enough men for a real game. Hell, we can't play high-low with only three men at the table. If I got a passion in life, it's playing seven-card stud, high-low.

I caught a second ace on the last card, giving me half the showdown pot. I still didn't care for the game. Ginwright won low, pulled in the pot, split it and gave me my half. I counted my chips. "Nine seventy," I announced first, being the guest. Not counting the five hundred I'd started with ,I'd won four hundred and seventy dollars. Hendley played banker, passing over a neat stack of bills.

"You coming back next week?" he asked, staring at me before he pushed Ginwright's pile over to him.

"If the reporters don't find me," I said.

"I got an extra fence gate. I'll drop it and a couple of posts off so you can block the road. Hell, I'll have a couple of hands put 'em in for you. Reporters won't bother you if they can't get at you. What do you say?"

I surprised myself by saying, "If I'm not run off. I'll stick around at least until next Wednesday, anyway. I'll let you know one way or another about sticking around longer at the next poker game." I'd picked up my winnings and walked to the door. I could feel their eyes on me, but no one said anything until I opened it.

"Would you mind telling me why you tore up those IOUs?" Hendley asked.

"I was walking point," I said. "We had the camp guards' rifles. I didn't relish the idea of a couple of dozen men owing me money walking behind me for a hundred miles." I shut the door quietly and went up to the bartender.

"I'd like a case of long necks, please."

"Coors?"

"That all you got?"

"We got Mexican beer . . . Corona."

"I'll take that," I said. I didn't know the brand, but it had to be better than Coors. As I waited, I looked around, surprised to see the place nearly full now. The back room must have a soundproof door, I decided. Interesting. I recognized the storekeeper sitting at a table by himself and realized he must be kin to the bartender. They had the same pug noses, lank hair and stubbly, unshaven look at this time of night. I carried the beer out of the bar and around the side of the building where I'd left my truck. A half dozen young Indians were standing around smoking under the porch light over the back door. I wondered if the old Indian's grandson was one of them. Too bad about that.

I placed the case of beer on the seat and locked my winnings and my discharge certificate in the glove compartment before driving back to my camp. The cat was sitting on the stump waiting for me. He stretched, arching his back, and walked over to greet me, rubbing his head against my leg. He wanted the piece of cheese I gave him before bedtime. My bedtime, that is. The cat went out hunting every evening, to wake me some hours later by jumping heavily up on the hammock and pinning my legs by flopping across them, carefully washing his face by licking his paw and rubbing his paw over his mouth. I assumed he was cleaning the blood off his mouth from a successful hunt. I went back to sleep with the certainty that both my legs would be paralyzed by morning. I hoped he was sleeping better than I was. Every time he twitched, I woke up, ready to fight or flee. I never moved, for that would give me away to the enemy, and there was always a short period of disorientation before I could recall where I was. At least I hadn't started having nightmares about being back in Vietnam like a lot of guys in the hospital had.

As usual, the cat woke me at first dawn to go fishing, walking up my body and rubbing his forehead on my face. I wondered how long I could go on taking as many fish from this short stretch of stream without their running out. I should have said so last night at poker. I knew that proposition Hendley had in mind must have some drawbacks.

Thinking the whole matter over carefully, I built a fire and started water for coffee. Spreading some hot coals beside the fire with my shovel, I cooked hotcakes on the overturned lid of the Dutch oven, another Boy Scout special. I used to wake mornings in Vietnam and stare up at the leaves, thinking for a moment, until reality hit, that I wasn't out camping again. I swore several times I could smell hotcakes. Anyway, you can cook four cakes at a time on a Dutch oven lid without spilling batter all over the place, and that's what I did.

I heard the girl, Lou Elwood's truck drive up as we finished breakfast. The cat must have recognized the sound of her Microbus, for he ignored it. I'd saved a hotcake for him, and put it on the clean rock next to the stump just as she stopped and opened the door. The cat hooked the hotcake with the claws of one paw and nibbled daintily at the edge, eyeing the girl as she came to stare at the two of us.

"You're feeding him hotcakes?" She sounded scandalized.

"They're pretty good. Like a couple? There's a little batter left and Mac doesn't eat more then one."

"You sure?"

I didn't respond except to scrape out the mixing bowl and make four more cakes for her. I set out one of the new plates and a clean cup along with the cheap metal knife and fork. With butter on them, the pancakes looked tempting enough, so I'd probably have eaten them myself if she hadn't shown up, but I handed them over.

"You know the way the John book starts, 'In the beginning was the word'? Ever wonder what the word was?"

"Not really," she said glancing up for a moment.

"Butter," I told her.

"The first word was 'butter'?"

"Sure. Then God had to invent pancakes to have some place to put it."

"Ah."

I watched her until I could see she wasn't just being polite and finished making the coffee, dropping some broken egg shells in the pot to settle the grounds. I handed her a key as she finished the cakes, all but licking the plate.

"Don't you eat breakfast?" I asked.

"Too much trouble," she said.

"I sometimes eat breakfast twice a day," I reproved her.

"Did you get hungry in the prison camp?"

"Did you read about that?" Damn! Everyone knew!

"Sure. The stories said you were all skin and bones when you brought those men out."

"I haven't seen it," I said, not answering her question.

"I have the papers in the truck."

I considered it, but shook my head. "You said stories. Were there more than one?"

"The account of your war record has been running for three days, with more coming out as new witnesses come forward. The reporters say the army wants to find you to give you a Silver Star Medal in a public award ceremony."

"I don't think so," I said. "You going to tell them I'm here?"

"No, but those guys that were with me, Keith and Kevin, want to. They said it would serve you right."

"They're pretty judgmental. What are you doing with them anyway?" I surprised myself. I shouldn't have asked that. It was none of my business.

"Keith is from the Anthropology Department down at UNM, like me. That's the University of New Mexico in Albuquerque," she explained when I raised an eyebrow. "His specialty is archeology. He's identifying old Santa Cala living sites to support an Indian Lands Claim case. Kevin is a law student, researching land titles to find who owns the land the sites are on so they can be dug. I'm not really with them; I just know them from school."

I suddenly felt good. 'Well, they sure don't like me. Want me to whip up some more hotcakes?"

She shook her head, then smiled at me, "The hotcakes were delicious and the coffee strong just as I like it, but I have to go."

The cat came over to her as she started to stir and jumped into her lap, putting an end to that nonsense. He rubbed his head under her chin.

"I guess the cat thinks you ought to come for breakfast every morning."

"I miss him," she said petting him. "What are you going to do if they find you? Getting a medal isn't like being beaten with a stick," she said, still looking as if there was something on her mind, probably the cat.

"They may find where I'm camping, but they won't find me," I said. "I just see the whole Nam thing from a different point of view than anyone out of Washington would. If there are a lot of reporters asking questions, I'm likely to give answers no one who was not there would like to hear and I'm not looking for trouble. If they don't find me, no one will know what I look like, and I can avoid it."

"There were pictures of you, along with the stories."

"That so?" I might have known. Probably my father was already starting to build a back story for the political career he was planning for me. "Maybe I'll just let my beard grow back," I added.

"Really?"

"No, not really. I was glad to get rid of it."

Another truck came up the road and I picked up my rifle and ran to the adobe house, saying "I'm not here" over my shoulder. The cat ran in the other direction, for the willows.

Hendley got out and tipped his hat to the girl. "Morning, ma'am. You a friend of Jack Kilroy's? I'm Hendley. We play poker," and he stuck out his hand.

"I barely know the man and haven't decided for sure, but I think so. My name's Lou Elwood," and she rose to shake his hand gravely.

"I see. Jack around?"

I walked around the adobe behind him and leaned the rifle up against the stump. "Morning, Hendley. You looking for me?"

He turned, saw me and the rifle and said, "You still a little spooky yet, son?"

"Some," I acknowledged, pouring him a cup of coffee. I was glad I'd thought to buy two new cups. He accepted his and squatted on his heels like the old cowboy he looked like.

"Well, I just dropped by," he said after an initial sip and a nod of approval. "Thought I'd better warn you there'll be a few workmen coming by the next few days to sort of spruce the place up a bit."

"I haven't said I'm staying," I said.

"I know, I know," Hendley said, "but this place has got more potential than meets the eye. You ought to judge it fairly."

"One of the reasons I picked it was for the quiet," I said.

"This won't take a week. You got my word on it. Just move your camp fifty yards down the river under that fine old cottonwood, and you won't even know they're here. I left a couple of men on the road to mend fence. You don't hear them, do you?"

I didn't, but I don't hear much.

Hendley rose and tossed the dregs from his cup into the fire saying, "Got some errands in town. I'll see you Wednesday," and touching his hat brim with his fingers in salute to Lou, he got back into his truck and drove off.

"What was that about?" Lou asked.

"I played poker last night with him and some of his friends down at San Ysidro. He wants me to hang around. They have trouble getting enough guys at the table on a regular basis," I said.

"Doesn't sound believable," she commented.

"No," I agreed. She'd believe it, though, if she played poker. Guys who like to play on a regular basis like to be able to depend on having a quorum.

"In the newspaper stories they wrote that you were an expert poker player," she said.

"What the hell," I muttered, then continued more politely, "I like the game. I'm not a professional. I can't do card tricks." I was a little irritated by her questioning manner, but tried not to show it. Actually, it was the newspaper stories that bothered me the most. She changed the subject, so I guess she picked up on my attitude.

"I guess Mr. Meph isn't coming back out. I've got to get to work, but I'll be out tomorrow. Don't leave without seeing me."

About the time I had my tarp ramada stretched and tied down under the cottonwood, following Hendley's suggestion, another pickup drove to the adobe and the old Indian who had brought me the wood walked down to talk to me. I'd recognized the motor sound with the bad piston and hadn't bothered to hide.

"Me and my grandsons are going to fix your house," he said.

When I shook his hand, I noticed that he didn't squeeze. He just touched my fingers like the ward guy in the hospital. Must be an Indian thing, I decided.

"It isn't my house," I said.

"It don't much matter. Mr. Hendley says he's going to pay us."

I could hear women talking and laughing.

"I brought my wife and two of my daughters down to clean the place and spread new plaster on the walls. My wife makes fireplaces; yours is all burned out. She's going to take it down and make a new one."

At lunch he invited me to eat with his family. We had a watery, chile-flavored stew, wheat flour tortillas and coffee. I wouldn't have been able to do a day's work on that, though it was a little better than what I ate in the prison camp. Along with the women he'd mentioned, there were a couple of young men that he said were his grandsons. Everyone grinned at me and the two men touched hands with me, but I got no names.

"Big hero," one of the grandsons said.

"Not really," I said, looking closely to see if he was trying to be funny.

"Oh, bad eye!" he exclaimed, in mock fear, raising his hands to ward off my glance.

"Stop that!" one of the women said to him. "That Jerry, he talks smart just because he's been to college. Indians don't stare; it's bad manners, but no way you could know that."

"I apologize," I said. "His tone of voice put me off."

The young guy shrugged and turned away, so I did the same, going for a walk to see what the fence repairs looked like. Mac joined me, once I was out of sight of the Indians.

The two cowboys said, "Howdy," and continued to work, talking to each other, but not to me. That was okay. They had pounded in steel posts that installed were about six feet tall and were stringing strands of barbed wire along them. The gate was already up. I left. They were not keen on having someone watch them work.

When I got back to my camp I saw that the Indians had brought adobe bricks that were over a foot long and more than half that much wide and piled them near the hut. They'd also started what looked like a mud pit that I guessed was for mortar. The trash inside the hut had all been loaded in the truck and the dirt floor had been swept.

"We got to make a new floor, too," the old Indian said.

"What will you use?"

"We'll make it out of mud and straw, just like the wall plaster. If it don't get wet it will be as good as a wooden one."

I'd have to see that. Didn't sound possible.

I walked down to the hammock under the cottonwood, itchy with all the people about, working and me doing nothing. The cat dashed past me, seated himself under the hammock and was washing his face when I arrived. Some wild cat. He didn't join me for a nap until I was nearly asleep, then jumped up and pushed my feet around until he was satisfied with their placement before curling up. I wondered if I'd ever get used to that. The cat let me sleep for a couple of hours before walking up my legs to crouch on my chest. The girl had said he weighed eighteen pounds. I'd bet he'd gained weight on the fish and night hunting diet he seemed to prefer.

I opened my eyes and saw that he was staring, not at me, but at the bridge upstream. Something was going on there, for sure. I moved him gently to one side, sat up and looked. A white truck had stopped on the bridge and, as I watched, two men poured the first of several metal barrels of fish over the rail into the river. It was a state truck. The fish hatchery was stocking my river! Mac ran off to investigate. It would be a few weeks in the cold water before their flesh firmed up and the hatchery taste disappeared. I guessed Joe Lima had arranged the delivery. He was the local politician. I had the uncomfortable feeling, not for the first time, that things were closing in on me.

The Indians left at sundown and I went over to inspect the work. The cabin was about twenty by sixteen with one good-sized room. The old rotting, peeled logs that had supported the flat roof had been removed and new adobe bricks placed where the wall had eroded. Hand-adzed planks that had formed the collar over the adobe had been salvaged. They'd support the weight of the new roof that had been planned. A dozen round, peeled logs would serve as rafters, vigas they called them, and were already piled beside the cabin, ready for placement.

As I was looking a new truck rumbled in. I stood my ground this time and a tall man with a wind-burned face got out and asked, "You Kilroy?"

"Yes."

"Here's the keys Mr. Hendley asked me to hand over. Usually there's just two with a lock, but he asked me to have a couple of extras made. He said you might want to loan one to Teno, the old man from Santa Cala, who's fixing your house. The boys stretched five strands of barbed wire around your whole parcel and put in your gate. That ought to keep anyone out you don't want in. The keys are for the padlock on the chain securing the gate."

"I'm much obliged," I said, accepting the keys.

"All in a day's work," he assured me, touching the brim of his hat, and left, driving backwards down the road. I heard him clang and lock the gate before he drove off. The thought of being locked in made me feel uncomfortable. Just like the prison camp. I had to think about it as others being locked out.

The next morning the Indians honked at the gate and I trotted down to unlock it. I shut and locked the gate back up after two trucks had driven through, walking back to offer one of the four keys to Teno, the old Indian. "You'll be in and out over the next few days and will need this. Keep the gate locked otherwise. I'm expecting some people I don't want to see."

He looked at me without expression, but I didn't explain further. Breakfast was ready to cook when I heard Lou Elwood's van. The cat recognized the sound of her motor, too, and walked down the road with me to the gate, ignoring the Indians who gazed on him with astonished eyes. I opened the gate, waved her through and relocked it. She drove on up the road and stopped to talk to Teno, the old Indian. He seemed to know everybody.

The cat jumped through the open van window, greeting Lou by standing on her lap, imprisoning her face with his front paws and licking it with affection. As I walked by, the cat jumped out and followed me, looking over his shoulder at Lou, inviting her to come along. Good host.

"I know Teno's family," she said. "All the Casaquitos have been nice to me."

"I didn't even know his first name until a little earlier today," I said.

"Teno doesn't like the name Casaquito. It means 'little house' or 'out house,' in Spanish. Last names are something white men forced on Indians to tell them apart. Indians don't even use their real names much in daily life. They mostly just use kin identifiers or what they term 'call names' to address one another. Even 'Teno' is a call name."

I'd heard them talk to one another using those call names while working on my house. The old woman, who worked on the fireplace, Teno's wife, was called Sofie. The young woman married to one of their sons was Elsie. The fat, jolly, lazy boy, Teno and Sofie's grandson, was Roy. I didn't know who his parents were.

"They seem to know Hendley," I said. "He sent them down here."

"Everybody in Santa Cala knows Hendley," she said as she parked the van and came over to the fire. "A lot of them work on his ranch. I'd never met him until yesterday."

"Well, I barely know the man," I responded, remembering what she had said about me.

"Un-huh," she said, picking up on the allusion. "Like I told him, I'll make up my mind about you when I know you better. With all the work going on around here, it looks like I might get the chance. You planning on staying around, after all?"

"Yeah, I'm thinking about it," I said, surprising myself. "How many hotcakes can you eat?" I asked, handing her a key to the gate padlock. I still had one extra left.

3

*T*he cat dug its claws into my belly and launched itself into the air, an effective if disconcerting alarm system. Without conscious thought, I rolled out of the hammock and swept up the 30-30, levering a cartridge into the firing chamber as I came to a fighting crouch. The coals from the fire were sufficient to dimly outline the figure that stood just beyond it, a man wrapped in a blanket against the cold, with a light glinting from his eyes.

"Roy's been hurt," he said.

It was Teno. It sounded like he'd said "Loy," but I was getting used to his "L" for "R" and "L" for "D" substitutions. Like, "Loy" for "Roy" and "miller" for "middle." The young, fat man who had been working on my house was Roy, Teno's grandson who drank too much beer from his army service. He was not the one with the fast mouth that had been to college.

"I'm sorry," I said lamely, not sure what the old man wanted.

"My truck is broken. I have to go down to the hospital in Albuquerque."

The old man needed help. "You want me to drive you down?" I asked, not believing that he really expected I'd do that in the middle of the night.

"Yes," he said. "Now."

"Oh," I said and fumbled for my boots, pulling on my army surplus store navy pea jacket against the chill. No wonder the old man had a blanket. He probably didn't have a coat and it was cold. High altitude desert air loses forty degrees of its daytime warmth overnight.

I put the rifle under the seat of the carryall, like its previous owner must have done, and started the engine, letting it warm up for a full minute before putting it in gear. It ran rough under any circumstances, but less so if given a chance to idle a bit before working. The old man climbed into the passenger side, silent, probably worried about his grandson. I wondered what had happened, but it really wasn't any of my business.

At the gate the old man got out and opened it with the key I'd given him, waited for me to drive through, then locked it before rejoining me. He must have climbed the fence from the pueblo side and waded the river to get to my place. I decided that the whole fence thing was a pain in the ass and wondered why I'd let them put the gate up in the first place. I also wondered what I was doing here in the middle of the night with this scared old man. And he was scared. I saw his face in the truck's headlights. I knew about being scared, well enough.

There were no lights in San Ysabel as we drove by and little traffic on the road until we hit the highway to Albuquerque. Even then it was mostly semis, overtaking and passing us. I drove at a steady sixty, about as fast as this particular vehicle was comfortable with. It was still dark when we reached the outskirts of town and the old man said, "Turn east on Lomas." They were the first words he'd said on the road.

He grunted and pointed with his lips at the building with the sign, "Bernalillo County Indian Hospital." I parked as close to the door as I could in a space marked, "Reserved for Physicians." There were a dozen of them, all empty, and nothing else even near. I wondered why doctors called themselves "physicians," when the term with the Latin root came so much easier to the lips of English speakers.

"I want to see my grandson," Teno said when we reached the information desk.

"I'm sorry. Visiting hours don't start until tomorrow at ten. You'll have to come back then." She dismissed us by turning her back and walking away.

"We're not visitors," I said loudly enough to make her frown as she came up to the desk again, ready to reinforce her ruling. "This man's grandson was brought here on emergency admittance," I explained.

"What's his name?"

"Roy Casaquito," I told her, using the last name that Lou Elwood had told me. I didn't want the woman to start looking under "L for Loy" and brushing the old man off again when she didn't find it.

The woman consulted a card, and the look on her face changed from annoyance to a grudging embarrassment. "You'll have to see the administrator," she said. "Take a seat and I'll inform him you are here. He'll be with you as soon as he can find the time."

The old man shrugged and complied. I had the feeling it was about what he'd expected. I found her manner offensive and had it been my emergency I would have raised enough hell to get better service. Or, maybe it was me she didn't like. Maybe if the old Indian had not been in my company perhaps she would not have been quite so disagreeable. I liked her even less than before.

Teno nudged me. There was a portly man in a white coat standing before me, staring.

"I'm sorry," I said. "I must have been dozing."

"Your eyes were open," he said argumentatively, a man with a grievance.

I gathered he'd been trying to get my attention. He obviously didn't like being ignored, a man of consequence like him, impatient to be off and doing.

"I sleep with my eyes open," I said blandly, lying. "It's a habit I picked up in Vietnam."

He appeared to be doubtful. So, to avoid a protracted discussion, I said abruptly, "We've come to see Roy Casaquito. This is his grandfather."

The man glanced briefly at Teno and then turned back to me to say, "I am very sorry, but I'm afraid that is impossible. He's in the morgue and there is no admittance there."

From the sudden bleak look on Teno's face I realized he hadn't known that Roy was dead. I leaned forward and looked straight into the administrator's face, "You officious son-of-a-bitch! Is this the way you tell everyone bad news, or is it just the way you tell it to Indians?"

He backed a step away and stammered, "I thought he was aware of it."

"I see. Well, he wasn't. You might have inquired first. Now bring us to where the boy is, or I personally am going to kick the shit out of you. That's before I go to the newspapers with this, mind!" I stood up, invading his personal space, and he backed away another half step, bringing his clipboard up between us as a shield. I tapped on the clipboard with my forefinger, eyeing him coldly.

"There's no need for that!" he objected querulously, "but, he won't want to see him."

I turned to Teno. He had already made up his mind. He had risen and adjusted the blanket over his shoulders. "Let's go," he said, and turned toward the man.

"You heard him," I said, placing my fingers lightly against the clipboard and exerting gentle pressure. "Let's go."

He turned and almost fled. I noticed the receptionist looking at us and talking excitedly into the telephone, calling security, no doubt. Well, they'd have to find us, I thought, as we followed the administrator through swinging doors, down a long corridor and through a door he had to unlock to open marked with the sign, Pathology Department, No Admittance, placed on it at eye level.

Inside, Bill Simpson, my sheriff poker buddy, was talking to a young man in a white coat stained with blood. "Ah, there you are," he said, nodding to me and going to Teno to take his hand. He held it gently saying, "I found him on the highway a mile south of San Ysabel. Looks like a hit and run. You know how these kids walk down the middle of the road when they've had too much to drink. Hell, he was even going the wrong way. He was still alive when I got there and I rushed him down to the hospital. He didn't make it. I'm sorry."

The old man nodded, disengaged his hand and walked past Simpson to the table where a still form lay under the sheet. He pulled the sheet off and looked at the body before the young doctor could prevent him. It was Roy, all right, bare naked. He'd lost a lot of skin and seemed pretty broken up, but his face hadn't been touched.

Something caught my eye, something I'd seen before. I leaned over the body and studied a section of the chest, stripped of skin where the road surface had abraded it, glistening red and white under the strong light. I ignored the doctor, who was annoyed by now, and ineffectively trying to pull me away. I straightened up and faced him, brushing off his hands. "What's the cause of death?" I asked.

"What business is it of yours?" he responded with anger. "Get out of here. I want everyone out of here," he told the administrator, appealing to authority.

Ah, good for you, Doc, I thought.

"Arrest him," the administrator demanded of the sheriff, pointing at me.

"What for?" Simpson asked calmly.

"He assaulted me!"

"That true, son?"

"Not yet," I replied.

"You threatened me," the administrator accused.

"You bet," I agreed, "but that's not assault. Look, Sheriff, look at the boy's chest about four inches below where his nipple should be. That's a bullet hole. This man's been shot."

Simpson walked deliberately over to the table and shoved the doctor firmly back to peer at the corpse. "Yeah, sure looks like it," he agreed. "What about it, Doc?"

The pathologist looked in turn and said, "It's a puncture wound, but not necessarily anything that can't be accounted for by the initial trauma."

"The bullet was the initial trauma," I informed him. "The flesh was bruised around the entry hole before the skin was scraped off. Turn him over."

"You heard him. Turn him over," Simpson ordered, no longer the laidback cowboy, but a grim policeman. The startled physician beckoned to an aide and together they turned the body. There were a half dozen exit holes. The bullet had fragmented.

Simpson pulled the sheet back over the body and walked to a wall phone. "I'm calling the coroner," he announced. "I don't want you touching that body again," and pointed a threatening finger at the pathologist. "If I thought this was a deliberate act to avoid the cost of a full autopsy instead of just incompetence on your part, I'd have your ass in jail."

The doctor turned red and left, ripping off his smock and throwing it on the floor. The administrator started to protest, but Simpson waved him to silence. "Shut up. Get the hell out of here. This is a possible crime scene," and turned away to talk on the phone.

A hospital security man pushed the door open just as the administrator was about to reach for it; the door caught the angry doctor full in the face. We could hear both him and the administrator berating the unfortunate security man all the way down the hall.

Simpson finished talking on the phone and walked back over to Teno, who had been watching everything but saying nothing.

"I'm sorry about this. I'll have the body cleaned up and released as soon as I can."

Teno nodded and Simpson continued, "I'll see he's brought up to Santa Cala for burial."

Teno nodded again and left the room.

Simpson detained me as I started after him. "Keep an eye on the old man, will you? He's got a bigger problem now than just a dead son."

"What's that?"

"These Indians believe about everything bad that happens in the world is caused by witchcraft. They think witches take animal shapes and can be shot, but not killed, when they're in the form of a deer or whatever. When they wash the body for burial they'll see the exit holes in the back. It'll look to them like he was shot several times."

"Even if he was, what difference would it make?"

"A death like this looks like a man was shot as a deer, maybe, more than once with all the holes, and turned back into a man. Like he let himself be killed by a car to disguise the fact that he'd been shot as a witch."

"They think a man would commit suicide to hide the fact he was a witch?" I asked in disbelief.

"A man isn't a witch by himself. It means his parents and his wife and kids are also suspect. They could be hounded with the suspicion for the rest of their lives."

"But there aren't any witches! This is all nonsense," I objected.

"Nonsense?" he repeated with a raised eyebrow. "It ain't nonsense to them. Me, neither, if it comes to that. But I got a problem of my own. That man was shot, like you said. And the body was found off the reservation, so it's in my jurisdiction. That's not going to keep the FBI hotshots from walking all over the case, muddying up the water. Damn! Worst thing is, I can't keep them away from the old man."

"I'll tell him he's welcome down at my place," I said.

"That reminds me. Here's your deed. Hendley asked me to drop it by, and I been so busy I forgot. Better go catch that old man."

Deed? Man, he worked fast. I took the envelope he handed me walked out after Teno. The old man was waiting in the lobby. I drove him back to Santa Cala without a word from him until we reached the pueblo. When I said I was sorry about his grandson, he just nodded and looked away. Then he directed me to his house, next to an irrigation ditch. I realized the ditch must drain into the river and would be a prime source of pollution. I'd continue to boil the coffee water; I was downstream. If I wanted something cool, I'd drink beer.

"The sheriff said the FBI will be bothering you if you stay here. You want to come down and stay with me for a while?" Hell, if he could ask me to drive him to town he might not be offended by the invitation.

"I'll get something to sleep on," he said, leaving me in the truck while he went into the house.

I could hear people talking inside, with raised voices and crying. Someone knocked on my window on the passenger side, and I turned to see Lou Elwood standing there. I opened the door and she slipped in.

"I recognized your truck. What's going on?"

"Teno's grandson, Roy, was found by the sheriff lying in the road south of San Ysabel. He'd been run over, but he'd been shot first. Teno asked me to take him down to the hospital. We just got back."

"He's dead?"

"Yeah."

"Poor Sofie! She's had such a hard life, losing so many children, and now this!"

"Yeah?"

"Twelve live births, and only four lived to grow up. One of those that lived to adulthood died of TB and another of pneumonia. Now she's losing grandchildren."

"Twelve kids? She's a little bit of a thing," I said.

"There's more. She has gray hair, a mark of great age here. Old age is not a blessing in the pueblos. People who live a long time are suspected of witchcraft, of taking others' lives and adding them to their own," Lou said.

"But, this is her own grandson!"

"That would just make her appear more wicked. And she's such a sweet lady!"

"The sheriff was worried that someone will claim Roy had taken an animal shape as a witch and was shot in that form, because of fragmented bullet exit wounds in the boy's back. They look like additional bullet holes. He said the hit and run accident was staged after the fact, but the interpretation the Indians would put on that would just reinforce the witch story."

She shivered in the cold, nodding as I spoke. "It would, too. Witches do that. What does Teno say?"

"Nothing. He's going to hide out down at my place for a while. If the FBI come looking for him, don't volunteer anything. The sheriff sounded like he believed in witches, and now you."

"Witches? Of course not. What would I know about witches?"

I had no answer for that, and she sat in silence, glowering, until Teno came out with his blanket and a goatskin rolled up together. What was this about witches that made people so uncomfortable? I wondered.

She got out and opened the door for him while he pitched the roll over the seat into the back of the carryall. She watched us drive off. I wondered where she was living.

Teno unrolled the goatskin on the ground and stretched out by the fire, covering himself with the blanket. He'd left his fancy one back at his house. When the cat woke me early the next morning, I found the old man gone, but the goatskin was still there. He came back to join me for breakfast.

"I have to watch the sun rise," he said. He didn't say why. Something to do with his religious obligations, I figured.

No one came to work on the house that morning, so I labored alongside of Teno, helping him lift the peeled vigas to rest on the walls so that they were horizontal to the ground like rafters, plastering them in place and nailing them to the four-by-twelve planks that had been laid along the top of the adobe walls to protect them from the rain. Rain melts adobe. These were new logs, fresh cut, and heavy. We used some of the adobe bricks that bad been unloaded the day before to fill up the spaces between the vigas so that the tops of the walls were level.

At noon a truck honked at the gate and Teno said, "That's my nephew, Virgil. He's bringing more boards from the sawmill."

I went down to let him in. There were two men in the car. One was the college kid with the big mouth, Jerry. He nodded as I opened the gate and the other man drove the truck on up to the house. When I came up, Jerry offered me his hand and said, "I want to apologize for the other day. I had no call to wise off to you. The Santa Cala say it's because I'm part Apache. My name is Geronimo. They call me Jerry." He offered his hand and I shook it, noticing that he gripped like a white man. We walked back together after he relocked the gate.

"Teno's wife's sister is my mother," he explained. I didn't need to know that, but I nodded. It seemed to be an Indian thing to identify oneself by who he's related to. I had a feeling it didn't matter much who I was related to, as if white men were all alike, anyway.

I helped unload the truck; it carried nearly a hundred rough cut planks, two-by-sixes, sixteen feet long.

"Where did you get these?" I asked.

"Mr. Hendley set up a sawmill for us up in the mountains. We can't sell the timber because the Indian Service won't let us sign a contract, but we have plenty for our own use."

"What's Hendley getting out of this?" I asked.

"Nothing. Oh, when he wants a little wood, like now, we bring it. He can't buy it, but he pays us wages. He can fish or hunt on the reservation any time he wants without going to the governor."

"He grow up around here?'

"No, he's from Oklahoma. He says us Indians got to help one another because no damned white man will. His grandfather was a Cherokee. He says it's just family."

I wondered if there were any Indians in the Kilroy family line. The

Kilroys came over from Ireland during the potato famine. Could be, maybe.

At Teno's direction, we placed the two-by-sixes flat across the vigas, side by side, clinching them tight against one another by prizing them over and nailing them to the vigas under tension.

"Tomorrow we'll tack on the tarpaper and seal it with caliche," Teno said.

"I'll bring a load in my pickup," the driver, Virgil, said. He'd shaken hands with me the way Teno had done, a mere touching palm to palm. I gathered he'd had less contact with whites than Jerry.

I gave him one of the keys to the gate. "Just come on in," I said, and he smiled at me.

"Virgil was in Korea," Teno said, after the man had driven off with Jerry. "His wife is up at the TB sanitarium in Colorado Springs. He flew up with her over the mountains in a little old one-engine plane. He said the wind bounced it around like a toy. He said it was the most frightening thing that ever happened to him, including Korea. His wife was seven months pregnant. She delivered as soon as they got her to the hospital, shook up the way she was, but she didn't even get to hold the baby. She's too contagious. It's still up there. She sees it through a window out in the yard from time to time."

"They still afraid of infection?"

"Yeah. They're going to fly Virgil up to get it next week. He's not looking forward to the trip."

"How will he take care of it?"

"The baby? Oh, that's no problem. His mother will take the child. But they won't let Virgil even see his wife. She's in isolation."

"They have a lot to say about it," I said.

"The US Public Health Service that handles Indian Medicine now is all right. When the BIA ran Indian health services we lost every second baby from infant diarrhea before it reached the age of two. The Public Health Service is a big improvement. Now it's just the BIA social workers that are so mean."

Next morning Teno and I had the ninety-weight tarpaper nailed down by the time Virgil drove up with his truck filled with gray-colored dirt.

"We scrape this caliche out of the irrigation canals when we clean them every spring," he told me. "It's waterproof."

It looked like ordinary clay to me, without much humus.

Teno insisted on laying two more rows of adobe bricks on the wall along the top of the edge of the board roof to contain the clay. Instead of shoveling the caliche directly on top of the tarpaper, however, he had us cut willows from along the river for the rest of the morning, waiting on top of the roof for Jerry and me to bring him bundles of branches. He carefully spread the willow withes over the black tarpaper so that none of it was visible before he let us add the clay. It was a long day, and I slept like a child through the night.

Teno was gone again when I woke up. I wondered how the old man got along with so little sleep. I caught a couple of hatchery fish for Mac; but Teno didn't eat fish, so I made cornbread and fried some bacon for us. It was ready by the time he returned from "watching the sun rise." That and coffee was all he wanted.

After breakfast I ate a couple of apples I had picked from one of the dozen trees still alive in the orchard. I was moving from tree to tree, each morning. There were several varieties and I wanted to try them all. They were pretty wormy but they tasted fine. If I stayed the winter, I thought I could split and dry some on top of the roof and have fruit all through the year. Have to get some mosquito netting to cover the roof and protect them from the birds though, I thought. I'd lived from day to day for so long that making plans was almost scary.

Most days, Teno and I sat around drinking extra coffee and talking. Mostly, Teno talked and I listened. He had my chair, so I occupied myself with making a bench out of a piece of the leftover roof lumber. He was trying to work out in his head what had happened to his grandson. Mac disappeared as soon as I started pounding nails. He didn't like the noise.

"All the young men were taken in the draft in World War II," Teno said. "When they came back they all had drinking problems. There were laws against Indians drinking then, even off the reservation, but when they were in uniform, nobody stopped them. They had money in their pockets for the first time in their lives, too." He shook his head.

"What happened when they came back?" I asked.

"Most of them didn't stay in the pueblo long," Teno said. "They went to the big cities like Los Angeles and lived on the twenty dollars a week they got in veteran's unemployment money. That was a bad program. It was supposed to ease veterans back into civilian life, but it made it impossible for most of them ever to come back. We lost that whole generation."

"Was Roy's father in that war?"

"No, but his older brothers and cousins were. There was no one to tell Roy how to behave except his father, and he wouldn't listen to him."

"Was that unusual?" I asked, thinking of how little I listened to my own father.

"You have to understand how it is with Indians," Teno said, shaking his head. "When girls reach puberty, everybody notices, the young men especially. Pretty soon they have a baby. Then their parents find a nice man for them to marry and they move in with one of the families, usually the man's, but not always. Roy's father didn't marry his mother. Roy was her first child. Unmarried girls leave their babies with their families if they go out to work. She did."

"That sounds good," I said. "He grew up in a family."

"It used to be good," Teno said. "The girls used to be different. They grew up pretty fast. As soon as they had a baby they stopped running around at night. Everybody respected them. The young men didn't grow up until they had a house of their own and started taking an interest in religious doings."

"What's changed?" I asked.

"Well, the young men used to look after the boys coming up and keep them from getting out of hand. They'd say who could go after what girl when they were breaking them in. There wasn't much drinking because there wasn't much money and no way to get to town. There weren't a half dozen pickup trucks in the whole pueblo before WWII. No cars. There were sports, boxing, baseball and track, mostly. And, of course, girls. It was enough to keep them busy."

I thought of my own days as a teenager. We had sports, too, but we had cars and music and dancing and movies and beer, also. And, of course, girls. Sports weren't as big for me; girls and training for sports didn't mix.

"Electricity came in during the fifties," Teno continued as I nodded encouragement. "Soon every house had a radio, and the young people listened to nothing but rock and roll, Fat somebody singing Rollolo Betollo. They didn't even come out to watch the corn dances any more. And there were suddenly children everywhere. The Public Health Services brought in penicillin to fight the infant diarrhea that used to kill our babies. A few years ago I could tell you the name of every child in the pueblo, and whose family it belonged to. Children were precious because they were so hard to raise. Now I don't know one from another. They're everywhere."

Rollolo Betollo? Could that be Fats Domino and *Roll over Beethoven, make room for Bach*, I wondered. I remembered that one. "Why didn't they introduce family planning and the use of contraceptives, if they were sponsoring a population explosion?"

"The pueblos all have Catholic churches from Spanish times. The BIA was afraid of the Church."

"Was Roy married?"

"Sure. I even offered to help him build a house. Roy was different. He left his family, moved to town and worked just long enough to buy a pickup before he came back home to live. Said he got hurt and had to leave his job. His family went on welfare; he just never grew up."

"Why would someone shoot him?"

"I don't know." The question cut off the stream of talk. I'd finished the bench and was sitting on it, feeling uncomfortable with the silence. A car came by, stopped outside the gate and honked. With a feeling of relief, I got up to see what they wanted, walking down the short stretch of road that screened us from traffic.

There were two men in suits, ties and hats standing by the gate and looking at the padlock.

I was carrying my rifle. "If you were thinking about trying to open that, don't," I said.

"Are you Sergeant John J. Kilroy?" one of them asked.

"Who wants to know?" I asked.

"We're from the FBI," he responded, and took out a black leather identification wallet from his breast pocket, flashing it too fast for me to see much. "Be careful where you point that gun," he added.

"I'm always careful where I point this gun," I said. "I want to look at your ID before I answer any questions. Just pass it through the gate." I raised the 30-30 so it rested against my shoulder with the barrel pointing straight up and reached out my hand.

The man gave me the ID folder and I looked at it, then at him, before handing it back. "All right, I'm Kilroy. Now, what do you want?"

"The army's looking for you."

"I read about it in the paper. I have no responsibility to make myself available to them. Is that what this is about?"

"No. We were told we could find Teno Casaquito here. We want to talk to him."

52

"What about?"

"Look, just open the gate," the second man said impatiently.

"Do you have a warrant?" I asked.

"We just want to talk to the man," the first agent said, frowning at his associate.

"Are you Teno Casaquito?" the second man asked, looking past me.

"No savvy," Teno said. I hadn't heard him come up behind me.

"He speaks a little Spanish, no English," I lied, following Teno's lead.

"You speak Spanish?"

"Yes," I said. "I do. I'm good with languages."

"Well tell him who we are and what we want."

I did, making a simple explanation, without any editorial comment.

The second man glanced at the first and nodded almost imperceptibly. I thought probably he understood Spanish and was vouching to his companion about my role as interpreter. It would be foolish to send out a team to interview Indians surrounded by Spanish rural villages without at least one member who could speak the language. If I could figure that out, so could Teno.

"*Sí*," Teno said and turned away, walking back up the rutted path.

I opened the gate. "Sorry about the reception," I said. "I just don't want to talk to a bunch of reporters."

The second agent snorted as he passed through and I relocked the gate. I gathered that was his comment on reporters, or maybe on the possibility of their telling reporters anything.

Teno sat back down in my chair and the two agents took the bench, testing it before committing their weight to it. I thought it was a pretty good bench, but not as comfortable as the chair. If Teno was going to stay around, I thought I might have to make another chair, maybe an Adirondack armchair. I could do that.

"Tell him we want to ask about his grandson," the first agent said. We did questions and answers in which Teno told them very little. One question interested me.

"What was your grandson doing south of San Ysabel? Shouldn't he have been walking back toward the pueblo?"

It was something I wondered, too, but Teno just shrugged, "*Borracho*." That meant drunk. Well, maybe that could account for it. I doubted it.

The question, "Do you know of anyone who might have wanted to kill your son?" elicited a shake of the head.

"Did he have any enemies?" got another.

"How about you?" the agent persisted.

"Do you have any enemies that might want to hurt you by killing your grandson?"

This time Teno hesitated slightly, pursing his lips before he shook his head.

The agent said, "You sure? Maybe something to do with your religion?"

At that, Teno got up without waiting for me to interpret and walked deliberately over to chop wood for the fire. The interview was over.

"He knows something," the second agent said, glaring at me suspiciously.

"If he does, he didn't tell me," I responded.

"We have a file on him. He was making and selling wine during prohibition, all through the twenties."

"Really?" I said, amused. I would never have thought of him as a bootlegger.

"Back then he threatened a Treasury man who wanted to inspect his house. He said, in English, mind, 'You may walk in, but if you do, you're not going to walk out.' We know he's lying with that *No savvy* bullshit. Tell him so."

"He answered your questions."

"He didn't tell us squat!"

"Well, he doesn't look like he wants to tell you anything more. If you guys are ready to leave, I'll open the gate for you," and I walked down the road.

As I locked it behind them, the second man told me, "We'll have to inform the army of your whereabouts, you know."

"Yeah, you have to do that, speaking of bullshit," I said. "Next time you come, you better have a warrant."

Tonight was poker night. Maybe I'd tell them I was pulling out. But, the deed to the place rustled in my shirt as I walked back up the road. Damn. This was not a restful place.

4

I shaved before driving down to San Ysabel to the poker game at about nine. I said, "Hi," to the bartender as I passed by on my way to the door at the end of the room. He didn't acknowledge me, but he didn't try to stop me, either. Sullen bastard.

They were all there, waiting for me. "Am I late?"

"Nah," Hendley said as the others nodded hello. "We generally talk a little business before we get down to the game."

I sat between Lima and Ginwright again. I pulled out my billfold and gave Hendley five hundred dollars for my chips.

"What do I owe you for the deed?" I asked Joe Lima. He took papers from the inside pocket of his jacket, leafed through them and handed me receipts for the back taxes, the warranty and the county court filing fee. "It comes to two hundred and seventy-eight dollars," he said, "Just about what I lost last week."

"Check that stuff later," Simpson said impatiently. "I need a poker fix."

"First one-eyed jack gets the deal," Hendley said, flipping cards around the table.

I stuffed the papers Lima had given me into my shirt pocket and paid him the money l owed him. "I better do this now," I said, "while I've still got it. And thanks. If I leave, I'll sell it back to you, same price."

"You still thinking about that?" Hendley asked.

"The FBI has been around. They're going to tell the army where I am. And that means reporters," I said. "I don't have a whole lot to say about Vietnam."

"You won't need to. Your buddies are talking for you," Hendley said.

I guessed that was true, I wondered if I could stop it.

"Deal!" Simpson ordered.

I don't talk much when I play poker, nor listen very closely to what others are saying unless it pertains to the game. I watch. Simpson played the same basic game I did, but without patience when the cards ran thin. Lima never seemed to fold, enjoying the fall of the cards whether he won or lost. His smiles and frowns gave away the strength of his hand. Consequently, he lost consistently. Ginwright was canny, smiling and friendly no matter what cards he held except when his cards were exceptional. Then he went poker-faced, trying to sneak one past us. I never called him then. Phillips was all flash and no substance. He bet big on good hands and bet bigger on bad ones, trying to bluff. He wasn't at the game on this night.

The only one who played nearly at my level was Hendley, but there was an almost imperceptible narrowing of his gaze when he looked at a potentially winning hand, a killer's stare. Too bad. I had him. I play automatically, about the way I drive a car. I tend to think of other things, so that the emotions that register are not necessarily relative to the cards. Professional card players watch for the dilation of pupils as an involuntary giveaway to an opponent's hand, but these guys all wore big cowboy hats that made that impossible. I never stare, anyway. Little details are more noticeable using peripheral vision. Besides, staring could get you killed in some of the games I'd played in.

I won big. Hendley won a little and Ginwright about broke even. Simpson and Lima lost again. I was just as happy when the two of them split the last hand of showdown.

"Fourteen hundred and sixty-five lucks," I said, letting the others cash out first. "I held good cards tonight."

"Two full houses," Simpson grumbled.

"Three, actually," I corrected him.

"And even that might not be true," Hendley drawled.

I shrugged. He was right, though. I'd had two that no one called. I also had bluffed on two hands, and won. I never bluff more that three times in a game unless no one calls earlier ones. I got caught on my third try this time, and had both Simpson and Lima bet into my full houses afterwards, with inferior hands. It helps to get caught bluffing from time to time.

"What do I owe you for the house, the fence and the gate," I asked Hendley.

"Nothing. I said I was going to do it."

"I know, but I'm not a charity case. I got a back pay warrant for eight thousand bucks locked up in my glove compartment. I always pay my own way."

"Well, everybody that works for me gets ten dollars a day. It keeps bookkeeping down. I settled up through today with the Indians. Teno and his relatives put in a total of thirty-two workdays. The two men who put up your fence and gate worked a week. So that's forty-two days, say four hundred and twenty bucks. The lumber was free, but the barbed wire costs sixty dollars a thousand feet. They used three thousand feet, more or less, with posts every ten feet. Steel posts cost two dollars apiece. The gate was twenty dollars, including the posts. The lock and keys were another ten." He started adding up the numbers.

"That would be six hundred and ninety dollars," I told him, counting out the money.

"Yeah, that's right," he said, after laboriously adding columns.

"You do that sort of thing all the time?"

"Just with numbers," I said.

"Hmmm."

I figured he was thinking it had something to do with my success at poker. As far as I knew, it didn't, but it was all right for him to think so. And it might help others to explain to themselves why I won and they lost.

"How come Phillips wasn't here?" I asked casually.

"He said he didn't want to play as long as you were in the game," Hendley said without looking at me.

"He say why?"

"He implied you were cheating."

"What do you think?" I asked.

"If you were, I'd have seen you. I saw him," he added. "He was upset when you went low instead of high after he'd given you three high cards. I damn near laughed out loud."

"If you knew he cheated, why do you play with him?"

"He never tried it with us. He ain't stupid. You looked easy," he said.

It was my turn to say, "Hmmm."

I asked Ginwright for a ride to town so I could see if I could stop the guys at the VA hospital from talking to reporters about me. I could get a bus back as far as San Ysabel. My truck was hard riding, and if I had to take that down, I'd have stayed here. Ginwright had a Volvo, the six not the four.

"The four gets a little better gas mileage," he explained, "but the six is hot. I don't like to hang around."

I understood what he meant by that when we went between eighty and ninety all the way to town, without any of the swaying or bucking you might expect in a light car. It was a lot smoother than my carryall, that's for sure.

Ginwright lived on one of the streets near the University, a big old adobe on a double lot. There was a Cadillac in the other stall in the two-car garage. "My wife's," he explained. "She feels safer in a heavy car, particularly when she's carting the kids around."

It was almost as if he thought he had to explain why he had a Caddy, him being black, but part of the educated elite. I don't give a damn about stereotypes, one way or the other.

"My dad drives one," I said. "My mother has an Alpha Romeo."

He raised an eyebrow, but I didn't explain. Let him think what he wanted.

On the way down he invited me to stay overnight at his house. He claimed it was too late for visiting hours at the VA hospital. His wife was up, waiting for him, dressed in simple but elegant clothes. She was tall, thin and her hair was straight. She looked more Indian than black to me. After greeting us and making sure I was seated comfortably, she said, "Ginwright says the FBI are pushing you. Has he explained how hazardous that can be?"

"Not really," I said. I wondered if Ginwright even had a first name. I'd never heard it; even his wife called him by his last name. "I don't understand what you're referring to." Sheriff Hendley must have told Ginwright about the FBI at the poker game before I got there.

"Judge Thatcher called me earlier," Ginwright said apologetically. "He appoints me as counsel for Indians when it looks like they're about to get into serious trouble legally because I understand federal law. The FBI has to get search warrants from him and that tips him off. He must have wondered about your friend."

"I was raised on Chicago's south side," his wife said. "When Martin Luther King was killed, the FBI flooded south Chicago with brown Mexican heroin. They used the Blackstone Rangers, the area's dominant gang, as pushers, supplying it for free and telling them to make it as available in the community as they could. For a while, you could get a hit for a quarter rather than the standard five dollars. Every potential rioter was strung out for weeks on drugs and some of them never came back from that. You don't want the FBI taking a special interest in you."

"I never heard about that before," I said.

"If you were black and lived in south Chicago at the time, you would have."

"I've only been out on my own for a few weeks, long enough to be called a baby-killer and be physically attacked by protesters because I served in Vietnam," I said, "but the FBI have been unpleasant only because I have this Indian friend whose grandson was killed. They were asking him a lot of questions, and I interpreted for him. They were just doing their job, I guess."

"Flag burners are ugly enough, but they don't have a patch on the flag wavers. They run to the FBI with every complaint. Tell him," she demanded, glaring at her husband.

"She's right," Ginwright said, handing me the bourbon on the rocks I'd asked for, and a scotch and water to his wife. He had what she had. I remembered that academics drank scotch. I hoped it was as good as the bourbon, after tasting it. It was my first real drink in four years.

"Tell him," she insisted.

"The flag wavers, as she calls them, at least the local ones, seem to be members of the John Birch Society. You heard of them?"

"My father was a charter member. I'm not," I replied.

"Oh. Well, they've become pretty aggressive in the last few years, a reaction to the Vietnam protesters. They hate hippies in particular and generally disapprove of anyone not like themselves."

"My father told me to shave and get a haircut when he carne to see me in the hospital," I said. "He seemed upset that there were black people in my ward. Said he'd have a word with the commanding officer. Said it fairly loud."

"Did it cause you trouble?"

"Nah. All the guys in my ward were from my prison camp. We're pretty tight. I did get kidded some."

"Birchers have complained to the University administration about a black man teaching Constitutional Law," Mrs. Ginwright said, broodingly.

"Does wonders for my image with all the future ACLU lawyers among my students," Ginwright responded lightly.

"They're not on the Board of Regents," she retorted.

"No, but I'm up for tenure. It's too late for anyone to interfere with the process now."

"You know the law doesn't apply the same way to black people as it does to whites," his wife said, anger edging her voice. "The FBI alerts the Birchers that you're obstructing justice and you can kiss tenure good-bye!"

"I'm not obstructing justice! At the request of a distinguished federal judge, I represent Indian clients pro bono. We almost never go to trial. No one's going to know anything," he said. "Federal grand juries are pretty closemouthed affairs." He looked to me for support.

This seemed to be a continuing argument, begun the Lord knows how long ago. What did he want me to say?

"Sheriff Simpson is going to be walking point on this particular investigation, as I understand it," I told Ginwright's wife. "The killing occurred off the reservation. The FBI has no jurisdiction. They're just nosing around. And, no one has been arrested, so your husband isn't involved in any way."

"The FBI doesn't need a reason. They'll invent one if they want to," she muttered.

"You sound like a lawyer," Ginwright said to me, smiling widely.

"I was in law school; I never finished," I said.

"Well, I'd grade that answer A plus," he said.

His wife was too gracious to press me further. I had the feeling there would be more discussion after I left. When Ginwright's wife independently invited me to stay over, I accepted. I'd stuffed a clean t-shirt, shorts and socks in my shaving kit, thinking I'd be spending the night in Albuquerque, so I would be presentable at breakfast. In the middle of the night the light was turned on in my room, and I woke up to see Ginwright was standing in the half-open door, dressed in red pajamas.

I sat up in bed and stared as he asked, "You okay?"

"Yeah," I said.

"You yelled."

"Must have had a nightmare," I said. "Some of the guys I came back with are doing that. Sorry." I didn't even remember dreaming. I apologized when I came down to breakfast in the morning.

Ginwright waved it off and said, "I just got a telephone call from Simpson. He's coming by to pick you up. Says he has to talk to you for some reason."

I ate breakfast with Ginwright and his family, his wife and two funny kids. Ginwright was the object of teasing by everyone but me. Maybe they were showing off, but I got the impression of a very solid family. Breakfast was hot oatmeal, toast and jam, orange juice, and milk for the kids, coffee for the adults. As a guest, I was offered other choices, but I like oatmeal.

Mrs. Ginwright drove the kids to school and Ginwright waited with me for Simpson to show up. "My wife was right about the FBI," he said grimly, after she was gone. "You want to watch those bastards." He took a sip of coffee and continued, "It doesn't matter what they say they're going to do. They pretty much do what they want. And they don't release their files even to federal courts, so you can't prove anything against them."

I'd grown up believing the FBI was the one incorruptible agency in the US government, maybe in the world. At Simpson's request, I'd tried to shield Teno from them without giving the matter much thought, and was surprised at the hostility I'd encountered from the agents who came to see him. Now Ginwright was saying they were typical, like authority figures everywhere that I'd encountered. It was depressing.

When Simpson came for me, it was just more of the same. "We have to stop by the federal building. Those sons-of-bitches have picked up Virgil Tewa for the murder of Roy Casaquito," he said over a cup of coffee in Mrs. Ginwright's spotless kitchen.

"And what sons-of-bitches are those?" Ginwright asked. "There are so many out there." He brought a cookie jar to the table and offered us round, fat sugar cookies. I took two.

"The sneaking FBI. Who did you think, the tooth fairies?"

"No, actually," Ginwright drawled, "I thought maybe the US Marshal's office."

"Nah, the marshal would have touched base with me before he started throwing his weight around in my county," Simpson said grimly. "Only J. Edgar's boys act like consummate assholes."

"That the Virgil I know?" I asked.

"Sure. Only pueblo Indian anyone knows named Virgil. Some teacher with a taste for the classics named him when he started school. Virgil is a war captain this year. When there's trouble in the pueblo, he's called to handle it. He took Roy down last week after he came home drunk and hit the old man, Teno, when he got bawled out. Virgil tied Roy up and left him in the yard all night to get sober. The deer flies woke him up at dawn for breakfast . . . their breakfast. Virgil came by about ten and sat on Roy for an hour, explaining what kind of behavior he expected of him in the future, before untying him. The boy was crying like a baby when Virgil released him."

"Why would Virgil kill the boy? He obviously had a different way of handling him."

"Virgil came home from the Korean War decorated. He'd been in heavy combat in the Marines. That's why they chose him for war captain; he's not afraid of killing, if he has to."

"But that's the point, isn't it?" Ginwright insisted. "He didn't have to."

"Well you see that and I see that, but Hoover's boys don't. Hoover believes that the biggest mistake ever made was Truman's desegregating the

61

army, and his boys better see it his way. Hoover says putting guns into the hands of black men and teaching them it's all right to shoot white men is going to lead to revolution."

"I'm familiar with the argument, but then Virgil is not one of us blacks, is he?" Ginwright said.

"You think blacks and commies are the only folks J. Edgar Hoover has a hard-on for? He doesn't like anyone too different from himself. He doesn't like women. He doesn't like Jews. He doesn't like Mexicans. He doesn't like unions. He purely hates hippies. If he hasn't got around to Indians before, it's only because he hasn't thought of it."

"Does Virgil have a lawyer?" Ginwright asked.

"How in the name of J. Edgar's silk dresses would I know that?" Simpson growled. "I just found out about the arrest this morning. That's one of the things I plan to ask, down at the federal building."

"Excuse me for a minute. I want to make a phone call," Ginwright said. "Help yourself to more coffee and cookies. I won't be long."

"What's a war captain?" I asked after Ginwright left.

"When the Spanish came into the southwest in the sixteenth century, they brought their priests with them. The priests objected to the native religion being practiced, so the Spanish authorities insisted on imposing Spanish-type village officials on the existing Indian governments, which were run by religious leaders. The religious leaders didn't mind. They just appointed the secular officials and escaped having to deal with the Spanish personally. The system still exists. Every year new public officials are chosen. This year it was Virgil."

"The war captains are like policemen?"

"It's more than that. They guard the pueblo from witches, too."

"Oh," I said, reaching for another cookie, "and if Roy was a witch, Virgil would have to deal with him in that capacity."

"Yeah, and they kill witches. At least that's the theory the FBI is going on, anyway, according to the phone call I had this morning with the area director. There has been a raft of killings recently, young men found dead on the highway, hit and run victims. Your finding the bullet hole changed that."

"You're saying I'm responsible for Virgil's being in jail?"

"Well, maybe not quite that."

"Close enough. What's his bail?"

"He hasn't even been arraigned, yet. The grand jury won't be convened until later this week."

"I reached Judge Thatcher," Ginwright said returning to us. "He'll have jurisdiction. He's just appointed me Virgil's attorney and I'm on my way to file a writ of habeas corpus. The damned FBI will leave him in jail till Christmas without a charge if we let them."

"I'm coming," I said, and Simpson slurped down the rest of his coffee and rose to join us, ready to go. He hadn't bothered to take off his big gray Stetson. In fact, I'd never seen him without it. He wore it to the poker table, too. I wondered if he were bald, or merely following cowboy custom.

"I'll run you down," Simpson said. "You'll never find a place to park. Besides, I want to see this."

When we reached the judge's office, we found the federal district attorney waiting for us.

"Judge Thatcher notified me you were on your way," he said. "I'm the DA, O'Brian," introducing himself to Ginwright. He offered his hand to Ted and Simpson but only nodded to me. I was not dressed for court. "What's your interest in this case?" he challenged me.

"This is Jack Kilroy, a friend of Virgil Tewa's," Ginwright told him.

"That's who you are? The hero? It's an honor to meet you," O'Brian told me. This time I got the handshake. I didn't say anything. I was related to half the Irish politicians in Philadelphia. I recognized the type.

"Seriously, I'm sorry your friend is in trouble, but these people have to learn they can't go around taking the law into their own hands."

"By 'these people,' you mean Indians?" Ginwright asked.

"Ah, yes. You know how they are."

"Taking the law into their own hands. Is that how they are?" Ginwright asked.

"Well, yes. Didn't they tell you? He was acting as village policeman and went too far."

"Did he confess to that?"

"Well, no. He even claims he wasn't in town when it happened."

"You check on his alibi?"

"No need. It was ridiculous."

A secretary interrupted us. "The judge will see you now." She walked before us to a paneled door and opened it for us. Seated at a desk was an old man with white hair, dressed in a dark suit and tie. He glanced in approval at

Ginwright, similarly garbed, and the sheriff with his bolo tie and neat western outfit. He glared at me in my jeans and blue shirt, but didn't say anything, merely waving us to chairs arranged before his desk. O'Brian took his seat in a chair beside the desk.

"You have the paper?" the judge asked.

Ginwright took a printed legal form from his briefcase and handed it over. The judge glanced briefly at it and signed it.

"After he's indicted by the grand jury and arraigned, he'll have to come up with bail."

"He has no money," Ginwright said.

"He's a flight risk," O'Brian said. "He could get on a bus to L.A. and hang out with the other Indians at Sixth and Main, and we'd never see him again."

"I've got a warrant for a little over eight thousand dollars," I said. "I'll sign it over to the court and take him home with me. He won't run away."

I handed over the warrant to the judge and he raised an eyebrow. "John J. Kilroy . . . I've been reading about you in the papers, young man. The army wanted to give you another medal."

"If they'd do it quietly, I wouldn't mind," I said.

"I see. I think I know your father. Met him in Washington when I was a senator."

"He's spent a lot of time there," I admitted. My father had been a well-paid lobbyist before he became a congressman. It was hard to tell from the judge's manner what he thought of my father. The judge would play good poker.

"This will be sufficient to secure a bond," he said, handing me back the warrant. "Bring it along to the arraignment. In the meantime, I'll release the man into your custody."

O'Brian didn't argue with the judge. Outside, he told us, "They're holding him at the county jail. I'll call down and have him waiting for you." He gave me a calculating look as if he knew something I didn't know.

"What was that for?" I asked when we were back in the car.

"He figures you're not aware that when you secure a bond, the bondsman takes a stiff fee. If the judge sets bail at eighty thousand, the warrant will cover only your ten percent share of the risk. The bondsman will get his cut from that just for issuing the bond, depending on how long the bond runs."

"He's wrong. I knew that," I said. "So, O'Brian thought I didn't and let me walk into it." I shook my head. "Did he think I'd pull out if he told?"

"Probably. He would."

Virgil was glad to see us. He insisted on riding in the back of the pickup when there wasn't room for all of us in front.

"I'll ride back there with him," I said. "I want to talk to him."

While Simpson drove Ginwright up to the university, I sat in the back with Virgil.

"Thanks for getting me out," he said.

"It was my fault you were in. I pointed out the bullet hole in Roy and insisted it couldn't have been a simple hit and run."

"I told them I was in Denver the night Roy was killed," Virgil said. "They didn't believe me. I flew up to get my baby and bring it home."

"In that BIA plane Lou Elwood told me about?"

"Yes. All they had to do was call and ask, but they didn't listen past my telling them I'd flown up. Why would they think I'd tell a dumb lie like that?"

"This the FBI?"

"Yeah."

"We'll tell Ginwright and Simpson. I think we're going to embarrass somebody. Judge Thatcher signed your papers. He doesn't seem to me to be the kind of man you involve in something this sloppy."

When we reached the university, I had Virgil tell Ginwright and Simpson what he'd told me. Their reactions were as I thought they might be, Simpson disgusted and Ginwright outraged.

"I'll check the alibi and get the charge dismissed. It won't go to the grand jury," Simpson said. "I think you ought to tell the judge about it, though," he told Ginwright.

"Don't worry. As soon as you've finished, let me know. I'm going to burn some ass."

On the way back to the pueblo, Simpson told Virgil why the FBI thought he might be involved in Roy's death. "They might light on the other war captain, now that you're cleared."

"Worse, they might go after Teno," Virgil said.

"Why?"

"War captains don't kill witches. They never did. It used to be that war captains put on the masks of the twin war gods, Mou-say-we and O-yo-yeh-we, if someone had to be killed. It used to be they'd cut off his head and kick it to the nearest sacred spring. When a man wears a mask like that, the mask wakes up and the god takes over. The only person who can make a man put on the mask of a war god is the Underworld Society chief. In the old stories, Badger dug a hole to lead the people out of the underworld, so now a man is chosen from the Badger clan to watch over the people."

"I thought the town priest, the cacique, did that," Simpson said.

"He does, but he is a holy man. He can't have anything brought to him that might disturb his heart. He's like a peace priest. The Badger clan man who is chief of the Underworld Society is the war priest. This is all supposed to be secret. I shouldn't be talking about it."

"Why are you?" I asked.

"As sheriff I know a lot. I have friends in the pueblo. But the FBI doesn't have any friends. Some one is talking to them. They're going to say that Teno is the chief of the Underworld Society, the war priest. They're going to tell the FBI that Teno ordered the killing."

It didn't leave much to say.

Simpson dropped Virgil and me at my gate. "I'll tell Teno what happened," he said and drove off toward the pueblo.

We found Lou Elwood waiting for us, talking to her cat. She was in my chair with the cat in her lap. The cat didn't bother to look embarrassed. I'm definitely going to have to make another chair.

"Virgil!" she cried. "You're out!"

"Kilroy came after me," he said simply.

"He shouldn't have been jailed in the first place. The FBI never bothered to check his alibi," I said.

"Do you know what they've been doing?" she asked. "Nurse Wilson is mad enough to quit over it."

"What?" I asked as I made lunch. I unwrapped the cheese and the bread and pulled three long-necked Coors from the stream where they'd been cooling.

As we ate, Lou told us that social workers from the BIA in Albuquerque had come up with the two FBI men and were threatening to remove whole families from the federal welfare roles if they refused to cooperate with the FBI.

"That has to be a violation of their civil rights," I said. "Ginwright is already mad about the way they've been acting. This will send him up in smoke."

"Nurse Wilson offered to speak for them, to protest. They said no. They said the BIA would wait until everything had blown over and then remove the families from the roles for some other reason. They can't risk it."

"The BIA is always here," Virgil said in explanation. "The Indians are always here. White people who want to help come and go. The BIA just waits the white people out and then does what it wants. It's happened before."

"Can you find out who the BIA official is who authorized this threatening? Maybe something unpleasant can happen to him for some other reason," I said. I wasn't sure what I meant myself, but I felt something should be done.

"I already know," Lou said. "He runs the place. His name is Ted Phillips, the superintendent. He seems to have taken a personal interest in the case.

"I know him," I said. "Why is he helping the FBI? He should be trying to shield the Indians from this sort of thing."

"He has a bad heart," Virgil said. "He hates Indians. He says we're stupid and dirty and lazy, even to our faces."

"Keith and Kevin are with them, too," Lou said. "Keith wants to join the FBI after he gets his law degree. Kevin is talking about changing his major to law. Archeology is too hard, and it takes too much time to get qualified to work professionally. Even then, jobs are scarce."

"I'm surprised the FBI men let them hang around," I said. "They didn't look that friendly to me."

"The boys know a lot of people in town. They're acting as guides. It was the FBI men who told them who you are. The boys are the ones who told the newspapers."

A wave of irritation swept over me. "Why did that seem to be a good idea to them?"

"They don't like you. They think if you are bothered enough, you'll run. They've been bragging about it."

I took a deep breath. "They'd have been right a few days ago," I admitted. "About now, though, I'm getting a little tired of being pushed. I think I'll stay."

Lou and Virgil looked at each other and smiled. I pretended I didn't see them.

5

*E*arly next morning Teno came by for coffee. "Okay with you if we harvest your apples and take them over to Hopi country to trade?" he asked.

I was peeling a long aspen sapling for a flagpole. As long as I was settling in, I decided I might as well fly the flag. "Sure, but they're wormy."

"It don't much matter," he said. "The Hopi cut them in quarters and dry them on their roofs. They eat them in the winter time."

"I'll help you pick," I volunteered. Dumb. I knew better. I growled to myself as I wondered how long it would take, while I tied the flag to the tall skinny aspen pole and lashed the pole to a convenient six-foot stump. I'd have to bring it down at night. It took four days, even with Teno's whole family working, for there were more trees scattered out in the brush than I'd seen. I was doing a lot less fishing than I'd counted on and had a lot more company than I really wanted, but I got the orchard cleared of brush in the process. Not a bad deal, I guessed.

We filled Teno's truck several times every day. The loads were taken to the village where they were to be sorted.

"We'll keep some for our own use," Teno told me. "I'll bring you back some dried fruit later on."

I'd wondered about that. I said to Virgil when the rest had left for the night the first day, "I thought Teno said his truck was broken."

"It was out of gas. If it won't run, it's broke, no matter what the cause," he explained.

I guess that was one way of looking at it.

There were enough spare boards to make an Adirondack chair and evenings I worked on building, using only my Swedish Mora knife and my axe. Virgil watched closely and made comments from time to time, wondering why I used wooden pegs rather than screws. I said that iron was scarce in pioneer times when the chair was invented and I wanted it to be an authentic reproduction. I don't know if he understood what I was getting at, but he didn't question me further.

The house construction process commenced again with Virgil, loud-mouth Jerry, Teno and me working. Virgil and Teno set the double-glazed windows in the south wall of the house with Jerry as mud man. I built a bedstead in one corner of the big room. I made it four feet wide, big enough for two people, according to the Indians, and much to their amusement. They offered to tell unattached females of their acquaintance about it.

"Better tell them it's not all that comfortable, unless you're used to sleeping on the ground," I said. "The hospital beds were too soft for me after Vietnam."

"Teno sleeps on a goatskin outside on the ground in good weather, just like he does here," Virgil said. "Most of us in Santa Cala sleep on the floor on pallets we unroll at night. Almost nobody has beds. We have no room for them. This is luxury."

"Yeah, well, I won't be using it for a while. For now the hammock is fine. Maybe by this winter I'll change my mind about the company. I'll let you know."

They thought that was funny, reciting it to one another and commenting on it in their own language. I don't know how anyone who spent much time around Indians could think of them as lacking in humor. They laughed all the time.

The honking at the gate announced visitors. I'd given a key to Lou, so it wasn't her. I didn't hurry on the way down to the gate.

"Tell them *no savvy*," Teno called after me. I turned my head and Virgil just grinned. Even so, I knew neither of them were interested in talking to anyone but family members.

I soon saw that these people weren't that. There were two cars and a TV van: reporters. I stayed around the bend in the trail and watched, shifting my rifle in my hand. They kept honking so I shot the rifle into the air. That silenced them. One of the car doors opened and a man got out in full uniform, an officer with rows of medals on his chest. He walked briskly to the gate and rattled it, calling out, "Sergeant Kilroy!"

Oh, hell. I shouldered the rifle and marched to the gate, standing at attention, saying, "Yes, Sir." It was a chicken colonel. I hadn't seen many of those in Nam. Two other officers joined him, a first lieutenant and a captain, aides, likely. The driver stayed in the car, and I figured him for an enlisted man.

"Open this gate," the colonel ordered. People got out of the other car and came to watch, some with cameras, snapping pictures.

"Rather not, sir," I replied.

"Do it anyway. This won't take long, and I'm under orders."

"I'll come out," I said, and proceeded to do that, shutting the gate behind me.

"What's the piece for?" he asked, eyeing my rifle.

"Habit, sir. Hard to break."

"It's a good set-up for filming," one of the reporters said. "The barred gate is symbolic of the prison and the gun is soldier-like. He needs a hat, though."

"I don't like hats," I said, objecting to the whole thing.

"This is special, a Stetson, complements of Channel 4." One of his associates came up with a hat box and the speaker opened it, handing me a new cowboy hat like Simpson's, but black. It had a silver band around it and looked expensive. It also fit.

"You can keep it after the interview," the reporter suggested.

It was a good-looking hat. "Okay."

Two men in the van got out and set up a television camera. One of them retreated back inside but the other aimed the camera at the colonel and me. "We're ready," he announced.

The lieutenant opened a briefcase and handed the colonel a sheet of paper. He glanced at it and looked keenly at me, shaking his head. "Don't you have a uniform, Sergeant?" he asked.

"No, sir," I said. "I didn't figure I'd have an occasion to wear one again."

"We can take him into town and have this done right," the captain remarked, not speaking to me.

"No, sir," I said, "I'm not going anywhere."

"Your country is conferring a signal honor on you, Sergeant!" he retorted, not appreciating my comment. "The least you can do is take it seriously."

"On the way up you probably saw the flag I fly," I said. "I take it seriously."

I glanced at the ribbons on the captain's chest. There wasn't one for Vietnam. "You weren't there, so you don't know," I said to him. "And if you don't know, I'm not about to let you tell me about how I should feel."

Before the captain could retort, as he obviously had a mind to, the colonel cut him off. "That will do! Please stand at attention, Sergeant, while I read this."

I grounded the butt of my rifle and stood straight while the officers at his side stiffened, the captain red in the face from suppressed anger. The colonel read:

"It is the pleasure of the President of the United States and Commander-in-Chief of the Armed Forces to bestow the Silver Star medal upon Sergeant John J. Kilroy for conspicuous gallantry. At the risk of his own life, Sergeant Kilroy led a revolt against his Vietnamese army prison guards, overcoming and killing them and leading fifty-seven fellow prisoners through a hundred and ten miles of jungle across enemy lines to the safety of American forces, without the loss of a single life."

He handed me the citation. It was signed, "President Lyndon Johnson." The lieutenant found a dark blue leather case in his bag and gave it to the colonel. It reminded me of a nurse working with a doctor engaged in some major surgery. The colonel opened it and looked at it closely for a moment as if he hadn't seen one up close before. Then he pinned it on my blue work shirt, shaking his head and frowning. Obviously he disapproved of medalling men in civilian clothes. He then handed me the case, saluted smartly and stepped back.

"Congratulations, Sergeant," he said, and turned on his heel, leading his fellow officers back to the car, leaving me standing at attention. Ass-hole. The driver had turned the khaki colored car around in the narrow road, and they left me with the cameras and reporters.

"How does it feel to be a hero?" I was asked by one of the reporters.

"I wouldn't know," I said. "All the heroes I ever saw were dead."

It went on. There were repeated requests to be let inside the compound, but I refused as nicely as I could, saying I was sleeping in a hammock and cooking over a campfire while I was fixing up an old one-room house for the winter. There was little to see, and that was a mess.

"Your father is an officer in the John Birch Society and you're flying the flag," one reporter said disagreeably. "Are you a member of the John Birch Society?"

"If I were, it would be my business," I said. "I've been out of touch. Is there a necessary connection between displaying the flag and the Birchers?"

"All the super-patriots like them are flag nuts."

"Well, I don't even know what a super-patriot is," I said.

"A super-patriot thinks the Vietnam war is not only necessary to keep Asia from going communist but should be continued until victory has been achieved."

"And you don't?" I asked.

"Jesus, no!"

"Did you serve?"

"Do you take me for an idiot?" the man asked, offended.

" I ask only because if you weren't there, you don't have a valid opinion, as far as I' m concerned."

"Well, my opinion is that anybody who gets a medal for baby-killing is as low as they come."

"Gee, and here I am with a rifle in my hand. If you think I'm capable of killing babies what do you think prevents me from shooting one into your fat mouth?" I was suddenly angry again. I'd started out that statement just being sarcastic and I finished it by snapping the lever on the rifle to crank a bullet into the firing chamber. Thank God I resisted the impulse to point it at the fool. As it was, he cringed. I laughed.

"A few years ago I'd have walked away from you," I said. "That's never going to happen again, for what it's worth, I never killed any civilians, let alone babies, that I'm aware of. I was on the perimeter line on the Cambodian border, assigned the most dangerous of duties, for mouthing off. I had a lousy attitude toward military service, and I still have. I never met an officer for whom I had any respect, but I was a good soldier in spite of it. I did my duty, and I take remarks like yours personally. I'll be glad to put this rifle down if you want to back up your words."

"Hey, hey!" one of his mates yelled and another, "What's the matter with you?"

Teno put an end to the occasion by tramping solidly down to the gate and telling me in Spanish that he and "Geronimo" needed help to hang the door. He deflected questions by shouting "*No savvy*" all the way back up the trail.

"You heard him. I have to go back to work now," I said. "Much obliged for the hat," I said as I opened and shut the gate, locking it behind me, ignoring other questions and comments that were shouted to me.

I found the door had been hung without my help and that Teno, Jerry and Virgil were sitting and drinking my beer. They'd opened one for me.

Teno was in my camp chair, again. "Nice hat," Teno said. Virgil just grinned, saluting me with his bottle.

"Nice medal," Jerry added.

I unpinned it and placed it back in its case, folding the citation and fitting it in as well.

"Your name really Geronimo?" I asked, taking a long drink of the beer. "What kind of name is that for a Pueblo Indian?"

"I told you. I'm part Apache," he answered dead-pan, which Teno thought funny, shouting, "Geronimo," as if he were about to jump out of an airplane.

"And that part would be your mouth?" I asked.

He grinned. "My Apache relatives hear that, you be in trouble," he said. "They always after me to live up to my great grandfather." I thought he was probably kidding. Hard to say for sure.

Mac came out and sat at my feet before beginning a ritual bath. That was his way of letting me know it was time to catch a fish for his supper. He never begged. I carried my beer over to the truck and put the medal in the glove compartment along with my discharge paper, my deed, the receipts Lima had given me, the title to my truck and the warrant for eight thousand dollars the judge had returned to me. Something new every day.

I took the beer and my fly rod down to the river, with Mac close behind. I was using a number ten gray hackle yellow dry fly as a lure. There was an old log with one end in the water that I'd been favoring where I could stand and cast upstream. Mac waited on the bank until I snagged a fish and brought it over to him, flopping madly. It was one of the rainbow trout the hatchery truck had dumped. I noticed the colors were darkening and the fish was livelier than ones I'd caught earlier. They'd be cleaned of hatchery taste and ready to eat in a day or two.

Mac made no distinction between one fish and another, interested only in that they were alive when he pounced. He pounced on this one as if it were the first fish he'd ever seen. I tugged on it, hoping to disengage my fly, but Mac took it as a challenge and backed away from me with the fish in his mouth, growling. He then pinned it with his paw and tore at it, leaving me the head and the backbone when he was through.

I unhooked the carcass and swished the fly back and forth in the air to dry it before letting it settle on the water along the far bank again. This time a fish struck on the first cast. I played it a while for the fun of it before bringing it over to Mac, who was still waiting. He was a two-fish cat. He eyed me suspiciously as if he expected me to try to sneak this one away from him, too, but I ignored him, only watching him out of the corner of my eye. He scratched dirt over the half-eaten fish before he stalked off, back to the camp, and I followed. Lou must have arrived. I noticed that Jerry had left.

She and Virgil were sitting on my bench talking to Teno, when I returned. Mac was washing his face again, sitting next to her where she could reach out and pet him from time to time. He didn't beg for pets, either. He accepted them as his due.

Lou smiled at me, briefly, but said, "The FBI is looking for Teno. One of his sons told me they've loaded the pickup with apples. He wants to leave for Hopi country tomorrow early."

Teno grunted in approval.

"Keith and Kevin are telling them that Teno may be down here," she went on. "I've been trying to get him to hide."

"Do they have a warrant for his arrest?" I asked.

"I don't know."

"If they have, I'll let them in and Teno can hide then."

"The reporters told the boys that an Indian was staying here."

"So. Virgil is here. He's an Indian." I was leaning up against the cottonwood as we talked, but I held out a cautioning hand when I heard a sharp "pong," followed shortly by another.

"Someone's cut my fence," I whispered. Teno was out of my chair and into the brush along the river in a moment. Virgil was about to join him, but I whispered, "Stay, and you, Lou. You sit in Teno's chair and take his beer. Pretend we're unaware of them."

They were lousy woodsmen. I could hear them breaking brush as they attempted to sneak up on us. I reached for Lou's guitar and strummed a few cords to give them some cover for the racket they were making, before entertaining my guests with my private version of "Red River Valley."

Lou broke into applause, saying, "Hey, you're really good!" as the two FBI men came around opposite sides of the cabin, guns drawn.

"Where is he?" one of them demanded, the mean one.

I tried to look surprised and succeeded only in looking angry, because that's what I was. "You two sons-of-bitches are trespassing!" I said.

Mac arched his back, his tail as big around as a baseball bat. He actually hissed.

"We have a warrant for the arrest of Teno Casaquito," the blond agent said, with a slight lisp, pointing his gun at Mac. "Is that wild cat yours?"

"He's mine!" Lou said, scooping up the cat. Mac wasn't having any of that. He struggled free and made for the willows. Some watch-cat.

"The warrant, let me see it," I demanded, holding out my hand.

"Where is he?"

"Teno? Do you see him? Give me that warrant," I demanded, hanging Lou's guitar by its strap on a tree peg.

"And point that damned gun someplace else."

"He's not here? We were told an Indian was living here."

"My friend, Virgil, is staying with me for a few days," I said, nodding at him.

"As soon as Sheriff Simpson gets the stupid charges of yours dismissed, he'll be going home."

Virgil still had his hands in the air, looking no happier about the guns than I felt.

"You have a strange affinity for criminals," the dark agent sneered, putting his gun back in his shoulder holster and taking out a warrant for me to see. His partner kept his pistol drawn, but pointed it up in the air as he looked suspiciously around him.

"And you have strange ideas of who constitutes a criminal," I retorted, scanning the document quickly.

"This warrant is not for here. It covers Santa Cala Pueblo. This is private land."

"We're in hot pursuit."

"Hot pursuit, my ass. You're out of line, and you know it. I'm going to make a formal protest to your superiors through my attorney. Now, how did you get onto my land?"

"We cut the fence," the dark one said sullenly. "We had reason to believe you were harboring a wanted man. I still think that."

"Cut my fence?" I asked raising my voice in outrage, as if it were new information. The outrage was real enough. "You can't do that! And I don't give a rat's ass what you think. After arresting Virgil, here, without cause and then this, I don't think your boss will care either. I'll have my lawyer complain to my congressman. You can try explaining it to him."

"Come on, Barr, let's get out of here," the dark one said sourly. "We'll be back, smart-ass."

"I'll be here. You cut my fence again and I'll be waiting. This time I'll be the one with the gun." I led the way down the path to the gate and opened it for them. The cut fence was right at the gate, the second and third strands from the top. I glared from it to the agents, but they left without further comment, indeed, without even looking at me again.

I tried attaching the loose wires to the post next to the cut and was joined by Virgil, saying, "You need a fence stretcher for this. Teno has one. We'll fix it later."

"I'm going to get a 'No Trespassing' sign to hang here," I muttered.

"A five-strand fence sort of gets that idea across," Lou drawled. She was holding Mac again and soothing him. The cat still looked upset. I wondered how she had coaxed him out.

"I borrowed some milk," she said in answer to the question she must have thought I wanted to ask. "He likes something to drink after supper, even if supper is raw fish."

If she could read me that easy, I wouldn't be playing much poker with her. And I'd better watch what else I'd been thinking.

Another voice, "Which way they go?" It was Teno. He'd sneaked up on me again.

"Toward town," I answered, leaving the wire repair for later, like Virgil had suggested. "I thought you'd high-tailed it out of here." Heading back to the camp, I thought maybe I could beat him to my chair. I'd figured without Lou. She took it as her right while waiting for Teno to roll up his goatskin.

"I got a doin's tonight. I'll leave for Hopi country tomorrow," he said. A "doin's" sounded like some kind of religious meeting. He was not ordinarily vague in speech.

"I've got a doin's, too," I said. "It's poker night."

Teno laughed his high, wheezy laugh and Virgil said, "Teno will make a prayer stick for you down in the kiva. You'll win big."

"If I do, I'll split with him." I wondered if he'd hold me to it.

Everyone but Phillips was waiting for me at poker that night when I opened the door into the tack room from the bar. I was greeted like a friend. "Saw you on television," Hendley said. "You looked good. Nice hat." I was wearing it.

"I like the band," Joe Lima said. "Like to trade?" His Stetson had a simple tooled leather band. It was a complement. It was also the first time he'd ever spoken to me other than to say hello and to hand me the receipts for my land. "Makes you look like a lawyer," he added with a sly glance at Ginwright. That wasn't supposed to be a complement, I guessed.

Hendley read it the same way. "Don't mind Joe," he said. "He don't like lawyers on principle."

"Actually, I thought about being one before I went off to Nam," I said, "but I decided I didn't want to. Too much arguing all the time. I like a quiet life."

"As the bard said, 'Kill all the lawyers,'" Lima murmured.

Ginwright laughed, "I might have agreed with you if I hadn't found constitutional law to be so interesting. But you're right, if I didn't have money of my own, it wouldn't have been possible for me to specialize in it. The people who need your services never have money."

"Like Indians?"

"Like Indians," he agreed.

"Are you counsel for the Santa Cala?" I asked.

"I'm counsel for Virgil Tewa and Teno Casaquito as individuals. Judge Thatcher says that the old men have formally instructed them to act for the Santa Cala."

"I see." I did, too. Teno was the pueblo war priest and Virgil the war captain, officials selected to deal with the outside. I wondered if Ginwright knew that.

"We going to play poker or are we going to talk?" Simpson asked. Strange man. He was good humored except when he was playing poker. He almost gave the impression of doing it to punish himself except that his style of play was so aggressive. He seemed to push marginal hands even harder than good ones. I'd already learned to avoid betting against him if he appeared at all affable.

"I feel I must warn you," I said, as I looked at my first hand. "Teno is in the kiva tonight. Said he was going to make a prayer stick for me. I promised him half my winnings."

Simpson looked at me sharply, but the others just grinned or shook their heads. Was Simpson as superstitious as all that? I wondered.

I won that hand and the next two before I folded a flush that didn't make. When we cashed in at the end of the night I'd won better than sixteen hundred dollars, my highest take yet.

"That's eight for me and eight for Teno," I remarked.

"Teno won't keep it long, with his legal bills," Hendley said with a glance at Ginwright.

Ginwright laughed ruefully. "If I'd known he was in partnership with our local shark, I'd never had taken him on pro bono."

"They don't have him yet," I said.

"Where's he hiding?" Hendley asked.

"Wait," Ginwright said. "I'm an officer of the court. I don't want to hear this."

"Neither do I," Simpson agreed.

"Well, you won't hear it from me," I said. "What I know is that the FBI cut my fence and snuck up on us with guns drawn looking for him before I came down here. They didn't find him. They also didn't have a proper warrant," I added.

"Cut your fence?" Simpson asked sharply. "The one thing you don't do in this country is cut fence. Shooting a man caught cutting fence is justifiable homicide for western juries."

"No warrant?" Ginwright asked, just as sharply.

"Their warrant covered Santa Cala Pueblo. They said they were in hot pursuit. They were lying."

"I won't ask how you know, but it isn't necessary. I'm going to register a complaint. Same two agents?"

"Yeah. Their names were Simon Padilla and Donald Barr. I got them off their IDs."

"Those two sons-of-bitches!" Simpson muttered, recognizing the names. My opinion exactly.

It was raining when we left the bar. The same little knot of Indians I'd seen before was standing out under the bare light bulb over the back door. There seemed to be some kind of argument going on, which quieted down when we started up our cars to drive to our separate homes. Simpson may have had a benign reputation among the Indians, but he was still the sheriff.

The rain came down in a steady sheet, no wind, but huge drops of cold water. I got wet just walking to my car, and wetter unlocking and locking my gate.

There was light in the window of my half-glass front door. Virgil had moved inside to get out of the downpour. He opened the door for me when I parked just outside. I almost stepped on Mac while getting out of the truck as he streaked into the house from wherever he'd been crouching. Virgil had tossed my hammock and bedroll on the bunk. I saw he'd unrolled his before the fire in the corner fireplace that Sofie, Teno's wife, had built. The blaze threw welcome heat into the chill air, burning board scraps stacked on end, leaning against the back of the fireplace. Mac was sitting on the bed, washing his face.

"I brought in both the chair and the bench," he said. "The bench will warp if left out in the rain." He eyed my rifle, but didn't say anything. He'd become used to seeing me with it. I'd pulled it out from under the truck seat.

"You saw the storm coming?"

"Sure. Teno is in the kiva, asking for rain."

"Not full time," I said. "He won eight hundred dollars at the poker table."

"Eight hundred dollars! He's never seen that much money at one time in his life."

"It will be my turn to laugh when I see his face," I said.

Virgil looked troubled. "He wouldn't ask for something like luck for playing poker, but if he said he was going to make you a prayer stick, he did it."

"Well, I thought about that while I played, and I won. I guess he won't refuse the money?"

"Eight hundred dollars? No, I guess not."

I put the rifle on the wooden bunk bed and stripped off my wet things, hanging them on pegs pounded into cracks between the adobe bricks that formed the wall. Unrolling my sleeping bag I slipped in to warm up. Mac joined me pawing at the canvas to move my legs into a conformation he approved of, as was his habit. I saw Virgil shake his head in disapproval. Lou had told me that Indians don't let animals into their houses. Witches can take animal forms. I was asleep before Mac settled down.

I was awakened by gunshots. I sat up and scooched into the corner of the bunk, my rifle in my hands.

"It's up by the bridge," Virgil spoke out of the darkness. The fire had died down to a dull glow of ashy coals. "I heard drunks go by a few minutes ago," he continued. "Then a truck drove up from San Ysabel."

As we listened, I could hear the truck's engine race as the driver gunned it, racing back down the road. Virgil opened the door and looked out.

"The truck turned down toward Albuquerque, stopped for a moment, and then went on," he said. "I could see the lights."

"We'd better check it out," I said, pulling on my still damp clothes. My dry ones were in the truck. "If it's another killing, maybe the man is still alive."

It had stopped raining. We were the first ones at the scene. We found a man lying dead in the middle of the road, with tire tracks across his body.

"It's Diego Aranda," Virgil said. "He's the other war captain. He wouldn't leave the pueblo, so he must have been waiting for them at the bridge."

"Why would he do that?"

"They must have stolen something to sell at the bar."

"He was set up, then. The truck came afterwards. What should we do with him?"

"Take him back to Santa Cala," Virgil decided. "The FBI still hasn't released Teno's son for trial."

"You're not going to tell the police?"

"That's up to the old men," Virgil said.

We loaded the body into the carryall and drove back to the pueblo. Virgil had me stop at the governor's house. Within five minutes, a dozen grim-faced men were standing around questioning Virgil. One of them was Teno.

"We'll take him," Teno said to me as several of the men moved the body out of the carryall, pull it on a wide plank and carried it off. "Virgil will have to stay here. You go on back to your place."

I didn't get back to sleep, even with the dry clothes I took from the barracks bag I'd left in the carryall. I finally climbed up onto the roof with my rifle in my hands and leaned my back against the chimney Teno's wife, Sofie, had built for my corner fireplace. The plastered adobe brick chimney stuck up a good two feet above the flat roof, a height necessary to create a draft for the fire, according to Teno. I figured I was invisible, which allowed me to doze some. At dawn, I climbed down and raked up the fire, putting coffee on to boil. I'd caught Mac a couple of fish and was sitting in my chair with my hot coffee when Lou drove up.

"They've arrested Teno again," she announced, taking the cup I handed to her before sitting in the other chair. "They pulled him right out of the kiva. I couldn't believe they could be so insensitive!"

"The FBI?"

"The same two agents that have been hanging around, yes. They had Phillips, from the BIA, with them, too. Right out of the kiva!"

"Get some beer, try out my new chair and tell me about it," I invited. "I'll make some sandwiches." I'd baked some fresh bread in the Dutch oven. The smell was still in the air.

Lou sniffed appreciatively while I cut slabs of bread and cheese. Mac rubbed his head on Lou's knees. I brought out the camp chair from the house and joined her, sipping beer and eating cheese and fresh-made bread.

"You'll make some lucky woman a great husband," she remarked, grinning.

I waved it off with mock modesty and told her about what Virgil and I had been doing. "What's this kiva thing?" I said. "I've heard several of the Indians use the word, but I didn't want to ask one of them."

"It's the pueblo ceremonial meeting room. Only men are allowed in, men and boys being initiated into the men's society. To have white men enter and haul a leader away in the middle of a ceremonial is equivalent of arresting a Catholic priest while he's conducting mass," she explained.

"They say why?"

"They didn't speak to anyone. Not even Nurse Wilson has heard the reason and she hears everything. Which reminds me, Phillips ordered her out of the pueblo. He said no whites could live there without BIA approval, which means I've no place to stay, either. I've been living with her." She eyed me speculatively. "Do you think I could stay here? It's close enough to the pueblo for me to continue my work. I'd chip in on the groceries."

"And it would make Mac happy," I said. "Sure, why not? You can use the house. I sleep outside, anyway, if it's not raining. If it does rain, I can sleep in the carryall. But the invitation doesn't include your two friends."

"They live in San Ysabel," she said. "They don't even have to know where I'm staying."

"Fine. You have your key. You can come and go as you will."

"Thanks. What are you going to do about Teno?"

"First I have to find Simpson and tell him about last night. There was another murder up at the bridge . . . Diego Aranda, one of the war captains. You know him?"

"I know his wife. That's what this was about?"

"I don't think so. The FBI weren't notified."

"Well, it wasn't Teno who did it, anyway. He was in the kiva. What are you going to do about him?"

"I'll go see Ginwright, my lawyer friend, and tell him that Teno was in the kiva when the war captain was murdered. Since they don't even know about that killing yet, they must be charging him with the first murder.'

As I drove past San Ysabel I saw the red pickup that Lou's friends drove, parked in front of the general store. I wondered who they lived with. They seemed to be popping up every time there was a new development. Did they have something to do with what was going on?

6

*N*ext morning I stopped off in Bernalillo to find Sheriff Simpson. He pushed aside paperwork to welcome me, standing and shaking hands. I hadn't shaken hands so much in my life as I had since leaving the army. Western folks seemed to require it.

"Good looking hat," he remarked. "Want some coffee? It ain't good, but it's strong."

"Sure. It can't be any worse than army coffee. You hear about Teno?"

"Yeah, the FBI are looking for him," Simpson said as he handed me a cup, eyeing me dead-pan.

The sip I took was so hot I spat most of it back into the cup. "Man! You couldn't get hotter coffee in hell!"

"Another fool would have swallowed it," he agreed with evident amusement. Had I just passed some kind of test?

"Well, they found Teno last night," I said, taking another, but this time, cautious sip. "Pulled him out of the kiva."

"They did what?" he shouted, scandalized, rising and slamming his own cup down on his desk with such violence that coffee slopped over some of his papers.

My turn for an evil smile. "True. Your poker buddy, the Bureau of Indian Affairs superintendent, Ted Phillips, was with them."

"That bastard is crazy as a shit-house rat," he said with disgust, sitting heavily back down in his chair and mopping up the coffee with a huge red bandanna from his rear pocket. He stuffed it back, damp. "He damn well knows better," he muttered.

"Maybe not," I said. "Anyway, I want to get Teno out as we did Virgil."

"You don't think he had anything to do with it?" Simpson asked hopefully. I could see that he liked the old man.

"I don't see how," I said. "There was another killing last night, and when Virgil and I brought the body back to the pueblo the town governor sent for Teno. The old man came out of a house in the middle of the block, along with half a dozen other men."

Simpson nodded. "It would be a society house, a meeting room for Teno's group. I'd hoped the old man would disappear for a while."

"His son has the old man's truck," I explained.

"He was planning on leaving for Hopi country with a load of apples to trade this morning. Teno was going with him."

"Ah, shit! What about the new murder?"

I told him.

"I can understand the Indians not wanting to hand the body over," he said, rubbing his chin. "They have certain rites they have to go through to send the dead man's spirit on, and they need the body for that. The damned FBI likes to put the dead in storage until a case is solved."

"They still have the body of Roy, Teno's other son," I said.

"Yeah, damn! I've tried to get it released. They're real hard-asses to deal with."

"What do you make of the fact that the man killed last night was a war captain?"

"He was probably on to something. Teno would know, for sure, but he might not say."

"Even if it meant going to prison?"

"That's right, if he had to reveal sacred knowledge he'd let them fry him before he'd talk. Most of these old Indians are tough and take their responsibilities seriously. As war priest, Teno has more than most."

"You know a lot about the inner workings of the pueblo," I said. "I learn something new every time we talk."

"I was going to be an anthropologist before my old man died and I had to take over the ranches. All I needed for my masters was a thesis. Never had time to get around to it." He seemed embarrassed. I wondered why. "You call Ginwright?" he asked, changing the subject.

"No. There's no public phone I know of between my place and here."

"You could call from the general store in San Ysabel."

"Yeah, I guess I could, but I don't feel comfortable hanging around that place," I admitted. "How did whoever was in the truck Virgil and I heard know that the war captain would be waiting at the bridge for the drunks from the bar? Did the bartender call someone? He's brother to the store owner.

"Good question. I may ask it a few times myself," Simpson mused. "Let me call Ginwright."

When he hung up, he said, "Ginwright will call back when he knows what's happening. He said you got to get a bank account. You'll need to be able to write a check for Teno's bond. You planning on doing that?"

"Sure. What will happen to Santa Cala if their war priest is in jail for any appreciable length of time?"

"Hard to say. His group should have a Badger Clan guy in training, but when they took Teno as a young man it was because he was the only one eligible. He'd been in a lot of trouble with the old men when he was young. Ain't no one tagged as an assistant war priest just like there ain't no assistant *cacique*."

"The war captain can't just fill in?"

"Virgil? No. He's probably not even a member of the old man's secret society. War captains are secular officials. The old men change war captains every winter solstice. The only exception I know of is the man who just got killed. He'd been in office for three years, out every night with his bow and arrow to shoot witches."

"He like the job?"

"Nah, he was about to go crazy. He was so pissed about being selected the first time, he got drunk and broke his cane of office. When he tried to turn it over at the end of his first year, the old men refused to accept it, even mended nicely. They said the earth power couldn't be passed on with a damaged cane. Teno finally took pity on him and planned to have all the canes retired this year and placed in one of the mountain shrines. It was going to cost the man hundreds of dollars in fees. I don't know who will pay for it now, but probably his relatives."

"You specialize in Santa Cala when you went to school?"

"I worked with Hawley-Ellis."

"Is that something special?"

"Special? She's the best damned Southwestern ethnologist we've ever had."

"So, you're a part-time anthropologist, part-time rancher and full-time sheriff?"

"It's the sheriffing that's supposed to be part-time," he said, looking out the window. "I'm a rancher full time, though it's hard to convince my boys of that. The anthropology is just a hobby. You need a Ph.D. to get a job, and I'm not up for that. Besides, I could never live on a teacher's salary. Don't know how Hawley-Ellis does it."

"What's your master's thesis going to be called?"

"The Socio-political Organization of a Middle Rio Grande Pueblo," Simpson said with a reluctant grin. I knew that look from the poker table when he knew he had a winning hand. He was lying. The son-of-a-gun had already written that thesis.

"Seems to me that you could testify as an expert witness and answer a lot of questions that Teno would be barred from answering by his need for secrecy," I said, draining my cup and putting it on one of the few clear places on his desk.

"I couldn't do that unless I was asked," Simpson said soberly. "Pueblo Indians don't like whites pushing into their business."

"Seems that Ginwright should know it's an option. He could ask Teno how he feels about it."

"Yeah," he agreed, swirling the dregs of coffee in his cup and staring down at the grounds at the bottom, like he was trying to read them. I wondered, could anyone do that? Like tea leaves?

"Something else," I said, "Could you take me over to your bank and introduce me? I want to open that account, cash my warrant and deposit it and some of my poker winnings. I've been carrying around more money than I've ever seen in one place before."

"Sure. They got a local branch here of the big bank in Albuquerque. One of their vice presidents runs it, a guy named Pete Ferenci. Hell of a poker player. He can go longer without blinking than anybody I ever saw, like a damned lizard. I've never seen him really smile."

"How come he doesn't play poker with you guys? He ought to be able to afford it."

"He and Joe Lima are political rivals in the state senate. Pete's a Republican," he added in a whisper as if it were a character flaw. "They don't spend too much of their free time in each other's company."

He drove us over to his bank, just down the block. We could have walked in less time, but I'd already got the idea that cowboys never walked farther than they had to.

Ferenci's office door was open and, without ceremony, Simpson led me up to it behind the rail separating staff and customers, nodding to the woman at the desk nearby. No one else even looked up.

Ferenci rose to shake hands when Simpson introduced us. He was about my height and gave me a thin-lipped grin that didn't extend to his eyes . . . coldest eyes I'd ever seen. Simpson was right about his not blinking, too.

Some kind of alien? I wondered.

"This is Jack Kilroy," Simpson said. "You must have read about him in the paper. Wants to open an account."

Whatever warmth there had been in Ferenci's face faded on hearing my name, but he said only, "Indeed I have. Sit down, please. What kind of account do you want?"

"Checking," I said. "I have a warrant for army back pay and about three thousand in cash to open it with. I'd also like a safety deposit box. I've been carrying around some papers in my glove compartment that I'd hate to lose," and I waved them at him: my discharge and the deed to my new place. "Probably not too smart," I added.

"No," he agreed without inspecting them, writing something on a slip. "Just hand that to one of the girls out front and they'll set you up." He rose, to show the visit was over.

On the way out, Simpson muttered, "What's got up his ass? He ain't the friendliest guy in the world at any time, but that's a little abrupt, even for him."

I shrugged and sat by one of the two desks near the rail, giving the woman the slip the banker had given me. Simpson went over to sit on the other side of the barrier to wait while I conducted my business. I saw him pick up a newspaper someone had left and then turned my attention to the woman who took my warrant, my cash and the papers I wanted to put away, handing the papers back.

When I was finished, I joined Simpson, stuffing my new checkbook in my shirt pocket and attaching my safe deposit key to my key ring. Simpson's face was stormy. He had the abandoned paper under one arm as we left; and out on the sidewalk he exploded, "I know what's on the bastard's mind. Read the lead editorial," he demanded, thrusting the paper at me.

It was the *Albuquerque Journal*, the paper that had been running the stories about my supposed adventures in Vietnam. The headline ran, "Hero's Feet of Clay." I scanned the text of the editorial. It was an angry denunciation, outrage at my using my status as a decorated veteran to attack the military, and consequently the country. Even my comments on the John Birch Society were misquoted, though not far from how I really felt. I was surprised; I'd not expected this to be in a reporter's story.

I handed the paper back to Simpson. "So?"

"They never talked to you, did they?"

"There were reporters with the TV truck when they gave me the medal. I did say I'd never met a commissioned officer for whom I had any respect after short acquaintance, or something like that. The truth is, I never got to know any personally. What difference does it make?"

"The damned publisher was an officer in the first world war. He's also a Bircher. He took your remarks personally. It ain't going to help Teno any, being your friend."

"Okay," I said. "Let's go down to the VA hospital. Most of my guys will still be there. We can call a press conference and explain about what I said and why."

"They'll go for that?"

"Sure," I said.

"Okay. Let's stop by the office and call Ginwright again. We'll tell him what we're doing and ask him what he plans for Teno."

Ginwright had returned Simpson's call by the time we reached his office and was waiting for the sheriff to call back. Between them they agreed to meet at Judge Thatcher's office in the federal courthouse in Albuquerque. Simpson drove faster than I would have and we were in the federal building in no time at all. Even so, we found Ginwright waiting for us in the lobby. He'd already seen the judge.

"O'Brian, the DA, wants Teno held without bail. Says he's a flight risk," he told us.

I asked in disbelief, "Where would he go?"

"Nowhere," Simpson answered. "His duties bind him here. "

"Tell the judge," I said.

"What duties are those?" Ginwright asked.

"Religious duties. Secret ones. I made a study of Santa Cala when I was in school. Teno is the head of an important ceremonial group."

"We'll have him testify to that," Ginwright said, nodding.

"That will never happen. The Indians got in trouble with the Inquisition soon after the Spaniards came to the Southwest and baptized them all. The Indians got hung as heretics for conducting their rituals. It's been a long time since they talked about their religion openly."

"That was hundreds of years ago," Ginwright objected.

"Things haven't changed all that much, except for who does the killing. When the big monograph on Santa Cala came out in the twenties the anthropologist who wrote it printed photos and the names of her informants.

It took a few years, but a guy from Santa Cala who'd been hung by the thumbs from a viga and beaten with yucca whips for giving away ceremonial secrets was given a copy of the book by an artist friend from Taos. All the man had done was take young people to county fairs to give harmless social dances in costume. He came into the plaza that night, roaring drunk and waving the book. By morning everyone knew that it was the old men who had sold the secrets. It was all in the book. The old men had known that bad luck was coming out of their actions and had fastened on the young dance leader as a scapegoat."

"What happened?"

"Within a year all the people who had sold secrets were dead. "

"No! Are you sure?"

"Yes. Ruth Bunzel had the same thing happen to her at Isleta and Ruth Benedict at Zuni. It shadowed both of their lives."

"What's a harmless social dance?" I asked.

"One that has no secrets. Rain dances are prayers for good crops and harvest dances thanks for the same. They're public. Women and children dance in them, as well as men. There are ramadas built to shade santos from the church and people pray to them."

"How did you get data for your research?" I asked.

Simpson looked embarrassed when he said, "I got it from drunks. By the time I was working in the pueblos, no responsible man from the pueblos would talk to an anthropologist. They knew the risk. Drunks were pretty much outcasts anyway and didn't care. They'd do anything for a few drinks."

"Doesn't sound like what they'd have to say would be worth much," Ginwright remarked in disapproval.

"Maybe not. I wouldn't do it now, but I was young and that's the way it was done back then. One of the great ethnographers, Leslie White, used to rent a motel room and keep booze on hand all summer long to entice drunks. Everyone thought the pueblo way of life would be gone in a few years and anything that was necessary to record it was permissible. In class one of my professors called it the 'rape, murder, arson' approach. No one was proud of it."

"Your master's thesis is finished, isn't it?" I asked. "You just don't want anyone to read it."

"Yeah, smart ass. The university library copy is kept locked up so it won't get into the wrong hands. The asshole at the graduate dean's office raised a stink about that. He said it was 'against scholarly ethics to hinder the dissemination of knowledge,' if I remember his exact phrasing."

"And?"

"Well, the anthro department chair was a friend of the president. It got done my way." He looked at Ginwright and added, "I'll testify if Teno wants me to, but not in open court and not unless he says so."

"I could arrange to have you testify in a closed session. All the judge would have to do is hold all parties to secrecy under the threat of contempt of court," Ginwright said.

"Okay. Talk to Teno about it and let me know."

We told Ginwright about the newspaper editorial and found he'd already read it. He followed us to the VA hospital saying I'd probably need a lawyer myself before we were through. That wasn't going to happen. We found that all my guys were still in the ward, though some were almost recovered to the point where they could be discharged. They were having enough fun, compared to where they'd been, not to want to rush it. The reception was as warm as I had expected, though it might have looked a bit odd to Ginwright and Simpson.

"Hey, Jackson," I said in greeting to the first man to notice us. "Hey, guys," to the others.

"Why, it's Mr. K, hisself!" Jackson said, in mock surprise.

"K stands for Cock," he confided to Ginwright and Simpson. "You wore out already?" he asked me. "White girls too much for you?"

"When did you ever see him with a white girl?" LeRoy, the sole Hispanic, asked. The others that clustered around when we entered the ward were all black.

To Ginwright, Jackson asked, "What's a brother like you hanging out with my walkie, old Bad Hand, hisself? He'll get you in trouble, sure." Jackson was bigger and darker than Ginwright. He lifted me up in the air and hugged me while the others crowded around, reaching out to pat me.

"Bad Hand?" Ginwright murmured.

"Oh, yeah!" my friend said, putting me back on the floor, but keeping hold of me. "Don't none of us shake his hand. Don't know where it's been," and the others joined in knowing laughter.

"An old joke," I said, glancing at Ginwright and Simpson. They were fascinated. Oh, man!

"Joke?" Jackson rolled his eyes toward heaven as if seeking support and moved his huge hand to my shoulder, pushing me down to sit on one of the beds.

"Have a seat, gentlemen," Jackson invited Simpson and Ginwright. "Only fair you know who you been associating with," and he gestured to the bed across from the one I was on. When the two were comfortable, Jackson told scurrilous story after scurrilous story about my supposed exploits with women, looking to the other soldiers for confirmation, which came as disciplined as a Greek chorus. Most of the stories were things that had happened to Jackson, or at least things he claimed had happened, but there were a few I hadn't heard before. Lord knows where they came from.

"So, you getting any?" he finally asked me, after graciously acknowledging the laugher his latest lie had evoked.

"My friend Jackson thinks I'm backward where women are concerned," I tried to explain. Wrong thing to say. The beds Ginwright, Simpson and I were sitting on were ringed by this time by familiar faces, all grinning.

"Backward? That the way you been doing it? No wonder you been having trouble," Jackson exclaimed. "Why didn't you tell me? I'd have straightened you out."

"Maybe a press conference with these clowns isn't such a good idea," I said. "It won't help my credibility any having them call me 'Mr. Cock.'"

"What press conference?" Jackson demanded. "Man, ain't you been reading all them pretty stories we been telling the reporter fellas? We know how to behave."

"Did you see this editorial?" Simpson asked, raising the paper he'd taken from the bank. Kilroy wants to talk to reporters with other veterans listening as witnesses."

"Yeah, we seen it," Jackson said, suddenly serious. "We be there. What's he going to say?"

"Well, the newspaper claims he's some kind of traitor, accepting medals and then turning on the military that granted them to him. How do you feel about that?"

"Mr. K speaks for the rest of us," Jackson said, after a glance at the other men.

"You don't care what he did?" Ginwright asked.

"Mr. K can do any damn thing he wants and it's okay with me," Jackson growled, "but that's not what I said. Mr. K explained how it was. He said if you weren't in Nam, you don't have any right to judge those who were."

"Well, both Simpson and I served in Korea," Ginwright said. "Explain to us how Vietnam was different."

"Probably wasn't," Jackson said. "Not if you were an enlisted men. If you were on the line, I'll bet Korea was one continual horror. Okay if you were back in headquarters maybe, a chance to get rich on the black market, smoke all the dope you wanted and chase easy women. I'll bet you had some term for them. We called them REPs for Rear Echelon Pukes."

"We called them REFs," Simpson said.

"So did we, mostly, but if we're going to have a press conference, I'm not going to use the 'f' word. My mama might read something about it and I'd never hear the end of it. How you guys know Kilroy? You wearing a star," he added, nodding at Simpson. "Our boy in trouble?"

"I've been playing a little poker with them, Ginwright, the sheriff and a couple of other guys," I said.

"I knew it! Let you out of my sight and you're playing poker again! How much money you lost?" Jackson asked in a fine display of outrage. "You need a loan?"

"You're talking to the wrong man," Simpson said.

"You look old enough to know better," Jackson said to him. "Why, I don't think gambling's even legal in this state. He been doing this?" and he pulled a pack of cards from his shirt pocket, fanned it face down and pulled out an ace. "I taught him everything he knows," he confided, shaking his head in dismay.

"Stop it," I said, then, glancing around at the ring of listeners, added, "Most of you guys, unlike Jackson, have homes to go to. If Jackson goes home, his several wives will put him in jail as soon as he hits Chicago's south side. If you want to come to the press conference, fine. But, there's a risk. It will be bad enough when you go home just being from Nam without being tied in the newspaper to an ungrateful traitor like me."

"Don't change the subject," Jackson said coldly. "Ain't no newspapers going to say anything about us one way or the other. We're black. They don't care what we do. What's important is you gambling without me to protect you. I should just let you get hurt, but I got more class than that." He turned back to Ginwright and Simpson. "How come you picked this boy up, leading him astray?"

"He asked in," Simpson said, a trifle hotly.

Jackson grinned, having drawn the sheriff out.

"We're a bunch of veterans who have attitudes we developed in service not too much different from those he's getting burned for now," Simpson continued more calmly. "I personally never met a commissioned officer I'd spend my spare time with, even now. We didn't know that about him when he knocked on our door, but we could guess. We were all sergeants, tough guys who served on the line like he did."

"Tough guys? Mr. K ain't no tough guy."

"Really?" Simpson asked. "He was an intercollegiate boxing champion in three different weight classes: welterweight, middleweight, and light heavyweight his sophomore, junior and senior years at Harvard. He added weight each summer, a shit-pack of muscle working on construction jobs in Philadelphia. The papers called him Mr. K, too, K for knockout. Maybe you didn't know that?"

And how did Simpson know about that? I wondered.

"Why didn't you tell us about you being a big-shot college boxer?" Jackson asked me. "Man, I'd never give you a free swing if I'd known."

I raised my hands and shook my head. "That's why, but never mind," I said. "These guys don't want to hear about that."

"I do," Simpson said. "I have a special interest in amateur boxing. I was lightweight champion of my division when I was in the Marine Corps. You're a pretty big guy," he said to Jackson. "You maybe six-two, two-ten? He hit you more than once?"

"Hunh!" Jackson grunted, shaking his head.

"I'll tell you about it," Leroy, the Hispanic, said. He and Jackson carried on a long-running pretend feud. "I can understand that Jackson is embarrassed."

Jackson just grinned, waving his hand for LeRoy to take over.

"When Mr. K led his squad into our camp, Jackson was camp boss. He called Mr. K over to explain camp rules and told him he would have to ask Jackson for anything he wanted. Mr. K just said, 'Whenever you're ready' and drew a line in the dirt with his boot."

"That happened?" Simpson asked me.

"Oh, yeah," I said reluctantly. "Taking orders from snot-faced second lieutenants was bad enough. I wasn't about to ask some lousy sergeant for permission to go to the john."

"Jackson came down to stand in front of Mr. K," LeRoy continued, nodding in agreement. "Jackson stuck out his chin and said, 'Take your best shot.' Mr. K just ducked his head, rolled his shoulder and hit Jackson so fast you could hardly see his hand move. He laid Jackson out for five minutes. Had to give him artificial respiration to get him breathing again."

"You do that?" Simpson asked him, enjoying the story.

"Me?" LeRoy asked in alarm, evidently appalled at the thought. "Not hardly! Jackson is way too ugly."

"Mr. K did it," Jackson said. "I came to and this white boy had his tongue halfway down my throat. Liking it way too much, you ask me."

"I thought I'd killed him," I said. "I was feeling a bit put upon or I wouldn't have hit him so hard."

"Hunh," Jackson said again. He was through with this topic. "We'll call a press conference here at eleven tomorrow morning," he said. "That way it can make the afternoon and evening editions. We already got the connections. You guys all be here?"

When we all nodded, Jackson said, "Okay. Go away now and let us talk this out. The brothers know this is serious stuff to mess with, but some of the white boys here may not. We got to tell them."

As we left the building Ginwright asked me, "How many are you counting on?"

"To back me? Everyone you saw today. There will even be a few white guys from my squad, probably, but I don't know. Things may have changed for them once we got back." I didn't try to explain that, but there was no need.

We drove down to the county jail where, between them, Simpson and Ginwright got us in to see Teno. The guards brought him into a small interview room where there were just enough folding chairs for us to sit around a dented steel table.

"Good to see you!" Teno said to each of us, reaching out his hand to touch ours in turn.

"They treating you all right?" Simpson asked.

"They not hurt me. Those two fellas from the FBI yell at me every day. I just answer them, '*No savvy!*' The louder the questions, the louder I answer."

"They don't try Spanish?" Ginwright asked.

"*No savvy* Spanish either," he replied laughing. "Only talk Indian and they not bring an Indian to me yet."

"The agency superintendent, Ted Phillips, will try to find them an interpreter," Simpson said.

"Nobody come," Teno said confidently. "They won't want to see me after I get out." The tone wasn't threatening, but the message was.

"Kilroy here thinks I should try to explain to the judge why you couldn't have done it," Simpson said. "Ginwright said he could get the judge to close the court so it wouldn't be public. We'll get you out and you can go back to what you were doing."

"Too late," Teno said. "They pulled me out of the kiva before we'd finished the doin's to start the new year."

"You mean there'll be no winter ceremonial season this year?" Simpson said in dismay.

"No summer either," Teno said. "Nothing until next year. "

"Is that bad?" Ginwright asked.

"If we don't hold the ceremonies there won't be any harvest next fall," Teno said.

"But why?" I asked.

"There's a regular order for the secret societies to go into the kiva," Simpson said. "The Indians believe the corn cannot grow unless the proper ceremonies are held. Even if the seed germinates, there will be something to stop it from maturing, hail or grasshoppers or drought. Jesus!" he muttered.

I smiled to hear Simpson sound more like a professor than a country sheriff as he talked from his academic knowledge. I didn't know if that last word was a curse or a prayer. "You believe that?" I asked him.

"It's happened before a few times," Teno answered for him. "We know it will happen again."

Simpson nodded. "Sorry about this," he said to Teno. "You want us to bail you out anyway?"

"It don't much matter now," Teno said. "The food here isn't bad. It'll be one less mouth to feed at home."

"Oh, that reminds me," I said. "I won sixteen hundred dollars at poker. What do you want me to do with your half?"

"Eight hundred dollars? You're giving me eight hundred dollars?" He sounded surprised.

"You said I'd win, remember? You were going to say prayers for me in the kiva."

"I made you a prayer stick," he admitted. "It wasn't for gambling, particularly. It was for good luck and good health."

"Close enough," I said. "I've already told people I was giving it to you. I can't back off."

"With that much money, I could buy food when the stored corn is used up," he said, half to himself. He was silent as he thought about it. Then he told Simpson, "Get me out if you can. I got to talk to the old men about the sheriff testifying for me, but they'll agree."

Judge Thatcher listened to Ginwright, Simpson and me in his chambers. I was there as the potential bondsman. O'Brian, the federal district attorney, was there as a matter of course and seemed open to the suggestion that Simpson testify for Teno, agreeing not to cross examine, letting Simpson appear as a court's witness in a closed hearing. Letting Teno post bail was another matter, however.

"This is a capital case, Your Honor," O'Brian said doubtfully when the previous matter was concluded. "I'm concerned about flight."

"He has no place to go," Simpson said. "He doesn't read or write and has inadequate English. Besides, his religious duties tie him to the pueblo."

"At the proper time, Sheriff Simpson will testify as to what those duties are and how they prevented Teno from committing the crime he has been charged with," Ginwright said.

"Save that for the trial," the judge said. "It is obvious to me that flight is not likely." He turned to me and asked, "You will post bail?"

"Yes, sir," I said, "provided it's not over ten thousand. That's about all I have free."

"Are you still living next to the pueblo?"

"Yes, sir."

"I'll put the old man in your charge, then, as I did the other man from Santa Cala. The FBI made a mistake about him, and it would not surprise me that they've made another here. Write me a check for the ten thousand." He signed the bond papers handed him by Ginwright.

"Do you play poker, Your Honor?" I asked.

He smiled. "I did when I was younger. Now, I pretty much limit myself to bridge. Among other things, gambling is illegal in this state. Why do you ask?"

"You have a good face for it," I said. "I couldn't tell what you were going to do until you did it."

"I see. I understand you had a reputation in Vietnam for being an excellent player yourself," he said, watching me.

"There was little else to do in the prison camp," I said. "It wasn't illegal there," I added, wondering if he knew that Simpson, Ginwright and the others were gambling with me. Why did he think I had so much money?

"Hmmm." he said. "We won't cash this check unless there's cause. If we do, the money had better be there."

I thought he might be referring to the possibility I would gamble it away, illegally, of course.

"I will replace it with a certified check, if you prefer it," I said.

"I don't think that will be necessary," he said and dismissed us.

"The judge likes you," Simpson said, after we dropped Ginwright off and picked up Teno. I nodded. I thought so, too. On the other hand, I thought O'Brian didn't.

Simpson drove the three of us to Bernalillo and Teno and I went on to Santa Cala in my carryall. When I pulled up to his door, I unlocked the glove compartment and offered him his eight hundred dollars.

"Give me twenty now and hold the rest for me," he said. People in the pueblos are expected to share good fortune, Simpson had told me. If it became known that Teno had eight hundred dollars there would be numerous requests for aid. This way he could give people a dollar now and then and still be thought generous. What I thought was that, at twenty dollars a week, I'd be doling out money for another nine-ten months. My commitment to staying was more binding every day.

I drove back to Albuquerque the next morning to the VA hospital and found Ginwright already talking to Jackson and the other men in the room set aside for press conferences. Simpson was standing off to one side as an observer. "The reporters will be here in half an hour," Ginwright said as I entered.

"Good timing."

"Thought he'd chicken out?" Jackson asked,

"Hmmm, no," Ginwright answered, matching Jackson's stare.

I'd taken an anthropology course once and learned that all primates stare in challenge. The dozen or so men ranged behind Jackson nodded in amusement. I gathered that they were the ones who chose to stand with me politically, rascals all, split between whites and blacks with LeRoy the one exception.

The press interrupted what might have been an interesting encounter between Ginwright and Jackson. I thought that maybe Jackson was suspicious of Ginwright's possible influence over me. That was funny. A half dozen reporters, some with cameras, came in a body, talking to one another and walking thick, to use one of Jackson's expressions. Indeed, they were huddled more closely than personal space might require under less intimidating circumstances. Even I could sense the hostility that emanated from the men behind Jackson.

"This the hero?" one of the reporters asked, unsuccessfully trying to push past Jackson to reach me. I was sitting behind a table with Ginwright on one side and Simpson on the other.

"We all be heroes here," Jackson said. "You want to stay?" The remark less a question than a threat as he clutched the reporter's lapels with both hands, lifted him off his feet and pushed him back to stand with the others.

"What are you doing?" the reporter asked, shocked, ineffectively pawing at Jackson's hands.

"Just explaining things," Jackson said, releasing the man and smoothing his lapels with his huge hands. "First I talk. Then you ask questions. Everybody got that?" he demanded, looking at the other reporters over the head of the man he'd assaulted. Without waiting for an answer, Jackson perched on the corner of the table with the other men from the prison camp behind him.

"We know this man, me and the brothers, here," Jackson said. "He ain't pimpin' no medal. Silver Star, shit! If an officer had been there to witness it, he'd have got a Medal of Honor. Did you know enlisted men's words ain't good enough with the army for a Medal of Honor? That's what they told us." The men behind Jackson nodded.

"Weren't no officers with us, and that's a fact," LeRoy added.

"Were you all in the same prison camp with Kilroy?" one of the other reporters asked. The man Jackson had pushed had retired to the rear of the group, seemingly half-inclined to leave, but fearing to miss something good.

"You think the Cong separated blacks and whites? Man, they don't give a damn," Jackson said with contempt that anyone could hold such a notion. "Sure, we all from the same camp."

"How long?"

"Most of us had been there a while when Mr. K led his squad in. They'd been beat up pretty bad and we sort of left them alone till they got easy with the rest of us. Took some time for us to make friends."

"Is that true?" the same reporter asked, looking at the other men.

"Most of it," LeRoy said. "Jackson was camp boss when Kilroy walked in. Ten minutes later it was Kilroy. Damnedest thing I ever saw. Maybe it took Jackson some time to come to terms with the fact, but the rest of it didn't make any trouble over the change."

Jackson shrugged, "Whatever," he said. "I'll tell you one thing straight. This white boy be the best man I ever met. He don't even know how to lie. Hell, he won't even cheat at cards! We all stand behind him here. No one else has a right to say."

Questions followed until Jackson cut them off after it was obvious nothing new was being asked. "You go write this up," he told them. "Do it right, you hear? Do it yourselves. It ain't for some fat boss sitting behind a desk to say nothing about Nam. And it ain't for officers to pretend to speak for us, neither. They don't know nothing about how we feel. They never talked to us there and they ain't talked to us since we got back."

Before I left I went to see the hospital social worker and chatted with her for a bit. I gave her my checking account number at Ferenci' s bank so the disability checks could be mailed someplace. I didn't need them, but I'd promised.

I thought about the newspaper interview as I drove back home. Man, the miles I was putting on the carryall. Anyway, I decided I didn't know what more could have been said. I did know I was sick of the subject.

7

I heard Lou singing as I drove the truck up to my camp.

She said she'd be moving in, but it had slipped my mind. Her voice was low and pleasant and raised in my father's favorite song, "The Wild Colonial Boy." I remembered he had sung it countless times at ward parties in Philadelphia and considered his voice one of his prime assets as a politician. I liked her rendition better.

When I parked the truck, I got out and sang the base line as I used to do for my father, at his insistence. Lou came to the door of the adobe and finished the verse.

"You do part singing!" she said with enthusiasm. She was in blue jeans and t-shirt. This one had a green label. "Save the Irish." I didn't know that we were endangered.

"Just Irish songs. Where's Mac?"

Mac came around from behind her and stepped up to greet me, rubbing his head on my knee. I stooped and scratched him behind his ears. Great cat.

"You ready to eat?" she asked. "I made supper."

"Really? Is there time for a beer first?"

"Sure, there's always time for a beer. Supper will keep. It's in your Dutch oven."

I fetched a couple of long necks from the stream, thinking what a great companion she was. When I got back I found her sitting in one of the Adirondack chairs, waiting for me. I took the other with a grin. "That the one you like? I just finished it last night."

"I like them both, but you made the other one first. I figured that one was supposed to be yours. We need a table for inside."

"Next project," I said, uncapping the beers and handing her one. I took a long swallow. "I could taste this all the way from Bernalillo," I said.

"Did you get Teno out?" she asked.

"Yeah. Took him home." I sat in my chair and relaxed and Mac jumped up on my lap demanding attention. Probably hungry. "He says it's too late. When they took him out of the kiva, they interrupted a sequence of prayer retreats by religious groups. He says there'll be no corn this year."

"Isn't it terrible?"

"You already knew about this?"

"There's a thesis in the library . . ."

"Simpson's? He said it was under lock and key."

"It's available to qualified students," she replied loftily.

"He doesn't know that," I said. "I think he lives in fear that Teno will be identified as his informant and come to grief."

There was an awkward silence. "Teno isn't identified in the thesis," she said in a small voice.

"I've done something stupid, haven't I?" I said, kicking myself. "You didn't know, did you?"

"No harm. I won't tell. Besides, I'm almost certain Teno isn't his informant."

"He said that, but I didn't believe him," I admitted. "Do you know who is?"

"I think so, but I won't tell that, either."

"Good. I don't want to know," I told her, which was the truth, but it didn't excuse me. I'd thought, from what Simpson had said, that identifying informants was required. I'd expected it to name Teno. Actually, it seemed unprofessional not to, somehow. How could information cited be verified otherwise? Didn't anthropology call itself a science?

"Has Mac eaten?" I asked, changing the subject. "He acts starved."

"I put his food out, but he refused it." This was said in a severe tone, and I glanced over to see her frowning at the pair of us. Mac stared back at her but gave it up and turned away, hitting me lightly in the face with his almost sheathed claws to get my attention.

"And he expects me to remedy the situation," I said.

"You can both have some nice chicken," she said. "I'll set it out."

"Need some help?"

"I can manage. Tell me what happened in town."

By the time I finished a somewhat expurgated account of our visit to the VA hospital, supper was ready. She dug the Dutch oven out from the coals and placed it on the stump. When she lifted the lid and as she doled out portions into my new plates, an almost indescribably delicious smell rose from the pot. Mac deserted me and went over to investigate.

"What is it?"

"Back home we call it chicken in a bean pot. It has half a dozen chicken breasts, a pint of heavy cream, a quarter pound of butter, four medium-sized onions cut in chunks, and salt."

"Sounds like sin," I said with a smile.

"As close to sin as I get," she quipped, eyeing me from under her brows.

"About that," I said. "Some of my guys have been talking to the press. They tell raunchy stories about me to whoever will listen, all more fiction than fact. Most of the guys have fairly full experiences of their own to draw on, and they have no hesitation in attributing their exploits to me. Sometimes I wish everything they said about me were true," I mused. Man, what a life I'd have lived! "Other times, like now," I continued, "I just wish they were more discrete, but I have no way to stop them outside of pleading, which would be out of character for our relationship and would embarrass them more than the good gained."

"And you're telling me this for what reason?"

"Two, actually. One, hanging out with me might not do your reputation any good, and two, you don't have anything to fear from me personally, despite what the papers are likely to say about me." I looked at her closely. She had her head bent over her plate, but she was shaking slightly.

"You're laughing at me?" I asked, incredulously.

"Yeah, some," she admitted, looking up at me, her face red from trying to hold it in.

"Uh," I said. I mean, what else could I say?

After she had herself under control again, she went on about the dish she'd made, which I was eating with relish, pushing Mac off, who wanted more than his share of it.

"My grandmother was a Cherokee. When she was on the reservation in Oklahoma, they got a lot of canned milk for rations from the Agency. Under the conditions of our treaty, the government is required to give the people food in exchange for their leaving their land. Lots of Indians can't digest milk; they lack an enzyme to break down the proteins. No one knew that then, of course, so they kept on issuing it and women like my grandmother tried to find some way to use it. She found her kids could eat it cooked and mixed it into dishes like this. There was always butter or cheese, neither of which need to be refrigerated past what a pot in the creek will provide, and when there was no chicken available, she could substitute rabbit or rattlesnake meat, both delicately flavored. And onions, of course."

"Of course," I agreed.

"You don't like onions?" she asked. suspiciously.

"On the contrary," I said. "The onions you cooked with are ones I bought. I was thinking more of the mention of rattlesnake meat."

"Oh, well, they ate what there was. And God knows, Oklahoma has a sufficiency of rattlesnakes, even now. She showed me how to prepare rattlesnake meat and it's good, really. Don't give me a problem with this," she added. "No one in their right mind argues with a Cherokee."

"Hmmm," I said, to forestall her offer to cook rattlesnake for me. Maybe later. And I'd ask Hendley about that arguing bit. He claimed to be part Cherokee. "I have a grandmother who lives in Oklahoma," I said, to get on safer ground. "She's not an Indian, though, as far as I know. She's a Kilroy; runs the Panhandle Foundation."

"Kit Kilroy is your grandmother? She's one of my heroes!"

"Mine, too," I told her. "She wants me to come see her, and I wrote promising I would when I got things around here straightened out."

"Take me with you," Lou said. "The Kilroy Foundation underwrites Panhandle College. It has one of the best programs in women's studies in the country."

"Sure," I said, holding out my plate for more chicken. I washed up, claiming the bits of food I rinsed from the plates in the creek attracted fish, and listened to her sing to her guitar, folks songs, some Irish, along with a few I didn't recognize that she claimed were Cherokee. She was still playing and singing when I sought my hammock, and I went to sleep with the sound of her voice in my ears.

Mac woke me up as usual, by jumping out of the hammock to saunter into the adobe house I'd loaned Lou. I realized the music had stopped, but I could hear the sound of voices coming from inside. They weren't loud so I figured there was no problem, still, I wanted to know how someone could come in without my knowing. Was my awareness of possible danger fading?

I picked up my rifle and ghosted over to the house, stopping just outside to reconnoiter. The two people inside heard nothing, but Mac spotted me and Lou noticed the cat's sudden alertness. I stepped in to find Jerry, the loud mouth, sitting in my chair and talking to Lou. He got up and offered me my seat. Well, that was an improvement.

"Thanks," I said, shaking my head, "but I don't want to interrupt you. I just wondered who it was."

"Teno sent me," he said. "If someone comes, I'm to hide and then go let him know. They'll be looking for him."

"I see. Okay, but how did you get in?"

"I came down the creek."

"Hmmm," I acknowledged.

I was getting in the habit of saying, "hmmm," just like Judge Thatcher. Dumb. I started to leave but Lou called me back.

"You've got to hear this," she said.

I turned at the door, retraced my steps and took the chair that Jerry still stood beside. He sank gracefully on the floor, legs crossed. I'll bet I could still do that if I wanted to, I thought.

"So, tell me," she said.

"It's nothing about anything you're worried about, but is worth hearing anyway. Jerry has been suspended from Stanford, not for drinking, like he tells everyone, but because some crazy professor accused him of stealing."

I looked at Jerry and he nodded. He took my silence for permission and started his story.

"My senior year project was to translate a letter I'd found, written by Heraclitus to the Persian king Darius back around 500 BC. My major is classics and my B.A. language is Greek, archaic Greek, to be exact."

"Heraclitus?" I asked, trying to remember in what connection I had heard the name.

"Heraclitus was the guy who spoke of not being able to step in the same river twice because the water was always flowing," Lou said.

"Oh, yeah. He also said 'the only constant is change,' right?" I added. That was out of Harvard Freshman Civ 101.

"Supposedly," Jerry agreed. "There is no exact source for attribution of that one. And the real water quote was, 'You can't piss in the same river twice.' That didn't sound elegant enough to the Victorians."

Attribution? That from smart-mouth? I hadn't remembered about the river thing, though, if I ever did. One-up for him.

"Where did you find the letter?" I asked, truly curious. I would have thought anything like that would be common knowledge to classicists.

"It was part of an uncatalogued collection of manuscripts borrowed from the Vatican. Students were helping the professors sort though the rolls of parchment, trying to identify the individual pieces," Jerry said, with no trace of an accent. "Of course, everything was in acid-free boxes and all of the good stuff had supposedly already been claimed for study, but some of the boxes were labeled miscellaneous. I was given one of those and assigned a cubicle in the library to work. I found the letter at the bottom of the box. Everything else seemed to be records of the Persian attack on Ephesus, lists of supplies, mostly . . . some lists of loot."

"The temple of Artemis at Ephesus was one of the seven wonders of the world," Lou said loftily.

"Gee," I responded, causing her to color up. They were ganging up on me.

"Well, I'll bet you didn't know that," she said defensively.

"Hmmm, no," I admitted. Who cared? I thought of going back to my hammock.

"The point is," Jerry said, "it is believed that Heraclitus and Darius had correspondence, but no manuscripts were known to have survived. Scholars think that just after Darius conquered Ephesus, he sent a letter to Heraclitus, who lived there, asking him to come to Susa, in Persia, to explain a book Heraclitus had written on nature and deposited in the temple of Artemus for safekeeping. The Persians had looted the temple, sending everything interesting back to Susa. Even among his own people, Heraclitus was called 'the dark one' or 'the obscure,' for his insisting that his readers work out the meanings of his writings from the texts themselves. It's also believed that he wrote back to Darius to say that Darius had nothing that would tempt Heraclitus to travel all the way to Susa. Not very diplomatic, seeing that the troops of Darius were in charge of the city."

"He got away with that?" Darius must not have seen the letter, I thought.

"From the manuscript I found, no, he didn't. Darius had sent a scribe to Heraclitus with a list of questions as an alternative to the visit. In the spirit of the times, a philosopher might say 'no' to the Emperor Darius once, seeing that the Emperor was enlightened enough to revere knowledge, but twice would be an unacceptable liberty."

"And the letter?"

"It gives both the questions and the answers to the questions of Darius. There's nothing else like it in classical literature."

"So, what did you do?"

"I made two Xerox copies of the whole thing, attached a cover sheet to the original identifying it as something of no interest, put it in one of the boxes that had not been issued to me, but had been catalogued, and restored both boxes to the archive. One of the Xerox copies I cut into strips, numbered serially, and pasted on cardboard, leaving space between the lines for translations. The other I kept to compare to the work sheets, in case I lost or misplaced stuff, as I have before. Then I translated the text and showed it to my major professor."

"Was he impressed?"

"Oh, I can't tell you! I mean, yeah. He was going to co-publish it with me, a great honor, believe me."

"Seems like taking credit for someone else's work," I said.

"Well, that's standard in academia, professors stealing from their students, but this time he'd earn the credit, retranslating and annotating it, using a lifetime of study that I couldn't begin to match. No one could question it, issued under his seal."

"So, how did you get into trouble?"

"The professor gave a preliminary talk about the manuscript, causing an enormous fuss, which he enjoyed, and before his critics could be satisfied, he died. The original manuscript couldn't be found and suspicion fell on me. I'm suspended until the matter is resolved, and may end up in jail."

"So, why didn't you tell them where to find it?" I asked. What was wrong with this guy?

"The problem is that the critics mostly are connected to the Catholic Church and hate what Heraclitus said in explanation of his book. With the original lost, and no way to check it, now they can say it was a forgery without having to prove anything. They don't want it found. Neither do I, for different reasons. It could get lost where only they could find it, if it surfaced."

"You still have your work copy?"

"Oh, yeah. And they don't know about the second copy, either, the unannotated Xerox of the original. They're both safe," he added.

"You sound more like a professor, yourself, than a man from Santa Cala," I told him.

"English is my first language. It's what my parents conversed in, since my mother didn't speak Apache and my father didn't speak Kiowa. Neither were Santa Cala; they were teachers. We had an Encyclopedia Britannica in the house, something my father thought necessary for a teacher's family, and I read the whole thing growing up. Finishing high school, I had a 1600 SAT score and could have gone anywhere to college on scholarship as an Indian freak. My dad said Stanford was the Harvard of the West, but more laid back and closer to home, so I went there. He's since apologized to me for pushing me to attend that particular school, but I have no regrets."

I'd had about enough lecturing on classics for one evening, so I excused myself and went back to the hammock. Mac stayed where he was. There was always a chance of something to eat where people were awake. My life was getting complicated, and all I wanted was simple quiet. The way Lou looked at me was as if I could do something about Jerry being suspended. I wasn't sure I even wanted to.

I was on the edge of sleep when Lou started singing again, this time with another voice in countertenor. Had to be Jerry, but countertenor?

I was up and had breakfast ready, fresh-caught trout rolled in yellow corn meal and stuffed with slices of apple, before Lou joined me, sleepy eyed. Jerry was nowhere in sight.

"I was up half the night," she explained. Who asked?

"I heard Jerry singing countertenor," I said. "Where did he learn to do that?"

"He calls it 'closed throat,'" Lou said, "and claims it's the way all Indians sing. His grandfather taught him when he was a small boy, he says."

"I learned to sing from my grandfather," I said, recalling a memory that had lain dormant many years.

"You have a nice voice," Lou said.

"All we need is a true tenor," I said. "With you singing third, Jerry at high and me at low voice, a true tenor would give us an authentic Irish bar sound."

"And that's good?"

"A matter of opinion, perhaps," I said, not wanting an argument. I thought it would be good, though.

"Both Keith and Kevin are tenors," she said, referring to her blonde buddies.

"Figures," I said. She let me get away with that. I was willing to argue about the two of them and she probably knew it and didn't want the hassle.

There was honking at the gate, and I went down to investigate. It was Sheriff Simpson.

"Teno got permission from the pueblo town fathers for me to testify for him," he told us after parking his truck and accepting a cup of coffee from Lou. He made no comment about her presence. "That asshole, O'Brian, begging your pardon, ma'am, charged Teno with second degree murder, but Ginwright, as Teno's attorney, wants to offer manslaughter one in plea bargain. Judge Thatcher is on record with thinking Indians ought to obey the laws like everybody else. Ritual execution, which O'Brian will charge, is murder in the judge's eyes."

"O'Brian is the federal DA," I told Lou. "He can't make that stick," I said to Simpson. "Teno was in the kiva when the second murder occurred. Did you get evidence on that? If he didn't do the second, he didn't do the first."

"They don't know about the second and neither do I, officially. The point is, he doesn't have to be present," Simpson said, shaking his head. "If he ordered the killing as war priest, he's as guilty as if he pulled the trigger."

"But he's surely not going to plead guilty to anything?"

"He ain't even talked to Ginwright about it yet."

"How does O'Brian know about Teno being the war priest?" Lou asked.

"Something I wish I knew," Simpson said. "It might be the key to this whole mess. How do you know, by the way?"

"Some of the women I'm working with told me," Lou said. "It's no secret in the pueblo."

"Well, it's not the kind of thing whites generally are made aware of. The FBI bastards, begging your pardon, ma'am, they knew it too. You tell anyone?"

"No, but a few days ago I found Keith and Kevin going through my notes," Lou said. "They claimed some of their own were missing and thought they might have gotten mixed up with mine. I told them to ask me, next time. Anthropology notes are supposed to be private. They know that. I'd never look at anything of theirs. If they looked at mine for that reason, they're going to be in trouble. I'll tell the lab director at UNM."

"That would get them booted out of school," Simpson said, shaking his head. "Anyway, the judge has set a hearing for this afternoon. You want to come? I'll drive you back in time for poker tonight." This was said to me but Lou decided the invitation included her, too, and both of us got in Simpson's truck for the trip to Albuquerque. I was thinking I spent more time going up and down that damned road than I did fishing. At least Simpson's truck was better sprung than mine.

Ginwright greeted us as we came in. "I'm just here as an observer," he said. "There are no evidentiary motions to be made."

Judge Thatcher's courtroom was big enough to play half-court basketball in. The acoustics weren't much, but I wasn't in a position to tell people to speak up. Deaf as I am, I was happy that Lou was along, because she whispered in my ear what people were saying. I gathered O'Brian was talking about what he called, in a condescending way, "simple native rites," in particular, asking about executions for witchcraft. Evidently he pissed Simpson off, for the sheriff raised his voice and from then on I could hear everything myself.

"Witchcraft may have a native base, but it was reinforced by the teaching of the Spanish priests," Simpson said.

"Witchcraft may have native base?" O'Brian asked, his voice all but squeaking. "You're saying witchcraft is Hispanic?"

"The Indians believe that everything that there is was created by the Great Spirit in the first times," Simpson said in his professorial voice, cold with the outrage of being challenged. "When the creatures he had formed carne to the surface of the earth, there were what are now called witches among them. All humans from the underworld could take animal forms. But while most of them lost this ability when they were baked and hardened from the heat of the sun, a few night hunters who slept during the day continued to be able to change from human to animal shape at will. When the Spanish came, the priests said that shape-changing was witchcraft and those who could do it were executed when discovered; the other Indians learned to shun them. The Spanish taught them that witches form covens, so anyone associated with a witch was probably also a witch and in danger of execution as well. So, native shape-changing practices became known as witchcraft because it paralleled the Spanish belief in witch behavior."

"Are you saying that witchcraft is Catholic?" O'Brian asked, outraged.

"The belief in witchcraft surely is," Simpson said. "It's part of dogma. Every diocese, including yours, Mr. O'Brian, has a priest especially trained in exorcising evil. The duty requires a man of more than ordinary rectitude, for dealing with evil is dangerous."

I noticed that Simpson sounded like a professor, going into that mode just as Jerry had, using no good ol' boy turns of phrase. Amazing. They both compartmented their behavior to fit the circumstances that prevailed.

"Your honor, I demand that the testimony of this witness be stricken from the record," O'Brian demanded, shouting and pointing at Simpson, who was himself red in the face.

"There is no record being made," the judge said. "Anyway, I think I have what I need. There will be no plea bargain. If the defendant is found guilty of ordering the murder, he is guilty of more than second degree murder, but I'll let the murder two charge stand," and he stood up, dismissing the court.

Simpson came over to us, saying, "I didn't help much. Lucky he wasn't up for murder one or I'd have got him burned, for sure."

"What made O'Brian so hot?" I asked.

"He's a religious nut. Had a mental breakdown a while back and got locked up. Claims he prayed his way out; still seems a tad shaky. Blowing up like that in front of Judge Thatcher will do him no good, though. O'Brian wants more than anything to be a federal judge, like his daddy was. They'll be asking Judge Thatcher about it, and I can't see him going along with it. Judge Thatcher takes his job serious-like." I noticed the good ol' boy talk was back.

Ginwright was seething after he gathered his papers together and had a few words with O'Brian before joining us. "That bastard promised he'd let Simpson appear as a mitigating witness. He had no right to attack him," he said.

"Teno will never plead guilty to anything," I said.

"I know that," Ginwright said. "At trial it could be said that he refused a plea of guilty to a lesser crime. That impresses juries. Now it can't be said because O'Brian broke his word and cross-examined Simpson. Every lawyer in the state will hear about it and no one will accept O'Brian's word for anything now, but that won't help Teno."

I wondered what would help Teno? Identifying the real murderers would, I guessed, but how would I go about that? I was aware that I had asked the question. of myself in such a fashion that maybe committed me to making an effort. Damn.

There were only five of us at poker.

"Phillips told me that he wouldn't be back as long as that baby-killer sat at the table," Hendley announced. He'd changed the story. No mention was made of the cheating accusation, or the belief Hendley had that it was Phillips, himself, who was doing it.

"Want me to leave?" I asked, looking around the table.

"No. He plays lousy poker," Simpson said. "I don't mind taking his money, but he isn't much of a challenge."

Looking at the others, one by one, I got winks and shrugs, depending on how well I knew them.

"I've been thinking I should do something about Teno's problem," I said. We'd talked about it between hands.

"You want to do some amateur detective work, start with the guy that runs the bar here," Joe Lima said unexpectedly. "I hear things about him and his brother I don't like. The only reason I haven't pulled my license before is that there's no other place to play poker."

"You get the power company to run a line to Kilroy's house and we could play there," Hendley said. "This table belongs to me, along with the chairs. They'd fit in."

Lima nodded. "We can meet there next week, then?" and he asked that of me.

"Sure," I said. Imagine that! Lou had her table.

The power company was honking at the gate early the next morning and had a pole installed beside the house, connected to the line along the road and metered by noon. After lunch, an electrician came by, courtesy of Hendley, and put in wall outlets and an overhead lamp, bulb and all. He turned it on just before he left, with darkness falling, and I was wired.

I wondered how long people had to wait for service, who were not blessed with friends like mine.

Lou ran me out of the house and created supper, a salad stuffed with more things than any salad ever made before. I did biscuits and apple pie in my Dutch oven and boiled coffee over the fire in time to catch Mac two fish for his supper. Mac didn't much care for salad, but Jerry, the loud mouth, did. He joined us.

"The governor told me to have you in his office as soon as your breakfast was over tomorrow," he said.

"I thought the BIA had closed off the pueblo," Lou said.

"That's what it's about. Hendley brought some lawyer paper over that makes Kilroy a member of the Santa Cala tribe, and the pueblo governor has signed it. The old men will then take him into the scalp society house and make him an initiate of the scalp society one of these days.

"Jesus!" I said.

"You're not safe to be around else, Kilroy," he said to me. "You've seen too much death."

I could believe that, but scalp society?

Next morning they were waiting for us at the bridge on the edge of town, made us stop the truck and get out. Some old man I'd never seen before swept me down from head to foot with an eagle feather fan, catching the evil in a red bandana neckerchief, tying it up at the four corners and throwing it over the rail into the water. "Water is sacred; it will kill the evil," he said.

Jerry was there, giving more explanation than was necessary. The old man did the same for Lou, and this time he did the explaining, saying that being in close association with me had contaminated her.

"We're just friends," I protested lamely, earning a grunt from him and a grin from Lou. Then they let us proceed to the governor's office, accompanied by Jerry.

"We Santa Cala don't adopt people the way some tribes do, who depend on tourism," he said on the way. "Their adoptions are honorary only. Yours is real."

"Why do they want to do that?" I asked.

"They said it's because you're going to keep Teno out of jail," he said.

"I don't know how," I muttered. "Beside, Teno said it's too late to do any good."

"That's for this year," Jerry said. "If Teno is imprisoned for years, the pueblo will die."

I could almost feel the bonds that were holding me to this place tighten. How did I let this happen?

The governor was all business. "We know that some tribes hold a ceremony to wash out your old blood and replace it with theirs, but our old men say that's impossible. The Badger Clan people have said they will let your name be placed on their rolls. They need some young men in their group."

The governor gave me a signed copy of the adoption paper, which I assumed had been prepared by Ginwright. "We have sent a copy on to the BIA," the governor said. "You can now come and go in the pueblo whenever you want."

"And you can move back with Nurse Wilson," the governor said to Lou. "The Public Health Service overrode the BIA ruling against her living in the pueblo."

"Good," Lou said. "This living in the same house with Kilroy is ruining my reputation. I've been contaminated."

She said it without cracking a smile, but I knew she was laughing inside.

I noticed a fish shocker in the corner, its handle leaning up against the wall. I'd been a summer ranger for the Adirondack League, a hunting and fishing club in New York. My father was a member. The club owned fishing rights along the river upstream from North Lake and guarded them from poachers.

"I've done fish counts back east," I said to the governor. "I'd be glad to help out, if you need it," and I nodded over to the gear.

"Good," he said, echoing Lou.

Jesus! Told off for presumption twice in the same day, I thought. The governor took me to a house on one of the wide streets. This pueblo had no central plaza, as most of the pueblos did, according to Simpson. Inside were a number of men sitting in a circle on wooden kitchen chairs, waiting for me. Some were my age, some maybe ten to fifteen years older, like Virgil, who nodded to me, and some my father's age or older.

"We are all men who have served in war," the governor told me. "Some of us were in World War II, some in Korea and some in Vietnam, like you."

I looked around and nodded to those whose eyes I caught. They were all serious.

"Now, did you kill anyone, or were you only around death?"

I thought of the guards that died when we escaped. I was sure about those. "I killed some," I said. "I don't brag about it."

"None of us do," the governor said. "We are all at risk of being refused entrance to the spirit world of our ancestors because of it. Killing let witchcraft into this world. It is our responsibility to protect those without our blood guilt from witches. Witches from outside the pueblo are after Teno. You must protect him."

"I will try," I promised. There, I'd said it. I was committed. But witches? How was I going to do that? And how did he know that they were from outside?

8

I hadn't seen Jerry come into the meeting of the scalp society, but he was there by the back door when the governor and I left, and he followed us back to the Governor's office where I'd left the truck.

"I didn't know you were in Nam," I said to him. He was too young to have been in Korea.

"I turned eighteen in my freshman year at Stanford," he said. "I registered for the draft there. When I got suspended, the school turned me into the draft board with a 'Do Process' tag. I was gone before I had a chance to go home, and spent my year in Nam as a grunt. Dark as I am, I passed as a brother. My last name is Bigbee. That passed, too."

"Doesn't sound Indian to me," I said.

"You expected 'Teepee'?" he asked. "It's missionary humor. In the old days, when they gave all the kids call names at the school, they called my grandfather 'Tom.' Tombigbee is a river in Choctaw country, so they wrote down Bigbee for his last name."

"I thought you were half Apache," I said.

"More like a quarter. I have an Apache grandmother," Jerry said.

"Huhn!" the governor said. I couldn't add anything to that. Inside the office I asked the governor what he knew about the murders that Teno was being accused of committing.

"There have been four in the last six months," the governor said. "Four is the sacred number for our people, and some of the old men say there won't be any more. The FBI heard about that. It's one of the reasons they charged Teno. Makes it sound like a ritual thing the old men would do. They know Teno would be mixed up in it if it were true."

"How would they know that?"

"Those two students helping with the Lands Claim case, Keith and Kevin, they told the FBI. It's in the anthropological literature of fifty years ago."

"I can't see Teno doing something like that," I said.

"No one would do that now. The people wouldn't allow it," the governor said. "I wouldn't allow it if it comes to that. And if I would, we got Pentecostal

Christians in the village, all women. They don't believe in the old ways. We do that kind of thing any more, they'd turn us in. They won't even help plaster the kivas. They won't do anything the preachers say is un-Christian. They will let the preachers take pictures of their kids standing out in the snow without shoes or coats so the preachers can show folks in California how the poor children of Santa Cala are being mistreated. Raise lots of money, from what I hear."

"Why are all the Pentecostals women?" I asked.

"Indian religious doings is for men," he answered, looking at me disapprovingly for having asked such a question. "At Pentecostal services, women get to listen to preaching and sing hymns. They participate like men do in the Indian ceremonials. Sofie, Teno's wife, is a Pentecostal, much to his disgust. 'She must think she's a man, going to meetings at night,' is the way he says it. If the old men were going to do ritual murder, they'd start with the Pentecostals. I might even help them," he added.

"You're not an old man," Jerry said.

"No, but I'm scalp society," the governor said.

"Teno isn't," Jerry objected.

"No, he's something worse, from their point of view," the governor replied, without saying what. It shut Jerry up. Whatever that was, I hadn't been able to do it.

"Well, who is being killed?" I asked.

"Young guys. Kids that never got drafted because they couldn't pass the IQ tests. The tests are based on being able to read and write English, and a lot of these kids can't do either very well. They all hung around the bar down at San Ysabel, swapping stuff they stole here in town for beer."

"Why doesn't someone stop them?"

"Some of these kids are pretty rough. They have the old men scared. Besides, if the old men complained, they'd have to talk about sacred stuff. They can't do that."

"I don't understand," I said. "The kids are stealing sacred stuff? What kind of sacred stuff?"

"Stuff for rituals. Anything Indian made. Kachina dolls the old men carve for the kids to teach them about the gods. Old pots even."

"Are there buyers for that?"

"You don't know? In Santa Fe I'd hate to name the high-end art store that wouldn't fence stolen Indian artifacts. Some of the rich folks in Santa Fe hang kiva items on their walls that are ritually so dangerous to handle that no knowledgeable Indian would even touch them. These kids don't know anything about the old ways and have no respect for them. The old men say that's why they died. The FBI men know that, too."

"And Keith and Kevin are telling them?" I continued.

He just shrugged.

"So why were the kids killed?"

"My bet is that they wanted to be paid twice, once for delivery and again for keeping their mouths shut. The people buying have connections."

"Does the FBI know about that also?" I asked.

"They're not stupid. Of course they know. But anything that would reflect on the collectors would be frowned on by people whose words carry weight with the FBI."

"The FBI aren't going to solve this, are they?"

"More than that, they're not going to let anyone else solve it, either."

"I've promised I'd try. Could I have mail directed to you?" I asked. "I expect to get a summons from Judge Thatcher."

"Sure, I'll hold it for you," and he gave me a business card. I couldn't have received more efficient service from my ward leader back in Philadelphia.

I decided I had to talk to Ginwright and drove down to Albuquerque that afternoon. Jerry came with me, saying the old men had appointed him my bodyguard.

"I don't need a bodyguard," I told him. "Besides, what could you do I couldn't do myself?"

Jerry slanted his eyes over at me as a switchblade knife appeared in his hand and clicked open. "I told you I passed as a brother," he said. "What did you think I was talking about?"

"You know how to use that thing, or is it just for show?" I asked, impressed despite myself.

He grunted, eyes back on the road, and the knife disappeared. I'd never fought with knifes, being content to use my hands when I needed to defend myself, but I'd seen knife fights on the streets of Saigon. People who talk about the violence of boxing have never seen a knife fight. I hoped I'd never see another.

We found Ginwright in his office at the university. I introduced Jerry to him and said Teno was his uncle and had detailed him to watch my back. Ginwright shook hands with him, but ignored him afterwards, which

I thought amused Jerry. If Jerry had chosen to talk in his Stanford mode, Ginwright would have been amazed. I wondered if Jerry was saving it up for a chance to discomfit the professor down the road. I wouldn't put it past him. I'd have to warn Ginwright. Fun is fun, but Ginwright was a good guy and he was representing Teno pro bono.

"They're picking Teno up," Ginwright said. "The grand jury has found probable cause. There will be charges of both first and second degree murder, so if he passed on one charge, there will be another waiting for him. Juries sometimes feel comfortable giving a lesser charge when they find a defendant not guilty on a heavier charge but want to do what they see as their duty. They think they've done a middle-of-the-road thing, particularly when there is only circumstantial evidence involved, as in this case."

"I thought the arraignment was for murder two," I said.

"That doesn't bind the grand jury. Murder one was O'Brian's pay-back for being embarrassed at the arraignment."

"What are Teno's chances to beat them both?"

"Not good."

"Have you talked to Teno?"

"I'll be informed when he's brought in," Ginwright said.

I told Ginwright about the scalp society and the charge laid on me by them. I also told him about what the governor had said. "The governor is pretty canny," I concluded.

"You're going to have to figure out a way to get the FBI out of the way if you're planning on leaning on the guys in San Ysabel," Ginwright said. "They're talking to the Bureau, cooperating, I hear."

On the way out I decided Ginwright hadn't been much help. I don't know what I'd expected, but any action that ensued would have to be mine, not his. I had to talk to Jackson. He knew more about crime than anyone should. And I thought I'd ask my mother to do a little research on who might be purchasing illegally obtained Indian artifacts. The same people who hung around art galleries in Santa Fe hung around them in L.A. Besides, her new gallery in Santa Fe on Canyon Road gave her access to the locals, though she didn't seem to be around much. As my father was fond of saying, when he had me employed on some task that would dirty his hands, "Why keep a dog and do your own barking?" I wouldn't mention that to my mother, she wasn't fond of hearing it.

I was surprised at the greeting Jackson gave Jerry when I introduced him as Teno's nephew. "Hey, blood, you passing?" he said.

Jerry grinned and said, "I can't help what Honkies see, can I?" and went through an elaborate hand-bumping ritual with Jackson.

"You said you were Apache and Santa Cala," I said. "If I'm misled, who's to blame?"

"I didn't mislead anyone. I'm Apache, Santa Cala and Choctaw. You just don't know about us Choctaw. We were slave owning plantation people at the time of what you Yankees call the Civil War. The Five Civilized Tribes, of which the Choctaw were the principal one, declared war on the Union along with the Confederacy. When Lee signed surrender papers at Appomattox, he somehow forgot about us, his loyal allies. We had to make separate peaces, and for the Choctaw, that involved putting all the slaves freed by Lincoln on the tribal rolls. You can figure those black folks didn't just disappear."

"So, you're an Indian, if people see you as an Indian, and a black, if they see you as a black."

"Works for me," Jerry said, shrugging.

"Hey, why not?" Jackson asked.

"Then you may be more useful than you appear to be," I said, sourly. "How long you going to hang around the hospital?" I asked Jackson. "Where are the rest of the guys?"

"They got discharged. I'm holding their back pay checks so they don't go crazy. They'll party some and get back in touch."

"You don't party?" Jerry asked.

"Hey, I invented party. I can leave any time I want," he answered, offended. "I been waiting for my man, Mr. K, here, to say, we're ready. The three brothers are casing out the town and LeRoy is getting his back pay warrant. I got mine," and he patted his shirt pocket.

"Well, Jerry's uncle is in jail for killing three guys and could burn if we don't find out who really did them in," I said. "We need some help. The old man is innocent."

"Never met a man in jail who wasn't," Jackson murmured, "me included."

"Sure, but this time it's me saying so," I told him. "Ask Jerry," I added.

"It's a frame," Jerry said. "The FBI knows who did it, but don't want to trouble no rich whites, particularly when they can't prove nothing. Just makes them mad. Who needs that?" His delivery had segued to black ghetto accents and rhythms. The guy was good.

118

"So, who did do it?" Jackson asked.

"It's a ring," I said. "There are Indian kids who steal sacred stuff and hand it on to fences, who pay them off and deliver it into the hands of art dealers, who sell it to rich collectors."

"Who's getting offed?"

"The Indian kids. There have been four of them in the last six months."

"The Feds think Jerry's uncle is the fence?" he asked.

"No, they say he's having them executed for stealing the sacred stuff," Jerry answered. "His position in the pueblo requires him to safeguard the traditional. In the past, the charge might well have been true, though Indian kids would never have been the thieves. Some of the old men, men who were responsible for taking care of things, sold stuff to anthropologists fifty years ago, both paraphernalia and information. When it became known, the sellers were killed. The man who held Teno's position then would have ordered it to be done."

"Did the anthropologists ever take responsibility for that?" I asked, wondering why he'd dropped the ghetto talk. And where did the word "paraphernalia" come from? I guessed he was showing Jackson he had another dimension.

"Not really," Jerry said. "Individual anthropologists regretted the death of friends and wrote about it, but none of them retreated from what they saw as their duty, the gathering of information on diverse cultures. A. L. Kroeber, the dean of American anthropologists, once said, 'I am a social scientist, not a social worker.' He has been much quoted."

"That ain't true this time?" Jackson asked.

"No. I would know. The war captains, who are appointed yearly to keep witches out of the pueblo, using night patrols, among other things, used to be the executioners. They'd put on the masks of the twin war gods, Oh-yo-yea-wee and Maus-a-wee, and filled with the persona of the gods, cut off the heads of such criminals. My cousin Virgil is a war captain this year; I'm his assistant. I'd have been involved."

"Why don't you tell that to the judge?"

"I'm not allowed to. Making sacred information public robs it of its efficacy."

"You just told me," Jackson said, wrinkling his brow.

"You ain't public," Jerry said, dropping back into black speech patterns. "If you told, dude, who'd listen to you?"

Jackson nodded. That made sense. "You got any ideas?" he asked.

"If we find out the truth and tell the judge outside of the courtroom, I think he'd listen," I said. "He strikes me as a man who is more interested in justice than law. As a federal judge, he can do pretty much anything he wants. He could just throw the case out."

"It's a gamble," Jackson said, "but that's what I do. What's the next move?"

"Let's stop by the bank and put your warrant and the ones you hold for the brothers in my safe deposit box. I'll get you a key and you can open it any time you want."

"We'll tell the brothers," Jackson said in agreement. "Soon as LeRoy is ready, we'll go meet them."

"You know how to contact them?"

"LeRoy gave them an address. He has cousins here."

LeRoy joined us shortly and approved of the plan to deposit the money in the bank. "I never had this much money at one time," he said. "It scares me."

The bank business took less time than it did when I came in with Hendley. I was a customer, I had Jackson and LeRoy sign for extra keys so they could deposit their warrants in the box for safekeeping. I'd trusted them both with my life. Giving them access to my papers was nothing beside that.

LeRoy directed us to his cousins who lived in an area called Martineztown in the northern part of Albuquerque. There was a corner bar he took us to first, where he introduced us around. We bought drinks and were on first name basis with the regulars in a couple of hours' time. They called LeRoy "Carlos." Jackson grinned at me.

"You got something to say?" LeRoy demanded.

Jackson just shook his head. We both still called him LeRoy.

I wrote the address and phone number for the governor of Santa Cala on a card that the bartender posted by the phone behind the bar.

"When the black men I told you about come in looking for me, show them this," LeRoy said. "I'm going up to Santa Cala with these guys. We got something we have to do up there."

I borrowed the bar phone to call my mother, promising I would come to see her as soon as I could get free from the responsibilities that had been thrust upon me. She, in turn, promised to find out about the sale of Indian artifacts, saying if I had anything really good, she'd get me top price. I'm pretty sure she didn't understand why I was interested, but that didn't much matter. She was a terrier. She'd dig it out.

When we reached my place on the river, the guys were impressed. "How did you promote this in the time you've had out?" Jackson asked. "I'm the best con man you ever met, and I couldn't do it."

Jerry squatted in the corner of the adobe and watched, his face impassive, as I explained. LeRoy was paying full attention to my answer. Neither Jackson nor LeRoy appeared to fully believe my story.

"Let's see if I got this straight," Jackson said, holding up one hand to count the points off on his fingers. "You horn in on this private poker game, win all the money on the table, and these white guys are so eager to lose more to you that they get you paper on this place, pay to have the house fixed up, fence and gate the property and bring in electricity? Good thing you got water in the creek or they'd have to dig you a well."

"I paid back everything it cost them," I said.

"You couldn't begin to do that," Jackson said. "Maybe you reimbursed them out of pocket expenses, but you sure didn't pay them for their time. These guys don't work for nothing." I hadn't thought about that.

"Can you get us into the game?" LeRoy asked. "You going to hog this all to yourself?"

"Darned straight," I said. "Not even I will play poker with either of you guys any more and I like you both. I've watched the two of you cheat each other shamelessly at cards for hours and never saw anything wrong. For me, poker is a game. For you it's hunting without a license. These guys aren't stupid and all of them have been around a lot more than I have. Chances are you'd get caught, be put in jail by the sheriff or just eliminated by Joe Lima. He has guys that do everything else. Why not that?"

"Don't worry about us," Jackson said.

"I'm not. I'm worried about me. I introduce either of you to the game and I'll be out of here in a week. I told you, we have to help Jerry's uncle. We can talk about other things after we handle that, okay?"

They grudgingly accepted my position and I sent them down to the little general store in San Ysabel to buy themselves blankets. "Get cots, if you want," I said. "I'm using the hammock and the bed is for guests."

"Ain't we guests?" Jackson asked, plaintively.

"No more than I am," was my answer. It was the right one.

As long as I wasn't putting either of them in an inferior position, they didn't care about the rural simplicity of the rest of the arrangements. I understood. I've spent years resenting the inequities of rank and privilege that I'd found in the army. It was at variance with my ideas of what should be allowed in a free country.

They left in my truck, coming back with blankets and some secondhand automotive tools that Jackson had bought at the garage. "I picked up spark plugs, cables and points while I was at it," he said. "This wreck you're driving needs to be tuned up. Man, it's rough."

"You know anything about cars?"

"I was the fastest hot-wire in Chicago," he said. "Me and my buddies could strip a stolen car in less than half an hour. Don't nobody know more about how cars are put together than me."

"Why didn't you get a job up in Detroit, you so good?" Leroy asked.

"You see many blacks in them unions? Membership is inherited, father to son, or nephew. I ain't got no white uncles."

"Nah, that ain't true," Leroy said. "Maybe the crafts work that way, but the assembly lines don't, that's for sure. Bro, I got relatives working up in Detroit."

Opening one eye, I interrupted, "How are things down in San Ysabel with Joe Lima closing the bar?"

"Man, like someone pissed in the family sink," Jackson said.

"Interesting allusion," I commented, opening the other eye as I continued to lie in the hammock. It was too early in the afternoon to fish. Mac had hidden in the willows, not coming out when Jackson and LeRoy parked and came to stand beside me, looking down and shaking their heads.

"All the booze was being loaded in trucks and hauled away by guys meaner looking than LeRoy, here," Jackson said.

"One was a cousin," LeRoy said. "He's handsome like me. He said he worked for Joe Lima. How come you know about Joe Lima? You mixed up with him?"

"I told you. He's one of the poker players," I said, "Why do you ask?"

"I didn't figure it was that Joe Lima. You ever hear of the Mexican Mafia?"

"Nope."

"Well, if there was one, it would be run by him," LeRoy "And you play poker with that guy? I take back what I said. I don't want in that game!"

"He's a nice fella," I said. "He's the one that fixed it up for me to buy this place for back taxes."

"Nice, huh? You think he don't cheat at cards?"

"He doesn't win more than his share. The only one that does that is me."

"And you're so transparent they could see right through you if you tried to cheat," Jackson said. 'I know how it is. They could all cheat, if they wanted to, but the others would know it. Your boyish honesty is the only reason you're still alive." It was a sobering concept.

"How are the locals taking it?" I asked.

"They ain't saying much," Leroy said. "They know who Joe Lima is. Mouthing off in front of his heavies would not be smart. I heard someone say the bar guy had hidden some of the booze. When Joe Lima does an inventory, he'll come looking for it. He'll find it, too."

"He keeps that close a check on things?" I asked.

"Joe Lima? I'd hate to have my life depend on betting Joe Lima don't know what's going on."

"We can't let him take them out until we can clear Teno," I said.

"You think he'll let such a thing slide, just to play poker? Joe Lima got where he is and stays there by taking care of business," LeRoy said. "You'd better move fast."

I drove up to the Santa Cala governor's office with Jerry, leaving Leroy and Jackson behind to nap. "I'll be home before dark," I said. "I have to catch some fish." I didn't explain it and they didn't ask. Neither of them had seen Mac yet, but they were both used to me doing things my way.

The governor was in his office. "I can't go to my fields while I'm in office," he explained. "It's hard; there's no salary connected with being governor, which means the man saddled with it had better have something saved up, or his family will go hungry. Even so, people will think you steal from pueblo money that comes through your hands, like fines for illegal fishing. Some men that get this job have to."

"Why do you take it?"

"The old men select the governors. You say no, they might hang you by your thumbs from the vigas of your own house and whip you with yucca whips until you change your mind. Reluctance to serve is admired. No one should want to put himself forward. But refusal to serve is not permitted."

"Are you doing all right?" I asked. "I have extra money. I could loan it to you."

"Thanks, but that would get out," and his eyes drifted over to Jerry, standing and looking out the window. "There's nothing you can do that would be proper in the eyes of the people. The sacrifice is expected of me."

"Well, we have to move fast on helping Teno," I said. "We heard that Joe Lima has pulled the license for the San Ysabel bar. He'll be around to check on discrepancies on the liquor inventory. The guys who run the bar and have been buying stuff from the young hoods here in town are likely to leave. If they don't they may not live to regret it."

"This would be a good time to burn the place down," Jerry said. "Joe Lima won't care, but you know there will be a new bar there with someone else's license in no time. The reservation is too handy."

"Burn it down? Flaming arrows like in the movies? I mentioned that once to Teno as a joke," I said.

Jerry just grunted.

"Joe Lima won't let someone else establish here," the governor said. "This is his turf. More likely there will be bootleg liquor coming in," the governor said. "If the BIA allowed us to have a bar on the reservation, it would be both good and bad. More adults would drink if it were here, but maybe fewer kids. For sure, there would be less theft." I noticed the governor didn't respond to Jerry's comment about burning the bar down, but that didn't mean he didn't hear it. I wondered if Teno had spoken to the governor about my suggestion. And what brought the idea to Jerry's mind?

"I have something else I have to do," I said. "I want to get the FBI guys out of here." I told them my plan and ended with, "Jerry, you stay here until the FBI men are in position. Pick up Lou Elwood and come after me. Don't tell her it was my idea, or she might want to think about it first, okay? We need her as an innocent witness."

They nodded and I went back to my place to catch fish for Mac. LeRoy and Jackson borrowed my truck to visit San Ysabel and plant the seed about being interested in buying the garage as part of the plan. The funny part was that they were actually considering it. That should keep the local crooks in town for a bit. It was nice to have the place to myself, for a change.

The next few days were quiet. Jackson and LeRoy worked on the truck, running back to town from time to time to look for spare parts and to push the idea of buying the garage. Mac introduced himself to the two of them at his suppertime the first night they ate with us, streaking out of the willows to jump on my fish. Neither of the men was inclined to make friends with something that looked like a wild cat, which was fine with Mac. I was getting impatient for at least one of my plans to mature, but got in some sack time, while waiting. Army guys sleep when they can. Mac liked it. Good cat.

I'd about decided my plan to trap the FBI guys wasn't going to work when Jerry drove in with Lou in her microbus, just after dawn. "The game's afoot! I need you, Watson," Jerry called. Oh, man.

Jackson and LeRoy were polite to Lou, but I could see them looking her over, wondering what she was doing coming after me.

"I'll be back," I told them. "Got to catch Mac a fish or two for breakfast. Try, if you want." I wondered how that would work out.

We drove through Santa Cala up a road along the river and stopped when mounted men blocked our path. "They're about a half-mile ahead," one said.

"You said you knew how to work fish-shocking gear," Jerry said. "I got waders for both you and Lou. She'll keep notes on the fish you count to make it look real. We don't want them to think this is a set-up. You're witnesses."

"Witnesses to what?" I asked, donning the waders.

"You don't need to know in advance," he answered and Lou smirked. Uh-huh. My plan was working out.

I picked up the shocker gear, strapping the power pack on my back and hanging the shocker from my shoulder by the strap. I felt Lou's eyes on me, checking to see if I really knew what I was doing, but I ignored her. When I was ready, I entered the stream and made for the first pool, testing the shocker in the quiet water. I was rewarded with a half dozen fish floating belly up, not dead, just stunned. "Rainbow, ten inches, female," I said, picking up an unmoving fish. I sorted out the others, and Lou wrote down what I told her on a clipboard. Jerry followed from the bank on a horse that had been brought for him. The other horsemen disappeared into the trees.

There was nothing much to see. There were no fish over a foot long, and most of them were rainbows or German browns from the hatchery. I did find a half dozen native cutthroat, however. They were better fighting fish than the hatchery stock, but never reached the sizes of the others. These were about eleven inches, but they were adult fish. I became so interested in what I was finding that coming upon the FBI men fishing from the bank was a surprise.

"What the hell do you think you're doing here?" one of them asked.

"Doing a chore for the governor," I said. "The Santa Cala want to know what they have in the water here."

"We've closed this pueblo to outsiders. It's a possible crime scene. Get your asses out of here."

"They have tribal membership," Jerry said coming up to them, waving his cane of office at them. "You do not. You are under arrest for fishing in tribal waters without a permit from the governor."

"You can't arrest us," one of the men said with a snort. "We're FBI."

"And I'm an assistant war captain," Jerry said. "Where is your car?"

"We're up the stream a hundred yards or so. We didn't know this was tribal land."

"It's posted," Jerry said. "I'll have to confiscate your cameras along with your fishing poles. I see you've managed to catch a couple of fish. Catch and release might have gotten you a warning, but you've killed fish."

"How do you intend to enforce your arrest?" the first man said contemptuously, spitting into the river.

"That's polluting," Jerry said, "another charge," and he raised his fingers to his mouth, whistling between them a shrill blast, than another. A half dozen men on horses, rifles pointing at the FBI men, came riding up from both sides of the narrow river.

"These are members of the scalp society. They function as militia. Do you wish to resist arrest, or will you come quietly?"

"You can't get away with this!"

"Maybe not, but we'll make a good start at it, anyway," Jerry said. "They'll be armed. Get their guns and their identification," Jerry ordered one of the mounted men. Ignoring the protests, the man dismounted and frisked both FBI agents, removing guns from underarm and ankle holsters for both men. He also took their camera and small tape recorder. He kept the guns, but handed the ID cases and other gear to Jerry.

"Which one is Don Barr?" Jerry asked.

The tallest one nodded. I had never heard him speak much, and when he had, he displayed a slight speech impediment. He had the injured air of one forced to associate with inferiors, which, I guessed, included his companion.

"You must be Simon Padilla," Jerry said to other man. "You senior here?"

"Yes, and I'm warning you. If you return our guns, cameras, poles and

Ids, I promise not to make an official report about this. You are wards of the government for which I am an officer. You can go to jail for interfering with an officer on official business."

"Fishing is business?" Jerry asked.

"If I say it is. Whose word do you think will be listened to, mine or a government ward?"

"Well, we have these two white witnesses who will probably testify as to the true nature of this arrest, haven't we?" and he waved at Lou and me.

"Do you have a written fishing permit from the governor?" Lou asked. "If you do, show it. If you haven't, you'd better not try to produce one later, saying you were never asked for one."

"What authority do you have here?" Padilla asked angrily.

"None, but I do," Jerry said. "Answer her question."

"Damned if I will. What I will do is have her charged for trespassing. And you, too," he said, frowning at me. "Now, I'm leaving. Better not try to stop me."

At a signal from Jerry, ropes snaked out from both sides of the narrow river, and the men were caught by loops tied to the saddle horns of the scalp society members, who started walking their horses up stream. When the FBI men stumbled and fell into the water, they were dragged along until they recovered their feet, screaming threats and imprecations with every step. Even the silent one found his voice.

"I'll go with them," Jerry said. "You backtrack to the van and I'll meet you at the governor's. Don't leave until we get there. Warn the governor about what is going on. He'll get the rest of the scalp society out." He gave me the tape recorder and the camera.

"Are we in trouble?" Lou asked me when we had shed our waders and she was driving us back down the dirt road to the village.

"How could we be?" I asked. "We were just onlookers."

"But we knew we'd find them there," she said.

"We did?" I said. "I don't recall that."

"Well, I did. I want to apologize to you for not letting you know what was happening," she said. "None of this is your fault."

"Were you told not to tell me?" I asked.

"I promised," she admitted.

"Then there's nothing to apologize for. I have no complaint. Had I known as much about it as you, I'd still have gone along with it."

She nodded, troubled. Speaking of trouble, I hoped she'd remember what I said if she ever found out that the whole scam was my idea.

We reported in to the governor's office, and he sent runners out to raise the other members of the scalp society. By the time Jerry drove in at about ten miles an hour, driving the FBI men's car, the street was full of armed men on horses. I saw men from each of the last three wars, including old men from World War II.

The governor had telephoned into FBI headquarters in Albuquerque, setting forth the particulars and asking that the men be picked up. He said he'd release them into the custody of anyone from there with credentials who could pay the fines of one hundred dollars apiece that he'd levied.

Out of sight of the men, I opened the camera and took out the film. I wondered what they'd been taking pictures of and decided I'd have the film developed myself. I wanted to see what they'd been up to, and if they'd kept a record. I also went through the briefcases that Jerry had brought around to the back of the governor's office. I also took the tape from their recorder, along with two spares from one of the briefcases. Everything else was replaced in the back seat of the car.

When two more FBI men came roaring up from Albuquerque an hour later, demanding to be informed, et cetera, the governor had Padilla and Barr brought out from an inside room, still tied up, each led by two scalp society men. The horsemen had disappeared. Only Lou, the governor and I were in the office when the outsiders arrived, but all of a sudden the small office was crowded. The men from Albuquerque demanded that the guns, cameras and IDs be produced immediately.

"Who do you think you are?" one of the newcomers demanded, tugging ineffectively at the rope binding his associates.

The governor had had enough. "Think? I know who I am. I am the governor of Santa Cala Pueblo, one of the domestic, dependent sovereign nations that Chief Justice of the Supreme Court, John Marshall, wrote of in 1831. You have no standing here except to investigate capital crimes. These men were fishing illegally. That is not a capital crime, even under Indian law, but it is a crime. The fine is one hundred dollars each. Their fishing poles have been confiscated because they were not registered on entry into tribal lands. You can have the IDs back when the fine is paid. The guns and cameras are in their car. And don't cut that rope," he said. "That's a horsehair lariat and expensive."

Jerry opened the door and said, "I heard shouting. You need any help?" Through the open door we could see that the riflemen were back. So could the men from Albuquerque. One of them pulled out a wallet and found paper money, which he handed over, requesting a receipt. The governor ordered the two captives released. As they were going out the door, Padilla turned and snarled at me, "You haven't heard the last of this!"

I looked him in the eye and said, "Neither have you."

9

*T*here were only four of us at poker. Hendley drove up in his dusty old Cadillac, Lima in his shiny new one, followed by Simpson in his diesel-engine, four-wheel-drive pickup carting the promised furniture from the bar. Jackson and LeRoy unloaded it.

"Better not leave this ride sitting around," Jackson said, patting a fender. "I'm tempted to steal it myself."

"If it's missing, I'll know where to start looking," Simpson drawled. The sheriff stepped out of the truck's cab and grinned without mirth while Jackson took in his badge and holstered gun in one brief glance. I kept my face straight, but I wanted to shout with laughter. Jackson's mouth had finally embarrassed him as it had me so many times. I saw LeRoy assume a sudden blank expression, different from his usual pleasant one. He and I would talk about this later, when Jackson wasn't around, or maybe when he was, I decided.

I helped the guys maneuver the table through the door and set it up. Even with the six chairs that we placed around it and the bed up against the wall, there was plenty of room in the twelve-by-sixteen house to move about in. The two-hundred-watt lamp hung right over the center of the round table, and we put the narrow table with one drawer that held the cards and money up against the blank wall.

"Couldn't have a better arrangement if you had an architect design it," Joe Lima said, giving his approval. He had joined us, making almost no noise at all. Useful trick, I thought, for one with Lima's interests. LeRoy all but tugged his forelock when Lima walked in. Jackson never missed much and he saw that. I could see some mutual heavy teasing in their futures. As soon as the furniture was arranged the guys left, and I could hear our truck going down the dirt road. It was lots quieter after they worked on it, but it was still an army vehicle.

"Where's Ginwright?" Simpson asked.

"End of term. He's got grades to deliver," Hendley said, seating himself with his back against the one-drawered table. He had a paper sack in which he had carried the cards, and this he put on top of the table, selecting a new deck to open to start the game.

"Been reading more about our hero here," Hendley said.

"Yeah Jackson called a press conference," I said. "That was Jackson rehearsing plans to steal your truck. I asked him to do it to counter that earlier story and he didn't let me talk."

"I saw that one, too, but what I'm talking about was in the *Philadelphia Inquirer*."

"My father?"

"Your father," he answered. "He seems concerned about the abuse the eastern press has been giving you."

"I didn't know the eastern press had even heard of me," I said, as Hendley finished shuffling the deck and began distributing the cards.

The first man to get a one-eyed jack took the first deal. It was Hendley himself, and he announced, "Seven card stud, high-low, ten ante," before saying, "Your father seemed to think the big newspapers were questioning your personal courage as well as your good sense in criticizing the military."

"So do you," Sheriff Simpson observed.

"Yeah, well, they were. That don't mean I do. I just don't like newspapers. I don't doubt our hero, here."

"Sure."

Hendley ignored Simpson's dry comment to say, "If your old man hadn't tied you to the University of Pennsylvania 'Baby-face Jack Kilroy,' I wouldn't have remembered your college boxing days. Simpson says he knew."

"Yeah, so he said," I muttered.

"My question is, if you had another year of eligibility, would you have gone heavyweight?" Hendley continued.

"I never weighed more than a hundred and ninety, even after army basic training," I said.

"Zora Folley weighed one eighty-nine when he fought Clay," Simpson said.

"And he lost," I said.

"Jack Dempsey weighed one eight-six when he whipped Jess Willard," Hendley said.

"His manager, Tex Rickert, had stuffed plaster of Paris in Dempsey's gloves. Rickert dipped them in water between rounds and when they hardened, Dempsey broke Willard's jaw in two places, knocked out several of his teeth and broke his cheekbone in the process of knocking him out. It's a wonder he didn't kill him," I said mildly. "Dempsey got bigger when he started to eat regularly."

"Max Schmeling weighed one eighty-four when he beat Joe Louis," Hendley said. They weren't going to stop, were they?

"And Joe Louis damn near killed him the second time they fought," I pointed out "What's this about? You want me to fight Mohamed Ali?"

"He ain't champion no more. They took his belt when he refused to go into the army. He said no Vietnamese had ever called him nigger," Simpson said. "They won't even let Ali fight now that he's out of jail. There's not a boxing commission in the states that will give him a license."

"Ginwright thinks he could fight on an Indian reservation and bypass the state boxing commissions," Hendley said. "We might be able to set a fight up if you're interested. We'd have to talk Stu Udall into signing off on it. He's Secretary of the Interior; I know Stu from way back. Used to date his aunt, Mary Udall. Prettiest girl I ever saw. Married I. O. Rasmussen."

"You're part Cherokee, right?" I asked Hendley.

"Yeah, a quarter. Where you hear that?"

"Lou Elwood. She says she's part Cherokee. I was giving her a bad time and she said, 'Only a fool argues with a Cherokee.' Said to ask you about it."

"That right?" Hendley said with a laugh. "I knew I liked that girl. Mostly that's something that Cherokee men say about Cherokee women, and anyway, we ain't arguing. I'm just asking."

"Well, talk to Jackson," I said. "If Ali can beat Jackson, I'll take him on." I thought I was safe. Jackson wasn't stupid.

Hendley and Simpson laughed, but Lima asked, "We going to play?"

That stopped the discussion for a time. I decided to alter my strategy a bit, using the classic fold or raise tactic on every hand, depending on whether I had a realistic chance of winning. By the end of the evening I was able to abandon it and successfully bluff big twice, getting caught on a smaller bluff bet to set up a kill on a full house.

I had made over a thousand dollars when the game was broken up by Jackson and LeRoy opening the door to tell us, "The bar in San Ysabel has burned down."

"Don't look at me," Joe Lima said, in response to Simpson's raised eyebrows. "I have an alibi." He all but smirked.

"The way it went up, there must have been some booze still in it," Jackson said. "We were down at the garage doing an inventory. We've about decided to buy it, but when I went to the grocery store to look for the owner, the guy's wife said he wasn't home. We were talking through the screen door when the fire broke out and she got hysterical. She said he was in the bar."

"You go look for him?" Hendley asked, standing and pocketing the few dollars he had left from the evening's play.

"The doors were locked," Jackson said. "By the time I got a sledgehammer from the garage to break in, the whole inside was blazing. Nothing in there could have still been alive."

"I better go take a look," the sheriff said.

"What do you think?" Hendley asked Joe Lima.

"I think he'd hid some liquor on me," Lima said. "I was going to tear the place down, if necessary, followed by doing the same to the garage and the grocery store until I found my goods, just to make an example. I can't have people thinking it's safe to steal from Joe Lima."

"Makes sense to me," Hendley said. "So, who did do it?" getting up to leave, himself. I missed Lima's answer as the two men went out the door together, and I stopped at the doorway to watch them talk quietly for a few minutes before leaving in their separate Caddys. Hendley told me he liked the fact that Cadillacs were heavy enough for the state's dirt roads, but he always bought them used. Lima's were always new. Both cars were black. I wondered if Lima passed his on to Hendley when the shine wore off. They had different image needs, but the black Cadillac answered for both of them.

"What's this about the fire and the missing man?" I asked Jackson, after the last two cars drove away.

"Missing men," Jackson said. "I think both the brothers were in that fire, the bartender and the store owner. They sure weren't anyplace else around."

"The fire was to cover up the killings?" I asked.

"That's what I think," Jackson said, and LeRoy nodded. "You didn't see anything?"

"No, but we heard a truck come in and leave when we were in the garage. Whined like four-wheel drive," LeRoy added.

"Yeah," Jackson agreed. "It was headed up to the pueblo."

No one in the pueblo would have a four-wheel drive, I thought. They'd cost too much. Lou's two blond buddies, Keith and Kevin, had one, though. I wondered if the FBI had arranged for passes to get them in and out of the pueblo, despite the prohibition against whites. I'd ask Lou. I hoped she wouldn't ask why I wanted to know.

"You could probably buy that garage in San Ysabel even cheaper than the asking price if you're right about the owners being dead," I said.

"Man, the sheriff's going to think that, too. You see the way he looked at me when I joked about stealing his truck? They going to need someone to arrest for that fire and those killings, and me and LeRoy here are just too handy."

"Who's this LeRoy?" LeRoy asked in mock indignation. "My name is Carlos. The sheriff will be looking for an ugly black man hanging around up to no good more like," he said, shaking his head. "I'd arrest you myself, for sure, I be the police. Me, I'm just a poor country Mexican guy who fell into bad company."

"You think white guys can tell the difference between us brothers and you Mexican guys? Ain't many blacks out here. You're the niggers around here."

"My grandfather used to say the Irish were the niggers of Europe," I said. "Being put down is not something any race has exclusive experience with."

"The difference is, when you got a little money you Irish started being white like the rest of them," Jackson said, brooding. "Ginwright's black funeral director grandfather got more money than your buddy Hendley, even, but he don't get invitations to join the country club. He's still black."

"The exclusive country clubs in Philadelphia won't accept Jews or Irish Catholics," I said. "My father is a congressman, and he can't get in. He pretends he doesn't care, doesn't like golf, but it hurts him anyway."

"You Catholic?" LeRoy asked, interested. "I never saw you go to Mass."

"I'm nothing," I said. "My folks battled about what I'd be, and I got a double dose of religious instruction while I was growing up, my father's Roman Catholic and my mother's Southern Baptist. Nothing stuck."

"Well, I'm splitting," Jackson announced.

"This sheriff and the FBI going to start talking to one another sometime. If I ain't here, I'm less likely to be the subject of conversation. Maybe LeRoy is all right, like he says, but I ain't."

"We'll go in tomorrow and get your money," I said.

"I don't need it," Jackson said. "If I have it, I'll just throw it away. Maybe I'll take enough to get some wheels, but that's it. You hang on to it until I ask for it. I'll check in with the other brothers and take off," he said.

Next morning LeRoy and I rode down with Jackson to Albuquerque. Jackson insisted on driving, saying he didn't trust either of us to stay on the road. "It may be okay when I ain't in the car," he said, "but when I ride, I drive." His confidence was well based. He was an excellent driver. I'm not a good passenger myself, but I actually got a nap in the back of the carryall while Jackson and LeRoy argued in the bench front seat. I wondered if LeRoy would go with Jackson when he left. They had been inseparable in the prison camp.

I dozed off wondering what to do about Teno. If the brothers that ran the bar and the store were dead, their murder could not be laid directly at Teno's door; but under the theory that O'Brian was operating on, Teno could order killings from wherever he was. I wondered why the brothers had been killed, if indeed they had been. Was there any tie between that and the deaths of the pueblo's four young men? Teno's grandson, Roy, had been one of them. Did Teno know more than he had told me? Was the bar burned down because I had suggested it to Teno as a solution to the problem?

We went out to the VA Hospital to see if any of the brothers had been there. We found messages for us to contact them at a bar on north Edith Street. We could get directions to the bar at the black Baptist church near there.

"Where you been?" was the greeting we received when we opened the door. The three friends came up to greet us with ritual hand-bumps. They differed each time I tried to master the routine, but that was part of the mystique, I thought. Whites can't bump. LeRoy did it all right, so maybe they were correct. You have to at least pretend to be black. It seemed important to them to believe it.

"I'm taking off," Jackson told them. "The fuzz be looking for me for burning down a bar. I can't buy that garage. I'm too handy."

"Yeah, we know. Don't matter. We got something else," one of them said.

"Ginwright talked to the brothers that run the funeral parlors in Albuquerque. We got a gig. We been waiting for you."

"What's up?"

"They want us to deliver cars for them. There are black funeral directors from California to Texas that have trouble getting credit with car dealers, and pay twice the asking price for everything they buy. Ginwright set up a corporation for us. With a white at the head, we can pick up cars wholesale and deliver them where they're needed cheaper than any of the brothers can buy them from dealers . . . a lot cheaper."

"You do the numbers, Mr. K, and we'll take care of the rest," one of them said, nodding at me.

"Numbers are easy," I said, "but I have no more business sense than a Girl Scout cookie seller."

"The brothers will take care of that," I was told. "We just need a front man."

"I'll have to wear a suit and tie?" I asked. I'd promised myself that would never again be the case.

"Only when you're talking to the bankers."

"We have to drive out to California," another said. "The brothers gave us contacts there."

"I have to try to find who is responsible for the killings that Teno was put in jail for," I objected.

"Didn't you hear? Your momma figured it out. She wants you to visit her. We can do that when we're out on the coast."

"How do you know that?" I asked.

"Ginwright told us. She called him. You got to keep in touch, man." I had given my mother Ginwright's number, but this was a surprise.

"I'll check in with him and see what he says," I told them.

If my mother really had figured it out, she was in some danger herself, I thought. There had been four men killed already for knowing too much. She was intuitive as well as being a shrewd judge of character. The artless, airy persona she affected might well protect her, but I was worried.

Ginwright had been charmed by my mother, making him no different than most men she encountered, even by telephone. Everyone who knew her called her "Jo," short for Josephine. She was most definitely not Philadelphia Irish. She was a North Carolina Scot, a daughter of the Old South and about as helpless as a mountain cat, despite her demeanor.

"Ladies with accents of that kind generally put me off," Ginwright said. "I tend to hear condescension, even where there is none. I mentioned that I was black, and she said, 'Me, too, dear, bless your heart.' Is she?"

"Black? Her hair is black, her eyes are black, but her skin is milky white," I said. "She was runnerup in a Miss North Carolina beauty contest a few decades back. She said it was her Scot's hooked nose that lost her the title. She had better legs than the winner and more talent . . . played piano as a soloist with the university symphony orchestra. Weren't any black women in the contest."

"Why would she say that, then?"

"To put you at ease, most likely. Worked, didn't it?"

"She lied?"

"Oh, sure. You figured out she was a southern belle all by yourself. Ever know one that didn't lie, when it would ease a social situation? Besides, she's less race conscious than you are. Being black wouldn't bother her at all."

"Easy to say."

"True, though. It's my father who is uncomfortable with blacks. There's a long history of bad feeling between the blacks and Irish of Philadelphia, going back to pre-Civil War days."

"An ethnic white thing?"

"Not at first. In Ireland, there was great sympathy for the plight of blacks in slavery in America. But on immigrating to America, when the Irish figured out that they could establish themselves as legitimate citizens by contrasting their status with that of blacks, they did. They became pro-slavery, even though they were too impoverished to hold slaves. They needed some group they could claim they were better than to rise above the despised status they had held in Europe. That's taking a while to establish in the social climate of Philadelphia, by the way. Still working on it."

"I grieve for them."

"Sure. So what did my mother say?"

"She said there were almost no pieces of ethnic art to be found in the San Francisco area except those in her shop. She mentioned that the Pakistani were making contracts to buy all the silver and turquoise jewelry that the Navaho, Hopi and Zuni could turn out and shipping it to markets in the Middle East. That part's true. Most of the 'authentic Indian jewelry' you can find in the Southwest is made by white craftsmen, unless it's crude old pawn jewelry. She also said that the rumors say one gallery with ready funds buys esoteric pieces, regardless of provenance, but they don't show up in the market. She's going to float a piece or two from her own gallery and watch where they go, but she wants you out there."

"Old pawn jewelry?" Ginwright asked

"Jewelry is like a savings account for old Indians," LeRoy said. "When you need money, you pawn something. If you get money, you redeem it. If you don't redeem it, it becomes 'old pawn jewelry.'"

"How come you know that?" Jackson asked.

"My grandfather owned a pawn shop," LeRoy said.

"You think my mother is on to whoever might tie into stealing of sacred paraphernalia at Santa Cala?" I asked, bringing the discussion back to the main problem.

"She thinks so, she said. She wouldn't tell me why."

"Okay, I'll have to go back to the pueblo and arrange for Lou to look after the cat," I said. "I also should check in with the Santa Cala governor and tell him there might be a lead here that could free Teno. How is Teno getting on?"

"Teno? He says he can't remember a time when he ate so regularly and worked less hard for it. He's all right," Ginwright said.

Sure. I doubted if Ginwright had ever been in prison. No one who had could so easily believe a statement like that.

In Santa Cala, I learned that the governor had given Hendley the recorder tapes and film we took from the FBI agents we arrested. From the tapes, Hendley told him that they identified the two young students from UNM as being the source of information on Teno that the FBI used. The punks had gone through Lou's notes, like she feared.

"Thanks," I said. "Tell Lou, will you? She'll tell the archeology lab boss at UNM, and they'll be called to account. And tell her I'll be gone a few days. Tell her to come see me before I go, if she can." When I explained to the governor about why I was going to San Francisco, he nodded without comment except to say that he wanted Jerry Bigbee to go with me. He said Jerry could ride down to my adobe with Lou. That gave me a chance to talk to Mac by myself and to fish for our supper. Mac hadn't missed me, if I could judge by the cold way I was greeted when I first arrived, but he jumped onto my lap after he had eaten and, eventually, purred. Some cat. No free reinforcement out of Mac.

Lou was on the verge of tears when she stopped by where I was resting in the hammock. I couldn't imagine what it took to upset her that much, but I was standing in front of her in a moment. She threw her arms around my neck and cried, not like I had seen women cry before, but as if her heart were breaking. I patted her back, not knowing if that's what she expected, but doing my best.

"What is it?" I asked, finally, when she was merely sniffing and gulping, trying to control the occasional sob.

She stepped back, leaving one hand on my chest and said, "It's Virgil's baby. She's dead." From the sudden intake of breath, I thought she would break down again, but she shook her head fiercely and turned toward the adobe saying, "I need some tea." She had left a canister of Earl Grey on a shelf, saying I could help myself to it if I wished, but I'm a coffee person, even after my army time, and hadn't touched it.

I brought water from the stream over to the firepit and poured it into the pot she had brought out. She was making a fire. I sat down in my chair and watched, knowing I'd learn what the problem was, in time. It was Jerry who explained it, however, not Lou.

"Virgil brought his baby down from the TB san in Colorado and gave it to his mother. The baby got infant diarrhea and the Public Health nurse took it down to the Indian Hospital. When she brought it back, she explained about boiling the water, but Indians believe illness is caused by witches, not germs. When the baby got sick again, the social workers put the child in foster care. It died there."

Lou broke in, "I'd offered to take care of the baby, but I wasn't on the approved list of foster parents, and they wouldn't consider putting me on. I was with Virgil's family talking to his mother when the BIA social worker came by a short time back to say that baby had died and been returned to the hospital. Virgil's gone down after it."

"By himself?" I asked.

"Yes. That baby was the dearest thing," Lou said, tears rolling down her face as she sat in the other chair to sip her tea. Jerry perched on the stump. "I went down to the hospital with Virgil, to see her the first time she went there. They had her in a crib, out in the hallway, and picked her up only to feed or change her. She was so alert and so happy to be held," and a fresh stream of tears rolled down her face, stilling her voice.

Jerry said, "The social worker warned Virgil's mother that they'd find the baby had had an autopsy, standard practice in cases of this sort, where a death had occurred with no physician in attendance. She said the cause of death was 'failure to thrive.' It didn't get enough love," he added, giving his own evaluation.

I could agree with that. I knew about the way the Indian Hospital did autopsies. I thought about Teno's grandson Roy, after his. Virgil would find the baby lying on a slab, rough stitches holding her tiny body together. If it had been me, I'd have found Phillips, the agency superintendent, and beat his face in, but Virgil had said the social workers would take his mother and sister off welfare if he complained. Those folks would literally starve. That was Ted Phillip's system. I'd find a reason to get him that didn't point to Virgil, but I swore to myself, I'd get him.

"The governor told me you were coming with me to California," I said to Jerry.

"I'm a trained witch hunter," he said, without cracking a smile. "You'll need me."

"You really believe in witches, a Stanford University man like yourself?" I asked skeptically.

"Saint Augustine believed in witches," he said. "Shakespeare believed in witches. Even today, the Pope believes in witches. What do you expect of me?"

"Something more rational," I said.

"Rational? I'm a Skinnerian behaviorist. You can't get more rational than that. I also believe that the behavior of some people is reinforced by contingencies that are intrinsically evil. We Indians call people like that 'witches.' Seems as good a term as any, to me."

"'Intrinsic evil' is an interesting category," I said mildly. "Sounds like my Jesuit uncle talking."

"You disagree?"

"No," I said shortly, after consideration. "No, I don't."

"Good thing. You're a scalp society member now. You're going to be hunting witches like the rest of us."

"I have one in mind," I muttered.

"Jack is so open that lying to him is unfair," Lou said. "Scalp society membership? Where's his scalp?"

"I gave him my medal," I said, "along with the citation. He said it was good enough."

"You want to be in the scalp society?" Lou asked, amazed.

"Teno wants me there," I said.

"We never used to have a scalp membership, like the Zuni did," Jerry said. "Teno said that the death and violence our young men were exposed to in World War II left them open to witch attack. The veterans tried to escape by drinking, but that just made them weaker. The old men had to drive the veterans away, finally, to protect the pueblo. We lost more young people that way than as war casualties. When the Korean War came, the old men decided to do something else. They borrowed the idea of a scalp society from Zuni. Now, they ritually clean returned soldiers and give them responsibility for protecting the rest of the people. So far, it's worked pretty well."

"But you're talking about men who have been initiated into a kiva as an adolescent, not some outsider like Jack Kilroy," Lou objected.

"Kilroy is hanging around, so he's as dangerous as I was, maybe more so," Jerry said. "Teno likes him, which explains why he was brought into the tribe and not run off. The kiva thing requires that someone have a clan membership, not that he knows the language. Clan membership comes through the mother, so if a man brings home a bride from somewhere else, her children will not be brought into a kiva."

"Teno said I was Badger Clan, like him," I said.

"He asked his sister to adopt you," Jerry said. "Clan membership comes though the mother's side. The initiation part will come during the right season for it. If you want, I can help you learn our language. It's not much more difficult than Greek."

"Sure; I'm good at languages," I said.

"I have what Margaret Mead calls a working vocabulary I could lend you to start with," Lou said. "It's just words and phrases, with directions for when they would be used . . . no grammar. But children learn to speak languages from scratch flawlessly without having a clue about grammar."

"I'd like that," I said.

"I used the six-hundred-word basic English list as a starting place, cut out about a third of it for being unusable, and added a number of other words and many phrases I have found useful. Some are women's words, used only by women. I'll eliminate those so you don't embarrass yourself," she said.

"Men and women have different words?" I asked in surprise.

"Not many, but a few," Lou said.

"Men tease women about them," Jerry, told us, "but only privately. We're not supposed to understand what they mean."

"Hunh," Lou retorted. I gathered that she thought Jerry didn't know everything.

"Tell me," I said, "is Teno telling me the truth about having nothing to do about the killing of the young men? And what about the fire at the bar? I remember saying that they should burn the place down. I thought he acted like that idea had never occurred to him before. Did my saying that get it done?"

"Teno lied to you about the bar fire, but not about the killing of the young men," Jerry said.

"Lying is institutionalized among Indians who deal much with whites," Lou agreed. "In the old days, telling the truth to Spanish colonial officials could get you killed. The Indian Service is not much more flexible. It was government agents that cut down the vines and fruit trees during prohibition to keep the Indians from making alcoholic drinks. Admitting you had children of school age meant losing them, not too long ago. BIA officials took them forcibly from their parents and enrolled them in school where they were beaten for speaking their own languages. Lying is not seen as a betrayal of trust among them in close relationships as it is with whites."

"I do not lie to Teno, nor he to me," Jerry said in disapproval.

"You're not white," Lou said in return and Jerry just shrugged.

I don't like lying, even when I can understand why others have had to do so for survival. The idea that Teno had probably lied to me made me uncomfortable.

Jerry and I drove down to Albuquerque the next morning, leaving Mac in Lou's hands, or perhaps vice versa. Lou was going to stay in my adobe house until I got back. I was happy about that.

We found the guys in the bar in Martineztown, waiting for us. "You taking Tonto here with us?" LeRoy asked.

"Who you calling 'Tonto'?" Jerry responded, whipping out his switchblade, flicking it open and leaning back against the bar's pool table, proceeding to clean his fingernails while glancing up at LeRoy over the rims of his dark glasses from time to time as he inspected his work.

"Look at the little brother do the Mau-Mau," Jackson said in admiration. "Better not mess with him, man."

"You bet," LeRoy said, grinning.

"Teno appointed him my bodyguard," I said with a straight face. "He's an assistant war captain for Santa Cala, and a member of the scalp society."

Jerry looked at LeRoy's thick black hair suggestively, and for a moment LeRoy allowed surprise to show on his face. It was enough. Jerry turned away to hide a smile, shut his knife and slipped it back in his pocket. Jackson laughed.

"Are we going in my truck?" I asked.

Jackson looked pained and said, "We're all driving limos back to Los Angeles for trade-ins. You think I'd be seen in that cool town in an army truck?"

LeRoy also looked scandalized at my question but said only, "You can leave the truck here with my cousin."

Under Jackson's eye, I transferred my pack and rifle to the trunk of a black Caddy. "You fixing on shooting someone?" he asked doubtfully.

"If I have to," I said.

Arranging for the purchase of new cars was simple. Joe Lima called his dealer in Albuquerque and vouched for me, guaranteeing my credit. Getting the cars was more complex. The dealers in Albuquerque didn't carry limos, but they could place orders for them in California. We were to drive the trade-ins to Los Angeles, where there was a market for the old Caddys and pick up the new cars there to drive back. We'd pay for them in Albuquerque.

We would leave Albuquerque for Los Angeles in a four-car procession. From there, we'd drive to San Francisco, once we had our new vehicles.

I was increasingly concerned about my mother, the more I thought about it. She was inquisitive to the point of foolhardiness. I hoped she hadn't alerted whoever we were going to question. She could be in danger, seeing a number of people had already been killed. Worrying about her being in danger was what she'd been doing about me for years. It was my turn.

10

*W*e found Jackson, LeRoy, the three other Nam guys I thought of as "the brothers" and four used black Cadillac limousines waiting for us at the bar in Martineztown. The only things that were delaying the departure to L.A. were our arrival from Santa Cala and the question of who was to drive the fourth car. The three brothers each had claimed a vehicle. The last one was reserved for Jackson, LeRoy, Jerry and me; the four of us were going on to San Francisco without hanging around L.A. We'd be picking up one of the new cars in San Francisco, all arranged for out of the Albuquerque dealership. That was the easy part. The hard part was picking a driver for the trip over.

"I know more about vehicles than all of you put together," Jackson told Jerry, LeRoy and me. "You know how I got Mr. K's beast tuned up so it almost makes no noise even in shifting gears." That wasn't quite true. This was an army four-wheel-drive carryall truck he was talking about.

"That engine makes more noise than my mother's old washing machine," LeRoy said coldly.

"Which is beside the point," Jerry said. "Being a good mechanic doesn't mean squat about being a good driver. I drove a taxi all the time I was at Stanford, seeing that personal expenses were a responsibility of the students and not the University. I may have been the only one there without rich parents."

"Oh, yeah," I said. "Being a taxi driver is just the kind of experience I want to see in someone who takes my life in his hands. Besides, I'm responsible for getting this car to San Francisco. I signed for it. I drive." I'm a fidgety passenger, not really trusting anyone but myself at the wheel.

Jerry ignored me, continuing his presentation to Jackson and LeRoy after he decided my interruption was over. I already knew that Indians thought respect required others to allow speakers to complete what they had to say before offering their own observations on a subject. It didn't mean they had to pay any attention.

"Based on my pre-army experience," Jerry continued, glaring at the others, "the army classified me as a truck driver and gave me extensive training. I'm the most professional driver any of you have ever met."

When the other two finally nodded, I decided it was pointless to continue my urging rights they didn't acknowledge and took a seat in the back. I leaned as far away from the driver as I could, to be as distant as possible from the disaster I saw coming. I sat alone; both Jackson and LeRoy insisted on being in front with Jerry.

"You can be the passenger," Jackson told me.

"I can sit in the back, you mean. You'd never know I was white," I countered.

LeRoy laughed and Jackson grunted. Jerry concentrated on starting the car and moving it out into traffic. I stretched out on the back seat and dozed.

It seemed to me that Jackson never stopped talking for the two days it took us to reach San Francisco, except for the rare times Jerry permitted him to take the wheel so he could rest. LeRoy kept insisting on its being his turn, a claim ignored by both Jerry and Jackson. No one asked me if I wanted to drive. I suppose I could have insisted, but what was the point? I separated myself in my mind from what was going on, a trick from the prison camp, and thought over what I knew about Teno's predicament. Certain patterns began to form for me. I wasn't ready to make any decisions about what I should do, except to gather more information, but I did have some thoughts about what kinds of information would be useful.

Once we reached the outskirts of San Francisco, I was happy someone else had the wheel. Jerry's experience as a taxi driver came in handy. He reached Palo Alto, where Stanford is located, almost without being checked by red lights or heavy traffic.

"Find a motel," I said. "My mother could put us up, but then we'd be working under her timetable, not ours. I suspect her real interest in all this is trapping me here and showing me off to her friends."

"That's bad? She knows artist's models, right?" Jackson asked.

"They belong to a different social circle than she does, I expect," I said. "You don't really expect my mother to pimp for you, do you?"

"I don't know this town. It might save time," Jackson said. Both LeRoy and Jerry sent Jackson scandalized looks. My mother would have been amused.

"Your mother . . . ," I said.

Let Jackson fill in whatever he wanted to. The silence stretched while Jackson considered the possibilities, finally saying, "Oh, my," in a faint voice, followed by, "I may have to kill you."

Jerry abruptly turned the car into a modest, one-story motel, saying, "I used to live here. It's clean." Inside, the motherly looking desk clerk recognized Jerry and came around the counter to hug him.

"You promised you'd write," she scolded.

"I did," he said, disengaging himself gently.

"Twice in two years?"

"I let you know when I was coming home," he said. "I told you when I was discharged."

"I worried about you," she said, shaking her head as she returned to her post.

"No need. Can we get rooms?"

"You like a kitchen suite?"

"Be fine. Four single beds," he told her. "He's paying," he added, indicating me by turning his head slightly and pursing his lips in my direction. Lou Elwood had told me that pointing with a finger was considered aggressive, even worse than staring at someone, a witch act, in fact. I nodded and offered to pay in advance, but she shook her head. Our being with Jerry was all she needed.

The space she showed us was shabby, but clean, as Jerry had promised. There were two separate rooms with two beds each, connecting with the combined living room and kitchen. The bathroom was off the kitchen. A television set and a telephone were the chief amenities.

"If you want to place a long distance call, you have to go through the office," she told us. "Local calls you do yourselves."

"I have to bunk in with Kilroy," Jerry told the other two after the woman had left. "Teno said so."

"Hey, that ain't no treat," Jackson told him. "He snores."

"I know," Jerry said, with a sigh.

I wondered, did I? I'd never find out the truth from either of them.

"We need groceries," Jackson said, looking at me suggestively. I took out my wallet and gave him two twenties. All the way across the country I had been giving Jerry twenties when we gassed up, never receiving any change. Lou had told me that among Indians handing something over was considered making a gift. An offered pack of cigarettes to a Pueblo Indian would end up in his pocket. A subsequent request for a cigarette would be honored by the same person by taking the pack out of his pocket, extracting one cigarette, offering it, followed by his repocketing the pack. I don't smoke, so I hadn't seen that, but the money thing was in the same pattern. I wondered if Jackson would bring back change. He had seen how Jerry operated.

All three went shopping, leaving me privacy to call my mother. I used the gallery number.

"Jimmie-Jack," she cried, when she head my voice. Most of the time she called me Jack, or even J.J., but at times like this, she'd revert all the way. I didn't mind. I used to. "I've found who's fencing your sacred artifacts," she said, excitedly. "Where are you?"

"Holed up in a motel," I said. "I'm with three other guys and expecting more to join us. They'll call you for directions," and gave her the telephone number of the motel.

"But why don't you bring them here? I have six spare bedrooms."

"I'll bring them over tomorrow after we've all had a chance to rest and clean up. We drove straight through," I said.

"Can't you come over this evening? I haven't seen you in years!" That was true. I liked my mother. I loved her, too, of course, but I really liked her as a person. She was funny and bright and good company.

"I can do that, but I'll just bring one of the guys, a Pueblo Indian who used to go to Stanford and drove a taxi for meal money. He can find your address. We'll eat here, so don't go to any trouble."

"Oh," she said in a mildly scolding voice. "That wouldn't be trouble!" She never cooked, never had, so far as I knew. She'd call a caterer. She had clothes at the gallery and could change and go out to dinner from there herself, usually escorted.

"I know," I said. "I'll see you tonight, about nine . . . ten?"

"Ten would be better," she said, made a kiss sound and hung up. She never rose until noon, so ten was early for her. I was asleep by then, most of the time. I'd slept for most of the trip over so I'd do all right, but Jerry might get sleepy.

When the guys came back, arguing over whether cigarettes were properly groceries or not, meaning whether I should be expected to pay for them, I told Jerry we would be going out in the evening and to sleep while he could.

"What about us?" Jackson asked, handing over the change from shopping. I expected his mother had taught him that. Jerry raised an eyebrow.

"The others will be calling in, any time," I said. "I'll need Jerry to drive me over, but someone has to stay here to give directions if the guys call tonight. Tomorrow we can tell the motel manager to take calls for us. I'll bring you all to meet my mother then. Okay?"

It was okay. On the way out to the car I told Jerry my mother's address.

"That's in San Mateo," he said.

"That a problem?"

"No, I can find it. But why did we stay here, in Palo Alto?"

"It was your choice, not mine," I told him. "You know the area, not me."

He grunted, refusing to take the responsibility for this.

It takes a long time to get dark in California in the summer. I could still see the color of the trees and shrubs when we pulled into my mother's driveway, and was reminded how much the area looked like Vietnam, hilly and green. My mother's house was one of the expensive ones that San Mateo was known for, built before World War II by old money. The house had been designed by a student of Frank Lloyd Wright's and was inspired by Wright's forest houses, with a high pitched roof and many gables. It was constructed of rough-cut redwood following the architect master's insistence on using local materials in building. It was huge.

The door opened before I could ring the bell, a Paulo Soleri bronze one that must have weighed twenty pounds, mounted above the doorframe, accessed by a pull chain.

"Jimmie-Jack!" my mother cried, throwing both arms around my neck in a fierce hug. She clung for a moment, pushing away to kiss me soundly before stepping back, but keeping one hand clenched on my wrist to greet Jerry.

"Jimmie-Jack?" Jerry echoed, faintly.

"Nickname," I explained, needlessly.

"Hey, us good ol' boys understand," Jerry said as if in admonition. I wondered if that would replace Mr. K once Jackson heard about it. Be kind of difficult to demand respect when everyone called you "Jimmie-Jack," especially with friends like mine. I might have to hit somebody.

"I'm Jo Kilroy," my mother told him, stretching out her other hand. My mother kept her married name after the divorce. She had already established it in a business sense, if not so successfully in the marriage one. I never knew what the problem was between my parents. Neither had remarried.

Jerry touched her hand softly, in the pueblo way, and I saw my mother do the same. I was surprised. How did she know that? Jerry did not offer his name. Pueblo people rarely do. Lou had told me that knowledge of a name gives a stranger some power over another, even if it's merely a call name, like Jerry, rather than his sacred, secret name, which I'd never heard. Witches can be found everywhere.

"Jerry is from Santa Cala," I told my mother. "He's my driver. He was a student at Stanford and used to run a taxi all over the southern area around San Francisco."

"I've driven you several times," Jerry said, unexpectedly.

"Why yes, of course, you have," my mother replied. She might even remember it, I thought. "Come in, come in. Could I get you something to eat?"

Jerry grinned. "There you sound like my mother," he told her. "That's the first thing she would say to a guest in her house."

"Mothers have much in common. I might even know her," my mother said. "I buy pottery in Santa Cala for my gallery in Santa Fe."

I had seen this before, when my mother used to charm my friends, concentrating on them as if they were the most interesting people she had ever met. And there was nothing insincere about it. To her each person was interesting in a way others were not, as unique examples of an ever-varying humanity. It used to annoy me because, while talking to them, she ignored me. This time, however, she had not released my wrist, taking a seat on a sofa where I could be beside her. From time to time, she looked fleetingly at me as if to reassure herself that I was truly there, but her conversation with Jerry went on unabated.

"Your aunt, then, is Annie Casaquito," she said, after listening to him speak of his family. "She insisted on making that revolting show-card color pottery, though she's one of the few who remember how to do the old work, using tufa from the mountains to waterproof the clay," and she shook her head in regret.

"She would do it the old way if she could get paid for her time," Jerry said. "It takes her weeks to gather clay, grind old potsherds for temper, mine the white clay for slip and the tufa you mentioned for waterproofing. The dealers aren't willing to pay her for the extra time and effort to do it right. She makes what sells so that she can realize a profit from what she does."

"I'd pay her to do it right," my mother said. "I told her that. I even offered her money in advance."

"Let me talk to her," Jerry said, "but I think the effort is what she is trying to avoid. She's an old woman. If someone gathered the materials for her, she might change her mind. I'll talk to Teno about it."

The talk shifted to Jerry and his experiences at Stanford, which led to his disclosing the entire story of his finding the Heraclitus document along with the subsequent scandal that followed the professor's death and the disappearance of the original.

"But who would take it?"

"I did," Jerry admitted. "I hid it back in the stacks in a dusty case labeled 'miscellaneous' that no one would bother to check. I was afraid something like what happened might come about. Academics have views on what is proper that differ from those held by less enlightened people."

"Could you find it again?"

"Of course."

"Why didn't you, when you were accused of stealing it?"

"Once I produced it, I could no longer protect it," he said. "It would disappear, and it would either be denied that I had brought it to light, or perhaps that it had ever existed at all. I would either be guilty of theft or hoaxing. Either case would destroy any chance I had to become a professional."

"Oh, surely not," my mother protested.

"You can't buck the system."

As the two fell silent, each thinking of what the other had said, I ventured a question of my own. "About the sale of stolen artifacts," I said. "You have some clue as to who is responsible?"

"Oh, yes," she said, looking at me directly. "Phillips' gallery deals with pre-Columbian artifacts. Most of his business is done with German buyers, but I have seen things in his shop that I recognize as contemporary religious items that no reputable dealer could obtain."

"Phillips? Ted Phillips?" I asked.

"No, Jax Phillips. It's short for Ajax," she answered.

"Does he look like Cary Grant with a broken nose? Maybe six foot, two?"

"And a three day beard," she said, "Yes. But he's not that tall. I don't know him well. He's rarely around. His shop is run by a blond woman who claims to be his wife. She says he spends all of his time buying."

"Could be a relative, but could also be the same man I know," I said. "Ted Phillips wears cowboy high-heeled boots. A dual identity would explain why no one ever seems to know where he is. His office at the Indian Agency is instructed to say, 'He's in the field,' when he can't be reached. Either way, I'll bet he's implicated. I've played poker with him. He cheats."

"My people say he has a bad heart," Jerry said. "He uses the BIA welfare program to punish those who object to agency policy and reward those who support it. He causes a lot of suffering."

"Would he have access to sacred artifacts?" My mother asked.

"Not directly, but there have been thefts of masks, pots and fetishes from Santa Cala. We found out who was taking the things but we don't know what they did with them. The thieves were killed before they could be questioned."

"The old man who is in jail was accused, you said," my mother recalled.

"Yes. He is innocent. I've been asked to find proof of that," I told her.

"He's my uncle," Jerry said.

"He'd be married to Sofie Casaquito?" my mother asked.

"Yes."

"I know him, too. I have to help with this! Perhaps we ought to set a trap for Phillips," my mother said, a faraway look in her eye. "He'd be fascinated by the Heraclitus document. It would bring a fabulous price in Germany. There are German collectors even more interested in ancient Greeks than they are in American Indians."

"My stack privileges have been taken from me," Jerry said. "I could never retrieve the document. I did bring the Xerox copy with me," he added. "It's back at the motel."

"Where had it been?" I asked. "You said you didn't have it but knew where it was and that it was safe."

"It was in the kiva," Jerry answered, grinning.

"Good place for something old," my mother said. "We can use it to advertise a sale. And we'll have to create a new identity for you. Would I be correct to believe that you can speak Greek? It would seem to be a necessary skill for one specializing in classic studies."

"I speak it fluently," Jerry said.

"So do I," I told them both. "There was a Greek guy in the prison camp with me. I like to learn new languages," I added almost apologetically as they both stared at me in surprise. Well, it was true.

"You never said," Jerry accused me, in Greek.

"Why would you care?" I responded, in the same language.

Before we left, the three of us had made a plan to go with my mother to Phillips' gallery as Greek buyers of pre-Columbian art. Jerry would be the expert, and I would be the money man.

"Come by around noon and I'll take you shopping to get the proper clothes," my mother said. "I'll arrange for a private showing for tomorrow evening. I've done this before. I get a commission when I bring customers there for things my shop doesn't stock. If there are any items from Santa Cala, will you be able to recognize them?" she asked Jerry.

"Some, at least. These items are very dangerous to handle for one not taught correctly," he said worriedly.

"Wear gloves," my mother said. "They'll have them. No one who deals with such precious material handles it with bare hands. Oils from your fingers can cause, damage."

Jerry didn't look convinced but told me on the trip back to the motel that we could undergo a cleansing ceremony when we returned to the pueblo.

"If we can return the items stolen, the old men will be so grateful it won't even cost us money," he added.

"Money?" I asked.

"I told you, handling ceremonial objects is dangerous. We'll be contaminated."

"You have to pay to be cleaned up?" I asked.

"Of course. Rituals are owned. You see any white doctors curing people for free?" I saw his point.

The guys picking up the Cadillacs had not checked in by the time we got back, and I gave out more money for expenses to LeRoy and Jackson, so they wouldn't get bored. They still complained, after hearing what we had planned for Phillips' gallery.

"You guys getting all the action," Jackson said.

"So, figure out a way to get into the library at Stanford so Jerry can steal the Heraclitus manuscript," I said.

"What he want with that?"

"It's worth a lot of money. We're going to offer it to Phillips with the understanding that it's hot. I'll get our sheriff back home to arrange for police coverage."

"Your mother didn't say we needed to do that," Jerry objected. "If I get caught with the actual parchment letter, my career will really be over."

"Man, you'll never even see it," Jackson told him. "Just tell us where it is and we'll take care of the matter."

Jerry drew out floor plans of the library stacks and explained which box the manuscript was in, muttering he still didn't like the idea.

"If this Phillips claims his brother, Jax, furnished him artifacts without telling him that they had been stolen, the gallery owner could go free," I said. "But, if he buys a stolen item, knowing it's stolen, he can't claim innocence."

"How will we know which document it is?" Jackson asked, interrupting Jerry's complaints. "We don't read no Greek."

"It will have a label showing it came from Room 69 in the Vatican, 'Vat. 69' in English," Jerry said. "It's a standard reference to a room in the Vatican. And it's the only one so labeled in the box. You can't miss it."

"Vat. 69 means something different to me," LeRoy said. "I used to be a bartender."

"Yeah, well, I didn't figure on a bartender finding it," Jerry said.

I wasn't sure that stealing the document was a good idea myself, but there might be a need to display it before we could hook Phillips. I hoped we wouldn't need it.

The next morning the guys with the Cadillacs showed up, having found our whereabouts by calling my mother. When they learned what we had planned, they opted to go with the library caper, all but Jackson.

"All you Greek millionaires drive Caddys," he said. "I'll just borrow one of these that the brothers drove in and be your chauffeur. I'll need a uniform, though, with a nice cap."

The brothers agreed to drop off our used limo and pick up the new one from the dealer in town, so Jerry handed over the keys, reluctantly. Jackson had ones to the new car.

My mother welcomed the change in plan and we spent the morning outfitting the three of us, Jerry and me in black suits, Italian shoes, white shirts and silk ties and Jackson in a natty black uniform, cap and all.

"We could rent this stuff," I told my mother.

"Don't concern yourself with that," she said absently. "These shop owners will get invitations to art openings that they could never hope to receive by themselves."

"Well, thanks for that. You have to promise me that I'll get the bills for all of this," I insisted.

"Nonsense. It's a business expense. Do you have any idea the value of exposing a crooked dealer to a gallery owner? It will automatically authenticate popsicles sold out of my shop, if I wanted to sell them."

"Nothing like a genuine popsicle," Jerry agreed.

When we drove up to Phillips' that evening, Jerry and I were speaking Greek to get into character. I corrected my accent, listening to him. My Greek was more colloquial than his, and definitely more profane.

"Is your accent that of classic times?" I asked. "That would be a mistake if anyone at the shop speaks Greek."

"No one knows how ancient Greek sounded," Jerry said. "My accent is upper class modern Greek. Yours hurts my ears."

"So, I'll be a functionary," I said. "I can talk numbers with anyone." That was true.

We were greeted at the door by a woman younger than my mother but older than me. Jackson came in with us and took a station by the door as if we were a bodyguard. He was big enough, I thought, to convince anyone, and his impassive face looked professional. The gallery manager was a little surprised to see him, but Jackson ignored her, looking straight ahead. Jerry barely nodded when he, himself, was introduced as the buyer by my mother. I wasn't introduced at all.

"And your name is?" the woman asked Jerry, for my mother had merely said Jerry was interested in seeing pre-Columbian art.

"What does it matter?" he answered rudely. "What do you have to show me?"

The woman colored up, turned abruptly and led the way to the rear of the shop, opening a door that led to a storage area.

"All of this is ready to be shipped to Germany," she said. "There are a few items you might be interested in that we haven't actually sold yet. They have to be seen before we could expect to receive the prices that are placed on them." One of the boxes was open, placed on a long table, and she put on white cotton gloves before she lifted out one of the wrapped bundles. Removing the wrapping paper, she held a square painted bowl up for inspection. The rim was terraced, and the top of each stepped center was pierced and decorated with feathers, sewed in with sinew.

"A Pueblo IV polychrome, very old," she announced.

Jerry helped himself to a pair of the white gloves from the box on the table and took the bowl in both hands, turning it and studying it. "Not that old," he said, shaking his head. "It's a Santa Cala fetish bowl, and it's alive, still in use, or would be if it was where it belonged. Not long ago it was on a ceremonial altar, filled with ground corn meal. The feathers are new."

"That's not what we were told," the woman said, flustered at last. I guessed that rudeness shown by rich European buyers was not unusual. Special knowledge was.

"We'll take it," Jerry said.

"How much?" I asked, earning an irritated glance from Jerry, but the woman recovered at the mention of price to say, "We're asking ten thousand."

"No," I said.

"Yes," Jerry corrected me. "My uncle will want it."

"Not at that price," I retorted calmly. "It's for his new young wife, not himself."

"She wouldn't know a fetish bowl from a finger bowl," Jerry said derisively in Greek. "When she shows off her new toy to her friends, my uncle would be embarrassed if it were not expensive. And anyway, the bowl will be around longer than she will."

"Prepare two invoices," I told the woman, "one for five thousand and one for ten. We're paying five." In Greek I said, "He can give her the expensive one so she can brag about it," and then to the woman, in English again, "Have you anything else of this quality?"

The woman showed us piece by piece a dozen other things, all of which Jerry wanted. We argued in Greek, and the way the woman listened, I gathered she was able to follow the discussion.

I allowed only those Jerry identified as Santa Cala to be set aside, nine items. "Make out two invoices, one at twice the amount of the other, with full descriptions and deliver them to Ms. Kilroy. I will wire a description of the items to our principal and he will arrange for a transfer of funds, through Ms. Kilroy. Deliver the items to her and she will see that they are shipped."

As we left, Jerry kept up a running comment on my lack of breeding, arrogance and general incompetence that amused the shop woman until I turned to him and said in Greek, "If you want to come again, shut your mouth. Your uncle thinks more of me than he does of you." With that, I got into the front seat of the car to sit beside Jackson. Jackson joined me after holding open the door to the rear seat for my mother and Jerry.

"What was that about?" my mother asked as we took off.

"A little playacting," I said. "The woman understood enough Greek to report to Phillips that Jerry was a bad mannered rich man's nephew and I was in charge of making decisions. You sure he wasn't eavesdropping on us, himself?"

"He's not in town. As I said, he rarely is," my mother replied.

Jackson drove us all to the motel to see how the others had fared. My mother was eager to see Jerry's Xerox of the Heraclitus letter. LeRoy and the brothers where drinking beer and celebrating a successful heist.

"Man, it was so cool," LeRoy told us, after I had introduced my mother. She was given the one chair in the room. "I got kin that work at Stanford, buildings and grounds, mostly. They loaned us white coats and building passes."

"Passes? Don't they have ID photos?" I asked.

"Aah, ID photos. The guards are all whites. They can't tell one brother from another, looking at them in the face. I could wear a photo of Mohammed Ali, and they wouldn't pick up on it."

"Did you get the manuscript?" Jerry asked.

"Right where you said it would be," LeRoy told us and pointed at a roll of parchment on the table, tied with red ribbon.

Jerry picked it up and inspected it. "It's the right one. What should we do with it?"

"I'll take it," my mother announced. "I have acid free boxes at home. I'll put it in my safe. Is it the actual letter?"

"A copy of a copy of a copy at best," Jerry told her. "But it is many hundreds of years old. Dr. Leippi, my professor, had a small piece tested by carbon fourteen dating and it came out at 600 AD, plus or minus a few hundred years. There is little or nothing extant that actually dates from classic times. The original of this manuscript was once probably at the big library at Alexandria in Egypt. There was a guild of copiers stationed there that prided themselves on the exactness of their work. Errors would have been noticed."

"I thought they burned that library."

"Three times, the last in 640 AD, but copies were made for collectors from pre-Christian times on. They could have gone any place in Europe or the Near East."

"How do you want me to let Phillips know I have it?" my mother asked.

"Wait until we complete the other transaction," I said. "We want to let the FBI in on the sting."

"You might as well take my Xerox copy with you as well," Jerry told her. "I brought it with me with the hope of using it in some way to clear my name," and he opened his suitcase, extracted a flat envelope, and handed it to her. "Be careful of it. The translation I made is there as well, and I have no other copy of either of them."

"I have a Xerox at my home. My real office is there," my mother told him. "I'll duplicate both sets of papers and return them to you. May I read your translation?"

"Yes, of course," Jerry said, embarrassed at her interest. Jackson drove my mother back home and announced that he would stay over and keep an eye on her. I was wondering how I could keep her guarded, and had planned on staying with her myself. Jackson would watch her at least as well as I could, and would have the advantage of being a professional, not a mere son. My mother seemed pleased at the arrangement.

11

I called Ginwright at home as soon as my mother and Jackson left. "I need some advice," I told him.

"Where are you?"

"In California. My mother found out who was buying the stolen Indian stuff, a gallery called Phillips'."

"Ted Phillips? He has a gallery?"

"No, Jax, short for Ajax Phillips I'm told, a brother, maybe? The family is Greek? Anyway, the description we have of the gallery owner sounds enough like our Phillips to be him except for his height, but I don't know. I thought the difference could be Phillips' cowboy boots. In any case, even if it's his brother, we've got him."

"Good! What do you need from me?"

"One of the men from Santa Cala, posing as a rich Greek, has identified a number of items as those stolen from Santa Cala over the last year and offered for sale by the gallery."

"Wait a minute. A man from Santa Cala posing as a rich Greek? You serious?"

"Yes . . . I'll explain later. The stolen items have been put aside for purchase, but probably we need an FBI agent to monitor it when we close the deal. We're also going to sting him into buying a manuscript that he will believe is stolen from Stanford University, so he can't deny culpability."

"Pretty complex. Let me get back to you."

I left my telephone number, expecting to hear something the next morning, but Ginwright returned my call within an hour. "I talked to Judge Thatcher," he said. "He has jurisdiction since Teno is already being tried for the murder of the artifact thieves. He's going to send out a special United States Deputy Marshal to represent him. Okay?"

I was more than happy. I had not been impressed with the FBI agents I had met. I was surprised the next morning, however, when Hendley and Simpson knocked on my door.

"Meet Special United States Deputy Marshal Simpson," Hendley said, "I flew him over."

Simpson grinned when I shook his hand, saying, "Me and Judge Thatcher go back a long ways. This ain't the first time I've acted for him."

I brought them in and LeRoy fixed breakfast for everyone, Spanish omelettes, shaking off any attempt to help that the rest of us offered. Just as well . . . LeRoy was a first rate cook.

"You looking for a job?" Hendley asked him. "I need a cook on the ranch the worst way. I'll pay about anything."

LeRoy shrugged. "Maybe," he said finally.

"We'll talk later," Hendley said.

"How we fixing to do this sting?" Simpson asked, impatiently.

"Whenever you're ready, we'll have Phillips come to my mother's house in San Mateo; it doubles as her business office. He'll bring the artifacts with him. She'll have cash for the purchase but it needs to be marked."

"I'll arrange for the cash," Simpson said. "How much do you need?"

"They rounded the bill to forty thousand. Phillips' agent said they wanted hundred dollar bills. She said Phillips was on a buying trip, but would return to close the deal."

"Okay," Simpson said. "Make the appointment for day after tomorrow. That will give Phillips time to return, but not enough to get suspicious. Now, what's this about a stolen manuscript?"

I let Jerry explain it, without saying that it had been hidden in the archives and just retrieved. "Not stolen, just hidden," he said, not giving the details of where.

"But, why did you hide it?" Simpson persisted.

"I feared it would be destroyed if it were available. If it could not be found, it would be safe."

"Destroyed? If it's valuable enough to tempt Phillips, why would anyone want to destroy it?" Simpson was being more patient than when he was at the poker table.

"The views expressed by Heraclitus are different from what classicists would expect from a Greek philosopher," Jerry said. "The point of view is almost modern, materialistic. Heraclitus was scornful of the concept of gods. He claimed a man was what he did, not what he thought. He said men were a part of nature and that their behavior was constrained by the same laws as those of other sentient creatures. Church dogma depends much on such Greek thinkers as Aristotle, after interpretation by St. Anthony."

Simpson nodded, "Okay, I know how academics think, close enough.

I'd have swiped it myself to keep it safe had I been in your position. Where is it now?"

"In my mother's safe, along with a Xerox copy of it," I said.

"Good. We'll deal with Stanford later. It'll have to be returned eventually, but we can put a hold on it as evidence in a murder trial. Ain't nobody will get it out of Judge Thatcher's safe, I promise you that."

"You think the agent, Ted Phillips, had some knowledge of the murders of the young Indian men?" I asked.

"Hard to say. Stands to reason whoever sold the artifacts to Jax Phillips knew about the murders, that's for sure. We can mine the brother for information. Where did he get the stuff? Religious artifacts are protected by the Federal Antiquities Act. Having a charge hanging over his head should give him a sharp memory. You don't get time off for good behavior in federal prisons, nor early parole."

"If the murders occurred on Indian land, they'd be federal crimes, too," I said.

"That's right. I guess you haven't seen this guy, or you'd know whether he was Ted Phillips or not." Simpson said to me.

"I haven't seen him in person", I agreed. "When he comes for the money, we can both look him over."

We took one of the other Cadillacs over to my mother's. LeRoy insisted on driving, leaving the black men watching television in our motel suite. My mother offered guest rooms to Hendley and Simpson, saying they needed to be close to plot the sting. I left them to it, promising to return with Jerry when Phillips was expected. LeRoy and I went back to the motel.

"Tell me about this Ted and Jax Phillips thing," LeRoy said on the way back.

"I don't know what to say," I told him. "I met Ted Phillips, the agency superintendent, the first time I played poker with Hendley and Simpson. He was a heavy loser that night, and I caught him cheating, though I didn't say anything. He knew I spotted him, however, because I crossed him, spoiling his take. It cost him hundreds of dollars in that one hand alone. He couldn't say anything, however, for he had no way of legitimately knowing what I had done. He told Hendley later that he wouldn't return to the game as long as I played. Said I was a sharper."

"Why did they keep you, instead of him?"

"Those guys aren't dumb. They saw what was happening. It's possible he was just showing off. Hendley said Phillips had never tried to cheat any of them. He said I looked like an easy mark. Said he might even have intended to give the money back at the end of the game, showing it was all a joke, but never got the chance."

"He ever say he had a brother?"

"Not to me, but I barely spoke to the man."

The next day the others took off, leaving just the one Cadillac for Jackson to drive back to Albuquerque. LeRoy, Jerry and I would travel with him. We got a call from Simpson that afternoon that Phillips wanted to close the deal that evening, rather than the next day as planned.

"You have the money ready?" I asked.

"Yes. You and Jerry come on over now. We'll eat here and wait. You'll have to hide since I'm still not sure there are two Phillips. The same goes for me and Hendley, but we'll all be within call, if needed. Jackson can protect your mother if anything goes wrong, can't he?"

"He worked for the Black Guards in Chicago before going to Vietnam," I said. "He's trained."

"Didn't know that. He'll do," Simpson agreed.

We went in the back door and found Jackson in the kitchen chatting up my mother's cook. She was an attractive Hispanic woman some years older than Jackson, but age meant nothing to him. He just liked women. He'd been overly careful in dealing with my mother in front of me, but I had few illusions about what he might be thinking. It was none of my business in any case.

LeRoy, Simpson, Hendley and I ate in the kitchen while Jackson left to watch the front door, ready to play butler for Phillips, and Jerry was sitting with my mother in her office study.

"You planning on arresting him tonight?" I asked. "You have a warrant?"

"Oh, yes," Simpson said. "Your mother is wearing a wire and we're recording everything. We can listen in to the conversation from here," and he nodded to some electronic equipment on a side table. "I have FBI men waiting out in the garage. They'll take him away. They'll be listening, too." We were on a third cup of coffee, following homemade apple pie à la mode for dessert when we heard my mother greet Phillips.

"Come in, come in," she said. "Take his hat, Jackson."

I grinned at LeRoy. The regal tone she used in addressing Jackson was one that LeRoy and I would imitate from time to time from now on, when dealing with Jackson and his somewhat peremptory ways. His responding,

"Yes, ma'am," was particularly amusing to the two of us. Knowing that he was aware we were listening in made it all the better.

"My man is bringing in the box," Phillips said.

I looked at Simpson and Hendley to see if his voice was familiar to them. They knew Phillips. Hendley nodded and Simpson said, "Got to be a twin, at least. But there's no law against taking on a second identity if ain't used for unlawful purposes."

My thought was that Phillips had a guard just as my mother did. I wondered if he was also trained as Jackson was.

"You have the money here?" Phillips asked.

"It's in the safe," my mother said.

"I must see the pieces first," Jerry said and Phillips addressed him in Greek, asking who his principal was.

"It is not necessary that you know that," Jerry said. "I have not asked how these items came into your hands. My principal does not intend to display them publicly and would be particularly upset if Interpol came asking questions."

"I have no dealings with Interpol," Phillips said, "nor is there any reason that Interpol would be interested."

"Good," said Jerry, "Would you open the box, please?"

We heard the click of a switchblade knife, followed by a rustling of paper. I didn't like that knife sound and left the kitchen to stand at the opening in the central hall leading into my mother's study. Standing there, I could overhear everything directly, and move quickly, if I had to.

"It is all there," Phillips said impatiently.

"I'm sure, but if something inadvertently got left out, it would be my responsibility, in the eyes of my principal," Jerry said. I could hear him take each item out of the box, unwrap it, inspect it and place it to one side on the study table.

"Where is the fetish bowl?" he asked finally.

"It is not listed on the manifest," Phillips said. "I had already committed it to another buyer at a higher price."

"It is the most desirable piece in the collection," Jerry told him. "I have told my principal about it; I must have it, or there will be no sale."

"Then I will just take it all back," Phillips said in a nasty tone.

"That you will not. You will call your shop and instruct someone to bring it here, now," Jerry told him. "Who do you think you are playing with?"

"Then you must meet the other buyer's price."

"And I will not do that, either. Move, Jackson!"

No one saw me as I looked quickly into the room. Phillips' bodyguard had pulled out his switchblade, but before he could raise his arm, Jackson had clamped a hold on it that broke the man's wrist, causing the knife to drop on the floor. As the man bent over in shock, Jackson hit him on the back of the neck and the man fell, unconscious. Jackson stood over him, watching. Jerry hadn't moved. He stared at Phillips, gestured at the telephone on the desk and said, "Make the call."

Phillips did as he was told and stepped back with his arms folded to wait. His back was to me, so I could not see his face and he seemed to be a couple of inches shorter than I remembered Ted Phillips being. My fantasy about Ted and Jax being the same man probably was just that, a fantasy.

I crept back into the kitchen and told the others what I had seen. "Unless Phillips pulls out a gun, I don't think there will be a problem. The money isn't on the table yet, anyway. I think this man is too short to be Ted Phillips."

When the doorbell rang, the cook went to answer it, and I recognized the voice of the shop manager when she was escorted into the study.

"I have the piece," she said.

"Unwrap it," Jerry said. "And Jackson, check her purse," he added, after a moment had passed.

The woman protested, but Jackson had evidently picked it up from the table. "It's a twenty-two automatic," he said. "Nice little gun."

"I have a license for that," the woman said.

"Not in this house, you don't," my mother said. "I hate guns."

That wasn't true. One of the things my father liked to do was to take the whole family to the city police rifle range when I was a kid. My mother was a crack shot and had always carried a twenty-two automatic in her own purse. She hadn't liked being dependent on male protection back then, and living alone, as she did now, I would believe she liked it even less.

"This is the right bowl," Jerry said. "You may give him the money now." He was speaking to my mother. "If you procure anything else of this quality, tell Ms. Kilroy and she will let me know," he added, addressing Phillips.

"You think I will do business with you again?" Phillips asked in outrage.

"Exclusively," Jerry said. "Unlike you, my principal does have dealings with Interpol. He would not like to hear you had sold something to someone else that he might find interesting."

"I have something else," my mother said. "Quite by chance, an original Vatican archival document, a letter written by Heraclitus to the Persian king, Darius, fell into my hands."

"The missing Stanford manuscript?" Phillips asked, excitement in his voice.

"You know of it?"

"Of course. It may be a forgery, of course, but I would be interested in seeing it."

"And I would not," Jerry said. "Jackson, repack this stuff. We're leaving."

"I have your money," my mother said, perhaps in response to a frown from Phillips. For a moment there was only paper rustling and the sound of a safe door opening. "There's forty thousand in hundreds, as requested."

"Give it to my manager," Phillips said.

"I want my gun back," the woman said. "I'm not going to carry that kind of money around without a gun."

"You can have the gun, but no bullets," Jackson said, and we heard the sound of his taking out the clip and emptying the chamber of its load. "You shouldn't carry it around with a bullet in the firing chamber anyway," he told her.

"I have the safety lock on," she said defensively.

"And pulling it out of your purse, the lock could be turned off. It's dangerous."

"Not to me. I want it ready to use, if I need it," the woman said dismissively. "Just give it here."

"Take this fool with you," Phillips said. "Drop him off at the emergency room of the hospital to fix his arm." I gathered the man Jackson had hit was no longer unconscious.

There was the sound of people walking around and finally being escorted to the front door before my mother spoke again. "I am sorry for the unpleasantness, Mr. Phillips," she said.

"Call me Jax," he responded. "If it had gone any other way, I would have been suspicious. To tell the truth, I am happy to have those particular pieces off my hands."

"They were protected under the Federal Antiquities Act?" my mother asked.

"Even worse. They were stolen, just as your document was, I believe. May I see it?"

"I'll show you a Xerox copy of it, first," my mother said. "If you are then interested in seeing the original, I can produce it."

"You are not contracting with a thug, like that young Greek man," Phillips said, amused. "I am an art dealer, like yourself."

My mother must have given him the Xerox copy of the Heraclitus letter, for there was a stretch of silence during which I assumed Phillips was studying it.

"If it is genuine, it is quite valuable," he said. "I could sell it in Germany. What do you want for it?"

"A commission, say forty percent of the sale price,"my mother said. "And I have a document for you to sign, guaranteeing it."

"Hmmm," Phillips said a few minutes later. "This paper would implicate you as well as myself. Show me the original now, please."

Again, there was silence.

"What is this square cut out for?" he asked.

"It was used by Dr. Leippi to carbon date the article. If you know about the document being missing, you know about that."

"Yes. Do you want a deposit?"

"A check for ten thousand would suffice," she said.

A moment later, Phillips said, "Here it is, along with the signed commitment."

"And here is the acid free box it belongs in," my mother said.

"I'll take that," I heard another woman's voice say. "I am Kit Kilroy, trustee of Stanford University. We have been looking for this."

Good God, it was my grandmother. What was she doing here?

I was down the hall and into the study before Phillips could do anything, followed by Simpson and Hendley. What I saw was my mother, her own twenty-two in her hand pointed at Phillips' belly, and my grandmother, my father's mother, holding an Irish blackthorn stick in both hands, ready to swat Phillips into the wall. He was crouched, all but snarling, but not moving.

I didn't wait. I stepped into Phillips and feinted a blow at his face, straightening him up so I could hit him in the belly, really hard. I try to avoid hitting people in the face. You can really hurt your hand doing that. My hand had ached for a week after I hit Jackson in Nam. Hendley grabbed my arm before I could hit Phillips again, a mistake on his part. I lifted my arm, tossing him backward over the desk, never taking my eyes off Phillips. He was on his knees retching. I shoved a wastebasket over to him with my foot to save the Navajo rug he was kneeling on from vomit stains.

Simpson brushed past me, seized Phillips by the shoulders and jerked him to his feet. "You're under arrest, you son-of-a-bitch," Simpson said, taking a card out of his shirt pocket and reading Phillips his Miranda rights. Two FBI men, who had been waiting in the hall, came in, produced handcuffs and led him away. Phillips had nothing to say, or at least he said nothing. Maybe he was having difficulty breathing.

When I looked around, my mother's gun had disappeared, and grandmother's blackthorn stick was leaning up against the wall. She held her arms out to me for a hug, saying, "You even move like your grandfather." My grandfather had a notoriously short temper, so it would have been difficult to see this as approval.

"I almost never hit people," I said, defensively.

Hendley, who had righted himself, snorted from the other side of the desk.

"Sorry about that," I said, looking at him. He was amused, I think.

"Wish you'd reconsider that fight with Ali," he said. "I'd put money on you."

"Later," I said and shook my head, knowing he was just talking and turned to my grandmother to ask, "You're really a trustee for Stanford University?"

"I'm a Stanford alumna and one of their financial supporters, as well," she said. "As Director of the Kilroy Foundation, I've given them millions for scholarships of one kind and another. Stanford likes to stay close to their money sponsors."

"Jerry didn't steal that Heraclitus letter, " I told her. "He'd hidden it in the archives. I arranged to retrieve it to catch Phillips. We hoped to use it to trap his brother."

"He ain't got no brother," Simpson said. "That was him."

"You sure? I thought the other one was taller," I said doubtfully.

"He was wearing low-heeled Italian shoes and a beret. He wore cowboy boots with two-inch heels and a Stetson in New Mexico. The beard couldn't completely hide the scar on his face. Ted and Jax Phillips are the same person," Simpson said.

"He's right," Hendley said. "The judge is going to have to let Teno go now."

"The DA, O'Brian, will claim he was working with Phillips," I said.

"Judge Thatcher won't believe anything O'Brian says," Simpson said.

"A Federal grand jury might," I said.

"Not with Ginwright for Teno's attorney," Simpson said.

"So, who did kill the young Indian thieves?" I asked.

"The men who ran Lima's bar and store in San Ysabel, likely." Simpson said. "The real question is, who set the bar on fire and killed them?"

I nodded, but said nothing. I was still pretty sure that it could have been done on Teno's orders, following my suggestion. In that case, Jerry was a likely culprit. I couldn't forget what he had told me, that when the war captains put on the masks of the twin war gods, O-yah-yeh-we and Mau-sah-we, the spirits of the gods enter them and it is the gods who act. I thought they donned the masks only to do executions, though, not arson. Simpson probably knew which from his Santa Cala studies, and as I glanced at him I saw he was quietly thinking. I hoped I was right about what that might be.

"What about the Heraclitus document?" I asked. "Will it be needed at the trial?"

"I'll take charge of it, as I said I would," Grandma Kit said. "I flew down from Oklahoma when your mother phoned me. I'll fly back and arrange to have it placed on loan to the Kilroy Foundation from there. If necessary, I will produce it at the trial, under subpoena. I don't want it stored in some evidence room."

"Take the Xerox copy, too," I said, "along with the translation. The translation is Jerry's property, but he might have difficulty in defending his claim now that his professor is dead unless the original, Xerox and translation are kept together. Jerry corrected his translation to conform to that of his dead professor's reading, annotating the reasons he differed right on the paper."

"Of course. Tell him I might consider having the foundation publish it if I can find independent experts to agree with Professor Leippi that the original is genuine."

We left, with me promising to visit Grandma Kit in the near future. She had something on her mind, I could tell. I also explained to my mother my feeling about all the green around her house and said I'd be back when the place was easier for me to be in. It didn't make her happy, but she understood. Grandma Kit's town in the Oklahoma panhandle was as dry as the country around Santa Cala, if not as colorful. The one color in Oklahoma was brown, in various shades.

"I'll be out to my gallery in Santa Fe soon," my mother said in farewell. "Jackson will drive me out. He's going to work for me." I should have seen that coming.

LeRoy drove my grandmother to Albuquerque in one of the Caddys. Jackson would stay in California with my mother. I settled up our bill at the motel and took off with Jerry driving our Caddy and me sitting beside him. I was more comfortable when I could stretch out on the back seat as I had on the trip over. Driving is no pleasure for me, merely less stressful than being a passenger. We talked some, but mostly not.

When we reached Albuquerque, we picked up my truck and left the Caddy at the bar to be collected and delivered by the brothers. I didn't argue with Jerry when he claimed the driver's seat in the truck. We stopped at the governor's house in Santa Cala and let him know we were back.

"So is Teno," he said. "Judge Thatcher vacated the charges against him."

Jerry stayed in the pueblo to see Teno and I went to my adobe hut by the river. Funny, I thought of it as home, now. Lou was in residence, along with Mac. Lou hugged me, but Mac didn't even come out of the willows until I had a fish on the hook.

"He's been eating expensive cat food for five days," Lou said, "grumbling all the time. He snooted it on day one and day two and is still sulking. I'm never going to get him back on a healthful diet." She looked disgusted.

"Cats are carnivores," I said. "The only time they eat vegetables in nature is when they want to purge themselves."

"You're talking about wild cats," she said, "not high-bred animals like Mr. Meph."

"Your Mr. Meph is descended from ships' cats that came ashore in Maine and Nova Scotia only a few hundred years ago at best. And they were descended from Norwegian forest cats not too far back. Mac isn't a descendant of Bastet, the Egyptian goddess, with a pedigree longer than yours, like a regular domestic cat."

"Bastet? You're talking about Bastet?"

"That was the name of the goddess, yes. The cats were merely her avatars, her embodiment on earth."

"How do you know so much about things like that?"

168

"I read; I know about a lot of things," I said, irritated. "My grandmother has Maine Coon cats like your Mr. Meph, for one thing. I saw her, by the way. She came in like a *deus ex machina*, at the last minute and claimed she was a Stanford University trustee. She took Jerry's senior thesis along with her and said she might get it published."

"The Kilroy Foundation has a scholarly monograph series that's very well respected," Lou said. "If she does what she says, Jerry won't have to worry about his career. He could get into any graduate school he wanted to."

"Except maybe Stanford," I said.

"You kidding? Especially Stanford . . . with your regent grandmother as a sponsor, Stanford would give him a graduate assistantship, which means a full tuition scholarship, like he had before, but this time along with a salary. He wouldn't have to drive taxis to eat."

"You tell him," I said.

"I will. I'm going back to the pueblo tonight to see some of my informants, and I'll look him up."

It was quiet after she left, with just me and Mac around. I was stretched out in my hammock and Mac was stretched out on me. His purring was the only sound I heard above the rushing noise of the river. The birds were quiet, as night fell. I went to sleep, awakened by Mac digging his claws into me. Only one thing that could be: visitors.

I rolled out of the hammock and picked up my rifle, freezing in place to listen. Mac stood by the hammock, twice normal size, staring off toward the creek. I could make out the outline of something at the edge of the light. The form materialized into the shape of a big yellow dog creeping forward, slunk low. He was snarling. Mac hissed a warning as the dog leaped at me, and I squeezed off a shot automatically. I hit it and it rolled over, scrambling to its feet to run off into the night. What was that?

I could see Mac wasn't about to back down to some damned dog. He hadn't moved. I could follow the dog's progress by watching Mac turn his head. The cat's attention stayed fixed, relaxing only as the sounds of his retreat faded.

As I was drifting off again in my hammock, my rifle cuddled close, Mac hissed again and I raised my head to see the dog attacking. I got off two shots before he reached me. He loped off again, into the brush. I was sure I'd hit him at least once more. Mac was on top of the stump, fluffed out to twice his size, an alarming sight

"Guess we showed him," I said. I laid back down, but I was jumpy and half an hour later either heard or thought I heard something down by the gate. I dug the hearing aid out of my pocket and put it back in my ear, squealing the damn thing as I always did. It might as well have been a siren.

"Kilroy!" someone shouted. "You there, Kilroy?"

Why would I answer a question like that? The voice came from down by the fence. Someone had cut it again. I crouched behind the stump.

The sound of several persons walking through the brush made me ease back toward the river. I could hide there in the willows along the border the way Mac did. I didn't fancy taking on more than one hostile at a time.

Flashlights lit from several directions caught me before I could complete my escape and I fired at them, high. Killing someone without knowing for sure who I was shooting at wasn't something I wanted to do.

The lights went off, but whoever it was returned fire. I hit the ground and rolled as soon as it was dark again, firing my gun and leaping up to dash for the river in the next instant. I almost made it. A bullet in the leg above the knee tumbled me on the bank, and I got off one more round before I dropped my rifle, my mind taken up entirely with the pain. I was aware of three men crashing through the brush and coming to a halt to stand over me, but who cared? God, it hurt!

"Bring the truck around," I heard a voice say. The voice registered. It was Phillips.

"The gate's locked," another voice called. And that would be either Keith or Kevin, I thought. Two guys whose names I couldn't put to the right faces, Lou's friends, one of whom was speaking, "Shoot the lock off."

"Move. We don't want to get caught here," the other speaker, Ted Phillips, again. Everything fell into place in my mind, a tad late, perhaps, but clear. Keith and Kevin, the two university student archeologists, were working with Phillips as well as the FBI. Being young guys themselves, they could talk to the young pueblo men, swapping money for stolen items, that Phillips, in his other role as art gallery owner, could then sell for thousands of dollars to European collectors. But what was Phillips doing out of jail?

The searing agony suddenly ceased and a numbness set in as I held my injured knee tightly with both hands. Phillips and I were alone. He reached down to me, grabbing my face to turn it towards his, a knife in his hand.

"I'm going to cut your throat, you meddling incompetent. Have you any idea what you've done to me?" He pressed his hand against his side, and it came away smeared with blood. Good, I'd got him. As he brought his knife hand toward me, I dropped my knee and seized it, pulling it forward, so that he fell across me, off balance. I hit him in the throat with my free hand as he came, a paralyzing blow. He dropped the knife as the willows exploded and Mac charged, leaping on Phillips' back, ripping at him with his hind feet as his front ones lodged their claws into the man's scalp.

Phillips rolled off me as I found his knife, hauling myself upright by clutching the stump and gritting my teeth; waves of pain starting again.

When the two students drove the truck up, they found me waiting for them, knife in hand, and Phillips in fetal position behind me. Mac, still puffed out to twice his size, crouched back on the stump and still hissing. They got back in the car and attempted to back out, smashing into Teno's truck, which had quietly driven up behind them. Jerry was driving with Virgil riding shotgun. Guys I recognized from my induction into the scalp society came pouring out of the back of the truck. They pulled the doors of Phillips' pickup open and had the two students upside down on the ground before they could react. A few kicks, judiciously delivered, I trust, quieted any protest.

"Got a tourniquet?" I asked. "The son-of-a-bitch shot me."

"Help," one of the students moaned. "I'm bleeding to death!"

"Nosebleed? Not hardly," Virgil said, shining a flashlight on him, "but you'll wish you were before Teno's through with you," and two of the scalp society warriors picked him up and threw him in the back of Teno's pickup to lie beside the other one they'd already dealt with. I turned to point out where I'd left Phillips, but he was gone. How did he do that?

The scalp society guys backed the truck away, hauling the two students back to the pueblo, leaving me with Virgil and Jerry.

"What's this about a tourniquet?" Jerry asked as Virgil took his knife and cut away the pant's leg over the wound.

"Not needed," Virgil said.

"The bleeding is not that bad and the bone has been jarred but not broken, I think. Can you flex it?" he asked.

"You a medic in service?" I asked, gritting my teeth as I tried to bend my knee. I could do it, though not without another wave of pain.

"I was an MP, but we were trained to give first aid," Virgil said, watching me closely. "You're okay."

That was easy for him to say. I held on to the stump as Mac rubbed against me. His tail was still bushed out, but he was back to normal size otherwise, which is to say, huge.

"Good cat," I said. Mac purred, proud of himself, no doubt.

"You need a tetanus shot," Virgil said.

"We'll take you up to the pueblo. Nurse Wilson is back in her house; she'll fix you up and keep her mouth shut. Or do you want to go to the hospital?"

"Hospital? Never again," I swore.

"Good. The scalp society has medicine men that know how to treat wounds. We don't want any kind of record of tonight," Jerry said.

I didn't ask why. Indians have little faith in the working of white man's justice in principle and here white men had debauched and finally killed pueblo kids in order to steal tribal secrets. I thought there might be three fresh scalps in the scalp society's collection before morning. I couldn't find it in my heart to care.

12

Jerry and Virgil took me to Santa Cala in the back of Phillips' truck and stopped at a house in one of the off streets. There were no windows in the front of the building, but the door opened even before Jerry shut off the motor. We'd been expected. Vigil had been putting pressure on the bullet wound on my leg, knowledge he picked up as an MP in Korea. Two men came from the house and helped me out of the truck, carried me into the lighted room and laid me down on a long table inside.

"This is the scalp society house," Jerry said, ever one to explain the obvious. There were scalps hanging from wires all along one of the walls. An old man brushed me down with an eagle feather fan, catching the evil in a leather pouch, and drawing it shut, said, "Throw this into the river from the bridge." He handed it to Jerry, who left without further comment. I'd have to learn how to shut Jerry off like that, I thought.

Virgil had already slit the leg of my jeans to get at the wound, and two older men inspected it, muttering in Santa Cala. "The bullet went through and did not touch the bone," one of them told me. "You're lucky."

"Yeah," I said. Lucky? A year of combat and two in a prison camp in Vietnam without any serious injury, and I get shot after three months back in the states. That was lucky?

The men covered the bullet entry and exit holes with sulfa powder and bound a clean bandage around my leg, cutting off the split denim trouser leg in the process. No mysterious native Indian medicine here. The pueblo governor had explained to me that all of the members of the scalp society were from World Wars I and II, plus the Korean police action and whatever Vietnam was supposed to be. "You been around death and are dangerous to associate with," he'd said. "You going to hang around Santa Cala, you got to join the scalp society." I'd already been made a member of the tribe, adopted into the Badger Clan at Teno's insistence. I hadn't been in any ceremony for either tribal membership or clan adoption. The same with the scalp society.

"We don't adopt whites with a lot of tourist shit," the governor had told me. "We just add them to the tribal rolls and notify the Indian Bureau. Doesn't happen often." He gave me a copy of the letter to the Bureau of

Indian Affairs. "The only other whites that are currently members of the tribe are Sheriff Simpson and the rancher, Hendley, and he's part Choctaw. They hang around Santa Cala and were in service the same as you." Why, when I played poker with them didn't I know about the Santa Cala thing? I wondered if I ought to mention it to either or them at the next game? Nah, probably net.

"Now, what happened?" the oldest man asked. I sat up on the table and everybody else sat down. There were a dozen men in the room by then. Even Jerry was back from his errand.

"I was asleep in my hammock and the cat that sleeps on my legs woke me up, hissing," I began. "I rolled out of the hammock and grabbed my rifle in time to shoot a big yellow dog that was charging us. I hit it in the side and it fled into the brush. An hour later I heard someone cutting my fence. I recognized Ted Phillips' voice as he called out. I played poker with him once. I even helped arrest him, so he didn't like me much."

"I was there," Jerry said. "You didn't mention you hit him in the belly hard enough to knock him out. He hated you."

"Well, I didn't like him either," I said. "He came into my place along with the two college kids from the University of New Mexico, who have been doing archeological research for the Santa Cala Indian claims case. Phillips shot me in the leg from the dark and ordered the students to bring the truck up. He was bleeding from the side and cursing me for shooting him. I hadn't. I never shoot at anything without seeing what it is I'm shooting at. Phillips drew a knife to cut my throat, but I hit him and knocked him off me just as Virgil and Jerry drove Teno's truck up and parked behind Phillips' truck. Guys jumped out of Teno's truck, grabbed the students, tied them up and drove away. Phillips escaped. Virgil and Jerry brought me here in Phillips' truck."

The old men questioned Jerry and Virgil for their versions and then said, "Take Kilroy up to Nurse Wilson's house for a tetanus shot." I was bundled out and into the back of the truck to ride over to Nurse Wilson's house, cursing at the bumps that I felt from every pebble in the road.

Nurse Wilson's house was a wood frame building, a little set apart from the adobe structures the Santa Cala lived in. It was surrounded by good-sized fruit trees, giving it an illusion of privacy. An illusion because there was little private in Santa Cala, according to Lou, who stayed with her most of the time. The guys opened the door and brought me into Nurse Wilson's clinic. The door was never locked, according to Lou. Jerry switched on the light and was about to call out, but I put my hand on his arm and stopped him.

"There's something wrong here," I said quietly. "I can feel it." Shaking myself free of Virgil and Jerry's support, I limped to the door that led into the living area of the house. Pushing it open, I stepped into a dark hall with several doors set into one side; the other side opened into a living room-kitchen area. I twisted the knob on the first door in the hall and found it locked. The second opened, and I thrust the door back, seeing in the dim light of a candle Lou stretched out on a bed, moving restlessly, eyes open but not focusing. I sort of hopped over and put my hand on her forehead. She was burning with fever! Virgil and Jerry followed me in.

Hovering over Lou, I heard one of the other hall doors open and then a jingle of keys. A moment later a large woman burst into the room carrying a ring of keys in one hand and a blackthorn cane not unlike my grandmother's in the other. Jerry and Virgil all but leaped out of her way. "What are you doing?" she demanded, the cane raised in threat.

I was still carrying my rifle and pointed it at her to stop her rush at me. "You're Nurse Wilson?"

"I am. Who are you?" She stopped several steps away, with her cane still waving at me.

"I'm Jack Kilroy. What's wrong with Lou?" I asked, lowering the gun.

"She has flu. She needs quiet; I'll have to ask you to leave. You have no business invading her bedroom."

"She was fine a few hours ago," I said.

"Well, she's not now. You must leave or I'll call the governor."

Lou turned to me and grabbed my hand in a grip hard enough to make me wince. "No," she said, gasping for breath. "No."

"I'm not going anywhere," I said to her and turned to the angry woman to ask, "What have you done to her?"

She swung her cane at my head hard enough to lay me out, but I caught it on the barrel of my rifle. Virgil and Jerry grabbed the woman from behind, but she shrugged them off like they were children. What was that about?

"Why, you're a witch!" Virgil said, while understanding flooded into my mind. Understanding, but not belief. I mean, witches?

"You've lived too long," he continued. "You're trying to take Lou's life to add to your own." She raised her cane again and I shot it out of her hand. Witch or no witch, that blackthorn was deadly.

"You keep coming and the next one goes between your eyes," I warned her, pointing the gun at her face. She hesitated, then turned to leave, brushing by Jerry and Virgil. I shot the clunky heel off her nurse's shoe. She crashed into the doorframe, throwing her back into the room, screaming curses at me. The key ring flew from her hand and bounced off the wall.

I re-aimed the rifle at her face to get her attention as she sprawled. She froze. "Let her go," I said. "I don't know what you're doing, but you have a choice. If I kill you, she'll be free of it. If you free her yourself, you'll live, for a little while, at least. Either way, she'll be free. I might add, I don't care which choice you make, but choose now."

"Shoot me? You wouldn't dare," she sneered.

"You don't know me," I told her quietly and cocked the gun.

Nurse Wilson took a moment to consider and then I heard Lou sigh. I risked a glance at her face. A sweat had broken out on her forehead. The fever was gone. How did she do that?

"You'll regret this," Nurse Wilson said to me, all sign of hysterics gone.

"As will you, if any further harm comes to Lou. I'll come after you. I'm in the scalp society. I'm immune to witchcraft." I couldn't believe I'd said that.

She looked at me, considering, but Virgil said, "He is. And you're a dead woman."

She shook her head, struggled to her feet and stomped out of the building, her broken heel notwithstanding. We heard her car start as she drove away. Virgil and Jerry were right behind her; I heard Virgil's truck fire up to follow.

I sat down beside Lou. "She won't make it out of town," I said.

"That was close," Lou said, one hand fastened into my shirt as I held her, sitting on the bed. She pulled me down, burrowing her face into my side. That was all right with me. As I had told her, I wasn't going anywhere right away. It had been a long damned day but it wasn't over yet.

"Take me home," Lou said.

As it was, she took me home. We used her van. She drove. We didn't follow Virgil and Jerry over the bridge in their pursuit of Nurse Wilson. Lou had had enough drama for one night, and my leg hurt. We didn't even have to discuss it. She took the road through the pueblo to the south exit, followed the San Ysidro road to my place, opened the gate, drove through, closed and locked the gate again and helped me out of the van and into the bunk in the cabin. We both slept in it, together for the first time, though nothing untoward happened. We just clung to one another.

Lou was up and dressed making breakfast by the time I woke up next morning with Mac in close attendance. "I want to look at that leg," she said, handing me a cup of hot coffee and sitting me in one of the Adirondack chairs.

"Not much to see," I said. "Virgil field-dressed it. He said it was a clean wound." Since the scalp society guy had cut away my trouser leg, Lou was able to unwind the bandage with little difficulty down to the last few layers of gauze. They were stiff with dried blood.

"It's going to hurt if I pull this off," she muttered.

"And I'll start bleeding again," I agreed. "Why bother?"

"Infection, that's why," she said. "You want to lose the leg?"

"Not much," I said, not making it easier for her.

She rose, found a basin and a clean rag and poured hot water into the basin from the coffeepot placed over the coals next to the cottonwood stump. Softening the stiff bandage with the clean rag dipped into the basin, she gently eased the bandage free. I thought about yelping but decided not to. She might object to being teased when she was being serious.

The bullet had bruised the leg when it penetrated and it looked worse than it felt, though it was sore enough.

"No infection," she said, "and the bleeding has stopped. That's good."

"Not as good as not being shot would have been," I offered. "Would you hand me my rifle? I want it near if Phillips comes back."

"Phillips? He did this?"

"It was him and your two buddies from the university," I said.

"Keith and Kevin? Never!"

I let it go. There was no point in telling her that the scalp society had taken the boys away. They hadn't captured Phillips, though. Lou handed me my gun and I laid it down by my side.

The governor came to see me in mid-morning, after I had finished breakfast and was indulging myself with another cup of coffee. He joined me.

"Virgil told me about the locked door," he said. "You got the keys?"

Lou handed them over from where they lay on the stump. The governor went off to inspect the locked room. It was early afternoon before he came back, grim of face. "It's half-filled with missing artifacts," he said. "I was dead wrong about her and everything else. She's been the one behind all the thefts from the beginning."

"She'd been in most of the houses in the pueblo on one errand of mercy or another over the past ten years," Lou said. "I've accompanied her on some visits. I've seen her praise something and have it given to her, but I never saw her take anything."

"When you praise an object, it is considered a request for a gift," the governor said, shaking his head. "It's part of the rules of hospitality. She knew that. She also knew that our medicine men do the same to get payment for services."

"Pretty cynical," I said.

The governor shrugged, but added, "There are things in that room that she wouldn't have been given, religious things. That's why she kept it locked."

"She was working with Phillips?" I asked.

"Probably. We'll never know. Phillips was found up near the bridge, dead. He'd been shot; you do that?"

"I shot at a big yellow dog that attacked me, and later, after I got shot myself, I saw that Phillips was wounded. He'd been shooting at me, but when I fired back I aimed high to keep him and those with him away. I never shoot at a target I can't see. He disappeared before the scalp society men reached my house."

"He turned back into the dog to escape," the governor said. "But witches don't die in animal form. They turn back into their human shapes to die. And you were wrong about being immune to witchcraft," the governor added. "Jerry told me to tell you. Anyone who has killed another person is more susceptible to a witch attack than a person who hasn't. One of the reasons we're all in the scalp society is to watch each other's backs."

I nodded. It was like being on patrol again. I could understand that. I kept my mouth shut about the witch thing. "Ask Wilson if she and Phillips and the students from UNM were in it together when you find her," I said.

"When we find her," he agreed. "No way to question the others."

I guess I knew why that pertained to Keith and Kevin.

He continued, "Wilson hit the bridge rail on the way out of town. Phillips evidently tried to stop her and she lost control of the car. Or maybe not. There were tire marks on him. He'd been run over. She wasn't there."

"You giving this to the FBI?" I asked.

"Sure, except for Phillips. We had to burn his body. He's a witch; else he'd keep coming back. The bridge is on pueblo land. Let the FBI figure it out. We'll take charge of the artifacts here and get them back where they belong. No need to complicate it for the FBI."

"Yeah," I said, "They'd probably appreciate it, if they knew."

"Yeah," the governor agreed. Neither of us believed it.

"Like some more coffee?" Lou asked, changing the subject. She didn't believe it either.

"Sounds good to me," I said and the governor nodded.

Our work here was done.

APPENDIX: The Heraclitus letter to Darius

*D*arius, styled the Great, King of Persia and Over-lord of Ephesus, Greetings, from Heraclitus, Prince of Ephesus.

I have forbidden your scribe to include the long list of titles that honor your name, or to begin this letter with the usual salutations due your person such as "I kiss your feet . . ." I am a son of what was the ruling house of Ephesus, and though in my forty-seventh year, was not the last to pick up a spear to defend my city's walls nor the first to lay it down when your army overwhelmed us.[1] I have nothing to gain from flattering you, for you have nothing that is yours to grant that I might wish for, but to be left alone.

Your scribe assures me I will be left in peace if I but dictate answers to the questions he asks in your name. While I well know that kings are not bound by the promises of others, it is with that understanding that I comply with your request.

You honored me with a letter inviting me to come to your court in Persia two years ago to explain in person several of the passages in my book on nature I had deposited in the archives of the temple of Artemis in this city. When your warriors conquered Ephesus, they took the book as spoils. I have no copy to refer to nor has anyone else since I wished it to be available only to scholars who would not hound me with questions.[2] Ephesus is filled with Pythagoreans, men and women who returned after spending the five years of probationary time as silent students in Pythagoras' school in Crotona and denied tenure at their completion. They have little to do here but dispute great questions. I would not have it done with me, for I need solitude for my observations and contemplations. For much the same reason I declined your invitation, explaining that I had a horror of display and no use for the riches you offered in gifts, being content with little in the way of creature comforts when that little was to my mind. Nothing has changed, but your scribe has suggested delicately that one does not say "no" twice to Darius the Great.

Your scribe stays in a room attached to my old quarters at the palace, as befits his free-born state, and has my leave to read the books I have collected there. I treat him as I might treat a pupil had I suffered such to plague me.

Every nine days I cease my meditations and return from my small hut high in the mountains for a hot bath and a day of rest at my old home. It is then that I answer your questions and read what your scribe has written from questions answered during my most previous visit, making such corrections as I deem mete.

The questions and answers are set out in the body of this letter as follows:

Question: My Lord Darius holds you to be the wisest man in Greece. He has read your book, "On the Whole," and believes it to be the most insightful treatise Ever written on human nature. Why is it not better known?

Answer: There is but one copy, the one his soldiers stole from the Temple of Artemis where I had it placed for safekeeping. There, it was only made available to scholars.

Question: You are called Heraclitus the Obscure by other philosophers. You must know that if you chose to speak so that all men could understand your words you would not be called to account now.

Answer: I must remember that this letter is addressed to Darius the Great and not his scribe or I might choose different words to reply. I speak only truth [Logos]. This truth, though it always exists, is not always understood by men, either before they hear it or after they hear it for the first time. For although all things happen in accordance with this truth, men seem unskilled indeed when they make trial of the words and matters I set forth in my effort to discriminate each thing according to its nature and to tell what its state is.[3] The proof is all around them but men fail to notice it for they make no effort to do so. Fortunately truth does not need believers to exist. Truth always exists for men to find. Eyes and ears are bad witnesses for most men since their minds lack understanding,[4] nor by learning do they come to know truth though they think they do.[5] Our knowledge is limited by the accuracy of our observations.

Question: Why are these truths evident to you that escape the notice of other men?

Answer: No sensible person asks "why" questions. If you mean "how," then what can be heard, seen and learned, this I prize,[6] though it seems to me that eyes are more exact witnesses than ears.[7] I have taught myself to observe, to see and to listen and then to consider these observations. In fact, I inquired of myself.[8] I observed the commonalties in the acts of men and assumed there were lawful principles underlying them. At best I can hope to arrive at an approximations of the truth that others may refine with better observations.

Question: By the way, what is wrong with "why" questions?

Answer: They can be answered only by guessing. Let us not make rash conjectures about the greatest things.[9] (In the Republic, Plato speaks of ". . . they see only their own shadows, or the shadows of one another, which the fire throws on the . . . wall of the cave.")

Question: But you speak of both God and gods; are they knowable to the senses or must they be approached through speculation, "why" questions, to be specific?[10]

Answer: I have no personal knowledge of gods of any kind. I know but one who has. My mother, a Jewess, concubine of my father, the late king of Ephesus, told me that she had such an experience when she was little more than a girl. On learning that she was to be a royal gift between rulers, she climbed a mountain to inquire of her Lord whether she should submit to this fate, or offer herself in sacrifice as Abraham offered his son, Isaac. She was blinded by a great light and a voice came from it saying, "I am the everlasting fire.[11] Good and evil are the same.[12] I say all things are good and fair and just; it is only men who suppose that some things are just and some unjust."[13] As a simple Jewish woman, and no god, she found little comfort in this, but sheathed her knife against some future intolerable situation. Now, this happened in Jerusalem and I usually do not hold with the present fashion of bringing forth untrustworthy witnesses to prove a point. To my mind, my mother is not an untrustworthy eyewitness.[14] The universe began in fire and the creator is the essence of that fire.

Question: Surely you learned about the gods as a student.

Answer: Oh, yes. Along with other Greek boys I learned Hesiod and Homer by rote as part of my education. What a waste of time! It is sad that Hesiod is the teacher of most men who suppose that his knowledge was very extensive, when he did not know the difference between day and night. There is no difference.[15]

Question: What?

Answer: Day is always changing into night and night becoming day, each a part of the other.

Question: Does this sound much like Hesiod's gods? Or Homer's?

Answer: Xenophanes is right in cursing Hesiod for his ascribing to the gods acts that would be a shame for mortals to do, stealings and adulteries and deceivings of one another. Homer is no better. In fact he is worse, for his poetry is touched by the gods. He deserves to be thrown out of the students' lists and flogged.[16] If he and Hesiod were correct in saying that the gods are like men, but with greater appetites and capacities, what would that mean? All sane men are totally selfish, each action calculated, knowingly or unknowingly to bring maximum benefit to themselves alone.

Since each man is unique, different from his neighbor, each with different personal histories against which to weigh each action, each man will weigh costs and gains to himself differently from his fellows. Acknowledging this truth in himself, each man must see it underlying the actions of others and be on the alert for possible damage to his self-interest in others seeking their own good. Much of what we term civilization arises out of disguising this.

Question: But aren't we taught that the gods watch over men?

Answer: Yes, but if men are truly like the gods, only less wise, perhaps, why should men assume that gods should care for any but themselves? If men dissimulate to avoid the consequences of their acknowledging selfishness, why would not the gods do so as well, only perhaps more effectively? If only selfish behavior is sane in men or gods, it follows that altruism is insane. Do we believe the gods to be mad? If not sane, why would we ask them for help? A sane god would be selfish just like a sane man. Do we really wish to come to the attention of insane gods?

Question: How can we know the gods then? Do they want us to or do they not care what we think of them?

Answer: The gods are manifest in what they do; Apollo's blinding chariot is not Apollo, but what else do we know of him? Only that the sun is new every day.[17] My father's singing an ode of praise to greet Apollo as the sun rises is not my father, but what else do I know of my father or indeed, of any man but by what he does? The character of gods lies in their works. The character of men lies in their deeds, god-like works writ small. One might best forget the gods, as they forget men. Character is a man's guardian divinity; he needs no god to monitor his behavior for him to behave correctly, no man either. [18]

Question: No one?

Answer: It is lawful to obey the counsel of someone when that someone is oneself.[19]

Question: In your book why do you equate God with fire?

Answer: By fire, I meant an unknown power as disinterested in men as whatever it was that spoke to my mother from the flame. So, when I wrote in my book "everlasting fire that always was and ever will be, created order in the universe, kindling according to fixed measure,[20] I meant an unknowable power like the God of my mother. This fire is the first cause. In my view, it is not only everlasting but constantly changing, transforming first into sea, then half that into earth and half that into lightning flash.[21] So began the universe. All things are exchanged for fire, and fire for all things, as wares are exchanged for gold and gold for wares.[22]

Question: You do not accept priests as servants of the gods?

Answer: Who are these men who pretend to guide our religious endeavors?

The mysteries recognized by men, and notoriously by women as well, are celebrated in a most unholy way.[23] If it were not to Dionysus that they make the procession and sing the songs with phallic symbols, their deeds would indeed be most shameful.[24] Of the sacrifices made to the gods, I see men attempt to purify themselves by defiling themselves with blood, as if one who had stepped into mud were to wash it off with more mud. Any man observing another doing so in other circumstances would judge him insane.[25]

Question: But, you Greeks love heroes even more than you love gods. Surely your heroes sacrifice themselves for others. Are they also insane?

Answer: Who knows what causes a hero to act like a fool? In all the tales of heroes you find them seeking adventures to win acclaim. Oh, they kill monsters, overcome enemies and release maidens from captivity, but they return home to bask in the approval and praise of the masses. It's very silly.

Question: But not altruistic?

Answer: The need for constant validation of self-worth is characteristic of children under the guidance of an adult. Most people grow out of it as they learn to monitor their own behavior. Exceptions like professional athletes and performers are tedious company for normal people.

Question: And politicians?

Answer: And especially politicians.

Question: It's a sour view of the world you hold.

Answer: Should I care? Asses prefer straw to gold [26] and only a fool is wont to be in a flutter at every word.[27]

Question: You speak of validation. My master, King Darius, will want to know how you come to hold these to be truths.

Answer: I suppose so. Thales of Miletus inspired them in me. Miletus is a only a few hundred stades[28] south of Ephesus and he was often a guest of my father's. Thales was the greatest of the Seven Wise Men of Greece. Of the others, I hold Bias, son of Tuetamas of Priene, of more account than others; he held men in low esteem.[29]

Question: But how did Thales inspire you?

Answer: I am not suggesting that my inquiries and his are similar. He was interested in the principles of being; I am more interested in the principles of becoming. Of the time I am speaking, he wanted to see the nearly completed Temple of Artemis, accounted by one and all as one of the Seven Wonders of the World, a monument visiting a monument, you might say. I was only a child, but my father encouraged me to question the great man.

"What do you like to do best?" I remember asking, expecting him to say philosophy, or something like that.

"Take naps," Thales replied. He was very old.

"What is the easiest thing for you to do?" I persisted.

"Give advice," and he smiled at that.

"What is the hardest?" was my next question. My father nodded at me, amused I think.

"What is hardest for everyone, to know oneself," he replied, sighing.

"Why are there only Seven Wise Men or Wonders of the World?" I was full of myself then.

"Ask Pythagoras that one," he answered laughing aloud this time. "He is always maundering on about numbers."

My father sent me off to bed then, and none too soon.

Question: That's it? He inspired you because he disliked Pythagoras?"

Answer: Not even I disliked Pythagoras! No, it was because he said it was hard to know oneself. That's where I started, attempting to know myself.

Question: Before we go to you, I want to know about Pythagoras. You disapprove of him, do you not, even if Thales didn't? King Darius was particularly interested why.

Answer: Pythagoras, son of Mnessarchos of Samos, undertook investigations more assiduously than any other man and from them made a kind of wisdom of his own–much learning and bad art.[30]

Question: But his school at Crotona was the most famous in the world. He had hundreds of students, even women.

Answer: He left his native city from fear of the Persians, taking a new name to hide behind. The name Pythagoras refers to the throat of the Pythian oracle at Delphi. The man claimed he spoke for Apollo. Is that admirable or mere vainglory? And he responded to the wrong questions, ones that attracted students, but lead nowhere. With his numbers he described a static universe, which does not exist, and went on to pose "why" questions about it. I'm being responsible for finding meaningful answers, he could talk forever of seeking them.

Question: Just talk? Didn't he live according to very strict tenets, inspiring his students to do the same?

Answer: If you mean he ate nothing but, bread and honey and fresh fruit and vegetables, drinking only water, I do the same, eschewing any meat but fresh fish. That is not holy, merely intelligent for a man of my years, or his when he started. The school at Crotona wasn't founded until he was over fifty.

Question: But didn't he also avoid eating beans?

Answer: A foolish practice. In the end, it killed him.

Question: Oh, come, now!

Answer: You do not know the story? In his travels, Pythagoras was a student of Zoratas of Chaldea for a time. Zoratas taught that beans were holy, the first living thing to rise from the slime when the world was still soft. For proof he offered the statement that if one chews a bean to a pulp, spits it out and exposes it to the sun, in a short time it gives off the odor of human seed. And further, that if a bean in flower is dug up, put into a pitcher of water to moisten it and then buried for a few days, it will exhibit the form of a womb with the head of a child growing in it.

Question: And these statements are untrue?

Answer: I couldn't get either of them to work for me. Maybe there's something different about Chaldean beans.

Question: Could you get back to how not eating beans killed Pythagoras?

Answer: Pythagoras' students became so arrogant, that they tried to take over the government of Crotona, deeming themselves better fit to rule than those not so educated. The people of Crotona burned Pythagoras' school, killing most of the students. It is said that Pythagoras escaped well ahead of his pursuers but was halted by a bean field, which he could not step into without profaning a holy place. He was caught and executed.

Question: And some say he escaped and went to Metapontum to live, finally starving himself to death at eighty because he had exhausted all problems capable of solution and thought his life was over. Why do you prefer the one about the bean field?

Answer: It's a better story.

Question: Who else among the philosophers holds your opinion on Pythagoras?

Answer: Xenophanes of Colophon, for one. He was even more widely traveled than Pythagoras. By the time he founded his school at Elea he was sixty-seven. Xenophanes has seen all the mystic fakery that Pythagoras had witnessed and came away believing none of it.

Question: Xenophanes is the one that said men made gods in their own images, that if men had looked like sheep, the gods would look like sheep?

Answer: Yes. Pythagoras was outraged by that, claiming it blasphemy.

Question: You use the word "soul" often in your writing. What do you mean by it? Pythagoras believed it was separate from the body, and lived on after the death of the body.[31]

Answer: Nothing like what Pythagoras means. I see each man, each animal, each plant, each rock as being unique, different from others with which it may be classed.[32] No two persons look exactly alike no matter how closely a few resemble others. It is reasonable to suppose that birds and animals recognize minute differences in appearance also. Their behavior towards one another would certainly suggest that. Not only are appearances dissimilar, but the experiences that build a person's character are also dissimilar at least in minor ways. When I use the word "soul," I refer to the essence of unique beings. I would not limit it to people and do not presume that it exists after death, except in the memories of friends.

Question: That sounds very little like Pythagoras.

Answer: True, the man was obsessed with rules. Two that he lived by were, "Do not pick up anything that has fallen on the ground" and "Neither laugh out loud nor show anger." He had a slave named Zosimus who did those things for him. That way the actions became part of the slave's history of experience, not Pythagoras' and did not detract from Pythagoras' goal of perfection.

Question: Do you mean that if a gold drachma escaped his grasp and fell to the floor, he would not stoop to pick it up? Zosimus would!

Answer: Exactly, and handed it to Pythagoras. Pythagoras used to say, "Why keep a dog and do your own barking." Pythagoras knew the value of money. There was nothing mystic about him there. The slave had a booming laugh and an extensive vocabulary of scurrilous words he picked up in following Pythagoras around in his youth that reflected well on neither of them.

Question: What happened to the slave?

Answer: Zosimus? He disappeared after the school at Crotona was burned. There are many stories. Some say he went north and taught the Celts Pythagorean wisdom. They account him the first Druid.

Question: Do you dismiss Pythagoras, despite the contributions he made to knowledge?

Answer: What would they be? Much learning does not teach one to have understanding; else it would have made Pythagoras and Hesiod wise.[33]

Question: Really? In your book you speak of the masses with contempt. Do you not believe in the wisdom of the people?

Answer: What wisdom? Even here in Ephesus no man deserves anything better than hanging. They cast out the best person in the city saying, "Let no one amongst us be best, and if one is best, let him be so elsewhere and among others."[34] Is that wisdom? They would do better for all the adults to strangle themselves and leave the city to the young people. The young people loved Hermadorus, my one true friend, but they banished him, the best man among them.[35]

Question: You certainly have definite opinions! Perhaps you will now tell how you came to know yourself?

Answer: How difficult that was! Nature loves to hide;[36] seekers for gold dig up much earth and find little of it.[37] At first I found that being so much in the company of others made the task impossible. Then I realized that being much alone we would have to limit ourselves to what we could discover as individuals and not accept what others said. In time I came to understand we are always alone even in the company of our fellows. What can we truly know of what others observe? All that we see as individuals is colored by the light of our previous experiences. As these experiences differ from person to person so our perceptions of those experiences differ even if seemingly similar.

Question: But men can tell you what they think, can't they?

Answer: You can't observe a man thinking, only doing. Is a man thinking when he is milking a goat, a task he learned to do as a young boy, or is he just doing? And is it not the experience of each of us that there is no true correspondence between what men do and what they say that they do? Men lie, exaggerate, misrepresent, fabricate, deceive . . . how many words are there to describe the unreliability of speech?

Question: What is thought, then?

Answer: Perhaps thought can be considered self-speech, directed at no one but the speaker.

Question: Since only men and the gods have speech, won't you admit that it is the most noble thing about us?

Answer: Because the gods do it? Are you suggesting that animals cannot communicate because they do not think, whatever that process may be? And yet a dog may lick your hand in apparent devotion one moment and steal meat from your table as soon as your back is turned. Are not such actions as vile as those of any man? I learned nothing of myself from what others told me, only from what they did. And I learned as much from watching animals.

Question: From observing yourself you learned that all men are selfish?

Answer: Oh yes, but first I learned that I was alone; there are only individuals. Each creature lives and dies alone.

Question: But isn't there often consensus among men?

Answer: Most men say the world is flat. Does that make it true?

Question: It's not?

Answer: No. It's a ball, like the moon.

Question: King Darius won't believe that. It's not reasonable.

Answer: Reasoned statements are common enough but most are not based on observation, and apt to be wrong, though most people live as though they had an understanding peculiar to themselves. Each man has a different history of experience to guide him and his experience informs his judgments. Of course there are commonalities in individuals' histories of experience as well as differences, but what may look like consensus may be more apparent than real.[38]

Question: How?

Answer: Have you ever seen men of a village practice for a spring festival? There will be old men patiently teaching children the proper dance steps, which the children learn gradually, with many an error. There will be young men practicing by themselves, exaggerating dance movements, stepping too high, strutting too much, hoping to catch the eyes of any maidens who might be watching. There will be men of middle age in groups, discussing the order of events and the responsibilities of individuals based on the relative importance of individuals in the village scheme of things. On dance day, they all seem to act as one with the elders to one side, singing and drumming, the middle-aged men leading out followed by the youths and the children. But are they doing the same thing? Are not the old men speaking to the gods, the men of middle age demonstrating their status, the youths dancing for the notice of maidens and the children intent on making as few mistakes as possible, little comprehending what the ceremony is all about?

Question: But even so, don't the gods see it as the performance of a group?

Answer: Not unless they are less wise than I.

Question: Do not our statesmen speak correctly then when they claim to express the will of the people?

Answer: In metaphor, perhaps, but when most politicians talk about "the people want this" or "the people demand that" as if some entity existed capable of joint perception and evaluation of circumstances, they speak nonsense. The "people" are a number of disparate beings groping blindly toward one another in the frustration of partial communication that is our reality.

Question: Not even words have meanings common to all?

Answer: Of course not. For example, to one person the word "mother" connotes a protective, loving presence, while to others it might mean one who punishes or who selects others from among her children for unfair, preferential treatment. There is room for confusion in any attempt for any two persons to talk about mothers, wouldn't you say?

Question: So we are each like islands, washed by a common sea, knowing only ourselves, but not knowing we know only that?

Answer: Well put.

Question: My mother was mean like that. I was the youngest.

Answer: Mine wasn't. I was her only child.

Question: But how can we even know ourselves?

Answer: If you accept that we can know only what we ourselves perceive and consider, then you have taken your first step toward wisdom. The next step is to undertake self-observation as a course of study, for ordinarily we are neither aware nor deliberate in the choices we make. Even with effort our conclusions may suffer from lack of attention, due to erroneous assumptions based on previous observations or self-delusion about our processes of deduction. However, it is all we have to work with. Practice helps. We must make a constant effort to see things as they are, not as they might be or should be or as we would have them be.[39] In my case I found it expedient to withdraw from the company of men so I would have less distraction.

Question: Did it help?

Answer: Yes. First, I acknowledged the constraints that limited my behavior. I could only do what other men could do, not what birds or fish or horses are capable of. In addition, I was an adult and not a child, a man and not a woman, a son of a noble house and not a slave. Second, I considered the possibility that others had done what I was attempting and that some record of it might exist. I found no writings that dealt with the subject, so I looked to what purports to be common wisdom. Classes freely mix in the taverns so I started there, drinking more than I wished, but in a good cause. Did you know that the poor sing in the taverns? I found that even slaves sing when their masters are not around, keeping a sullen quiet at other times. They even have a saying about it: Slaves don't sing in public; the rich don't sing in private. Another, somewhat at variance, went: Sing only when you're working; then when you sing the overseer will think that you're working. They both can't be true. I found many such sayings that supposedly encapsulated experience, but little to explain how they become so widely held.

Question: You listen to the talk of slaves? In King Darius' court, slaves never speak aloud. This is most interesting. Do you know any other slave sayings?

Answer: It will not get us any farther along the road to understanding.

Question: But it would amuse King Darius. Please? I doubt if he's ever listened to a slave just talk.

Answer: Oh, very well. Two similar ones I remember are: Don't trust ice until you see a bear walking on it, but then don't trust the bear. Bears are not dangerous unless they're hungry, but bears are always hungry.

Question: I like those! More please?

Answer: If you insist:

Freed-men wear iron rings to remind themselves they once wore iron collars, but only free-born men need reminding.

Slaves have masters, poor men have patrons, rich men have gods and gods have illusions.

It is hard to watch over old vineyards and young girls, for young men steal the fruit.

And remember that I said that even Pythagoras used slave sayings such as, "Why keep a dog and do your own barking?" That's enough, surely, to make my point.

Question: Well, say for the purposes of argument that to understand how people come to act as they do you must first find how an individual person comes to act as he does. For that you proposed to study yourself. What did you learn?

Answer: What I told you before, that I am selfish. I undertake no action without hope of a reward of some kind. Like now. If I answer your questions you will finally go away and leave me alone. You will, won't you?

Question: Are you sure of that?

Answer: You are never sure of reward, but if you do not hope you will not find that which is hoped for. You have to make an effort.[40] In time you learn what conditions are necessary for any effort to be successful and what kind of effort is best to make. If the consequences of an effort are beneficial one is more likely to make the effort again while seeking that benefit, when in circumstances similar to the last time the effort was successful.

Question: I would think punishment was as strong a force in controlling acts as rewards. It's also easier, isn't it?

Answer: Easier, yes. And the avoidance of punishment is beneficial, is it not? On the other hand, punishment itself is effective only when the one doing the punishing is around.

Question: I see. We have a saying, "When the cat's away, the mice will play." But tell me, do you have to go all through that in your mind each time?

Answer: Of course not. I became aware of what I was doing only when I carefully observed myself doing it and saw how it could come about. To test my conclusions, I spent time in the royal nursery watching children. Their first efforts in learning to crawl, to walk, to speak, to feed themselves were pitiful to see. Spurred on by praise and admonitions of their caretakers and others they finally come to approximate behavior. So it is at each step in life. We become skilled in weaponry, in reading, in oratory only gradually, being given time by our fellows to reach proficiency. We do not make such allowances for those who come later to the feast. You have only to observe the scorn we heap on strangers who attempt to speak Greek as we speak it to know the truth of that.

Question: Didn't you say that society was an illusion?

Answer: It is. We each learn to behave as we do as individuals. Each action we undertake has some consequence, though not always an intended one. We impose changes on our surroundings when we act, accepting speech as an action. Perhaps speech is the easiest example for it includes other people as part of the speaker's surroundings. The words one utters change the surroundings in the sense that before the utterance the words were unspoken. The reactions shown by others makes it more or less likely that one will use such words again in such a gathering. Why do some individuals tell the same jokes over and over to the same audience?

Question: And the listeners finally stop laughing as they come to regret laughing the first time, which means that eventually that joke will not be told by that person again?

Answer: Precisely. The joke-teller is part of each of the listeners' surroundings and the listeners learn not to laugh. And so it is with all behavior. The wise man learns to escape the consequences of his folly sooner, rather than later. Even the fool must learn eventually, or perish.

Question: So men learn to act in certain ways under certain conditions because of what happens afterwards? Are you saying that behavior is both shaped and maintained by its consequences?

Answer: I guess you could put it that way.

Question: It seems to me that there must be some initial action for patterning to take place. What brings that about?

Answer: Each creature swings between hunger and repletion, always in the process of reaching one state or another. It's always hunger and repletion, want and satiety.[41] In nature, the only constant is change. All is flux, waxing and waning, coming and going. Remember I said you could not piss into the same river twice, for fresh waters are ever flowing on to you?[42]

Question: Yes, but what if the results of an action are not immediately apparent?

Answer: True learning requires that they be immediate so that the connection between act and effect is evident. Every beast is tended by blows,[43] but learning takes place only when the blows occur immediately after the unacceptable actions. For instance, a dog will not learn to stop killing chickens unless caught in the act and punished immediately. And then it will only have learned not to kill chickens when the punisher is present. What is true of dogs is also true of men. However, as I have said, it is better to build good behavior than to punish bad, for punishment for bad has bad side effects; the punisher is feared. Praise is better than gold to reward the actions of men. It's cheaper, too.

Question: When you say "praise" do you mean flattery?

Answer: If you like. Flattery is effective because we all believe ourselves worthy of praise. If it is not believed, however, it has no power.

Question: If you are correct in this, wouldn't it be possible for you to manipulate others to obey your will by selectively praising and scorning their actions?

Answer: Do we not all attempt to do so? Is knowing not to do it effectively make the practice more odious?

Question: Are you doing this to me?

Answer: Probably, but not on any level of awareness. I am not aware of caring what you do past making an accurate record of my words.

Question: Your words have great significance for one like King Darius. Can these practices help him to know how men come to act as they do and so bring stability to his realm?

Answer: Hardly that. There is no such thing as stability. I have already told you, change is the order of nature. All is flux. like a child's see-saw, as one end goes up the other goes down. Everything is in a state of becoming or expiring, not of being. Time does not stand still. It is night and day, winter and summer, war and peace, satiety and hunger, one becoming the other and assuming different forms just as when incense is mingled with incense.[44]

Question: Is there no wisdom in governance, then?

Answer: Wisdom is truth and is apart from all other things.[45] But everything that is done can be done with wisdom if one comes to understand the intelligence by which all actions are to be steered through consequences. If understanding comes, it can be applied to governance as to much else; what I was doubting was whether it can be taught as a skill as other skills are taught.

Question: And how are other skills taught? Give me an example of how Pythagoras might do it.

Answer: Pythagoras might ask, "What would you do if a battle elephant loomed before you, raising his trunk to trumpet, preparatory to stomping you into the ground: one, take off your cloak and flap it in the beast's face, hoping to startle it; two, draw your sword and stab its descending foot; or, three, appeal to it as one reasoning creature to another?" Do you understand?

Question: Well, I know the Pythagoreans are forbidden to injure any beast that does not prey on men, but useful as an elephant is, one trained to battle might be considered a predator, so number two might be right. Is that it?

Answer: There is no "it." No matter what you'd decide, you'd be already dead. Sometimes it's best not to think too much. Remember, learning takes place when consequences immediately follow the action taken . . . but if you're dead you can't learn anything.

Question: How is that helpful?

Answer: Having some idea how men are likely to act in certain circumstances may help you plan courses of actions that you might call wise governance, but in specific cases there are usually too many variables for prediction. You must think of dealing first with men one at a time,[46] and that is not what most people mean when they say governance.

Question: Can you predict what a single man will do?

Answer: Yes, if you have observed a person long enough to watch him perform in different situations so that patterns emerge. A man will act as to best bring consequences he considers beneficial to himself. He does not have to be aware of what these are, but you, as observer, should be able to see them. And knowing what he may do in certain situations is next to being able to control his actions if you can arrange to have the consequences take place.

Question: Could you give me another example?

Answer: If you see that a particular man consistently acts generously when he is in the presence of one he considers a superior but only then, never ask him to be generous except when he is in the presence of one he'd consider a superior.

Question: I see! But, that's governance. How would you teach me that?

Answer: One of the first exercises for a philosopher who wants to study human nature is to watch children as I did. It is indolent and instructive, both valuable conditions for contemplation. If one spends time in the company of children, one can learn to see what governs their behavior. There are fewer aspects of a baby's surroundings competing for his attention than is true for an adult. Surroundings have no significance for any person unless one has learned to use them. Babies lack this sort of history of experience. Babies first try their social skills on their mothers, smiling, flirting, pouting, laughing, crying and all the time watching their mothers. You can actually see the babies change what they do in response to their mothers' reactions, either approval or scolding. Approved actions are likely to occur again under similar circumstances. Mothers can quickly determine what it is each baby desires at specific times: the breast, diaper change or merely attention. Behaviors may differ from baby to baby because different mothers react differently to crying, calling, laughing and so on.

Question: Could not a despot learn to control others by threat after torturing them to discover what it is they fear?

Answer: Or prostitutes by teasing after discovering what others fancy through practice. Are you surprised by this? In my book I explain this under controversy."[47] As a man learns to act in certain ways to gain desired ends, so do other men in observing him. A man acts to bring about certain changes in his surroundings, which we may call a "good," and his surroundings contain other men, like as not. Inevitably, conflict arises as they strive against him and against one another in obtaining that "good," if it is in scarce supply. So, as men learn to act to gain some good, they also learn to act so as to avoid losing it, once obtained. The fear of loss, whether it's gold, honor or health, is as powerful a force in molding the acts of men as the hope of gain.

Question: Do the things babies learn persist in later life?

Answer: Oh, yes, if there is no compelling reason to change. Babies will extend their actions as they grow up, earning praise, for example, for being obedient. They learn, too, that there are limits in the amount of praise available . . . a mother has only so much time available for children, and may have to spread it among several of her own. A new baby would displace the last one, in any case, and the child would learn that old behaviors no longer bring the same consequences as they once did.

Question: So a child will learn that his brothers are rivals for their mother's attention? That may explain why so many brothers hate each other.

Answer: Very good!

Question: Praise from you? Am I a child then?

Answer: In philosophical inquiry, perhaps.

Question: Isn't freedom a philosophical ideal?

Answer: Understanding leads to freedom. Despots are despots regardless of whether you approve of them. Knowing how they come to power is the only safeguard you have.

Question: I assume benign rulers learn just as mothers, or for that matter, despots do. But as with praise from a mother, might not praise from a king have limits? A king has only so many honors to bestow. Rivals for the king's attention might learn to hate one another and act accordingly.

Answer: And a king who is aware of this may well be able to create rivalries when he deems it better for two powerful subordinates not to be friends. This, too, is governance.[48]

Question: But is it wise not to give men what they want?

Answer: It is not good for men to have everything they desire. Disease makes health sweet and good; hunger, satiety; toil, rest.[49]

Question: I see strife between men of your city for even the smallest of advantages. How can a king bring harmony?

Answer: Why would he want to? Opposition unites. From what draws apart results the most beautiful harmony. All beneficial changes take place through strife.[50] Only the strongest survives, to the betterment of the race.[51]

Question: That's exactly the kind of explanation Darius wanted. Even I can understand that. Why didn't you say so?

Answer: Didn't I? I said that which draws apart agrees with itself; harmony lies in the bending back, as for instance with the strings of the bow or the lyre and is made manifest on their release.[52]

Question: Now I understand the simile. You did not mention release in your book. Let me return to Ephesus and pose the question differently. It appears to me that the civil society of this city is sick. Put the king in the position of a physician. How would he cure it?

Answer: The king as a physician? One who cuts and burns and in every way torments the sick yet complains that he does not receive adequate recompense?[53]

Question: That is not an answer, is it?

Answer: Well, how is it helpful to label our civil society as sick? It is the only one we have. If men are behaving in destructive ways to gain recognition it would seem intelligent to offer recognition to them for non-destructive acts.

Question: Would you give rewards to those who break your city's laws?

Answer: Never! Men should defend their laws as they would their city walls,[54] but you must unite the harmonious and the discordant, things whole and things not whole.[55] Justice arises from accommodation of the whole to the not whole.[56] All men should have opportunity to share in the civil good.

Question: Why do you say that it is recognition that men desire? A thief steals money.

Answer: And brags about it in the tavern to his fellows to bask in their admiration. Thieves are rarely caught in the act, but after the fact when they talk about it. Like as not the money stolen is used to pay for the drinks of the listeners. Give him another way to earn the regard of his fellows and a thief need not steal. But you should not plan to give a thief money, for that would have come from taxes and would not gain general acceptance.

Question: But what of those who do not break the laws? Are they to be ignored?

Answer: They have already found ways in which they can earn the regard of their fellows, perhaps as members of craft associations, sitting through long dull meetings only to be able to say they belong.

Question: And that is not virtuous?

Answer: Virtue has nothing to do with it. Have you ever known such a group to accomplish any good except picking up the cost of burial for its members? It is the talking about doing good that is praised. If such talk brought about real change in civic behavior, it would be labeled destructive. Men fear to lose the benefits of custom-approved acts.

Question: Have you any advice for King Darius, apart from the answers you have given to my questions?

Answer: As Thales said, giving advice is the easiest thing to do. Have him know that it is necessary for those who rule to hold fast to the commonalties men agree upon in governance, as cities hold fast to their laws.[57]

Question: Are you saying he should hold by his laws or by the laws the city gives itself?

Answer: It would be arrogant to choose which laws should be enforced. Arrogance must be quenched more than a fire.[58] What he should not do is visit punishment upon disobedience where there is a conflict unless he is willing to destroy the city before changing his laws. Where there is principled resistance, punishment will lead to further resistance until finally annihilation may be the only recourse open. As I said, justice arises from accommodation; constant change is the order of civil arrangements as well as of nature. It will overtake forgers of lies and witnesses to them.[59]

Question: That is wisdom for a king?

Answer: For anyone. Wisdom is not one thing to one man and another to his brother.

Question: But you said everyone's understanding is different from others' based on different histories of experience.

Answer: True, but understanding is only the road to wisdom. Wisdom is apart from all other things.[60]

Question: You, at least have found wisdom. I have no more questions. Have you anything else you would want King Darius to know? You can advise this king; isn't it one of the beliefs philosophers hold, that only the wise should rule?

Answer: That's Pythagoras that says that, not me. What's the point? Who would listen? It is better to conceal ignorance than to put it forth into the midst where men who know less can scorn you for knowing more.[61]

Question: That's happened to you?

Answer: Yes, oh yes.

Question: Perhaps you would be more forthcoming if we went down to the tavern and had a glass of wine.

Answer: You buying?

Question: Yes.

Answer: Then probably, but again, it is also better to conceal stupidity, an effort in a time of relaxation over the wine.[62] To be temperate is the greatest virtue.[63]

When a man gets drunk he is led about by beardless boys like yourself, stumbling, not knowing where he goes.[64]

Question: But haven't you found that understanding is sharpened by discourse and that a tavern releases the constraints that inhibit a man from expressing himself in daily life?

Answer: It is harmful to contend with passion, for whatever is won is paid for with cost of soul.[65]

Question: Ah, soul again. You called it the essence of a being. What happens to it at death? Remains with the body?

Answer: Corpses are more fit to be thrown away than dung.[66] The essence lives while the being lives. What comes after? No man knows.

Question: Do you believe that there is life after death?

Answer: There waits at death what men do not expect or think.[67]

Question: Maybe nothing?

Answer: Who knows? How could it be discovered except by experiencing it? And who has come back to life to report his experiences? Man, like a light in the night, is kindled and put out,[68] but the limits of the soul you could not discover through traversing every earthly path.[69]

Question: At least your words will be immortal, won't they? King Darius will preserve this letter for the ages.

Answer: You think so? Maybe I'll have that drink after all and I can tell you about what I'm working on now.

Question: Didn't the last book cover all knowledge?

Answer: No I only dealt with four of the five basic mysteries: the creation of the universe, the origin of life, the descent of man, and the nature of learning.

Question: What else is there?

Answer: Well, I've discovered . . . No, don't write this down . . .

NOTES

*H*eraclitus' letter to the Persian King, Darius, written circa 500 BC (upgraded from Laertius to "Selections from Early Greek Philosophy" 4th Ed. by Milton C. Nahm, Appleton Century Crofts, 1964.)

1. Heraclitus was born in 540 BC. Ephesus fell in 493 BC.
2. A Latin rendering of Heraclitus' one known book, "Peri tu Pantos," would be "On the Whole." The manuscript no longer exists. Until the discovery of this scroll our knowledge of his writings have been limited to one hundred and thirty quotes gathered by Diogenes Laertius, Greek philosopher, who lived in the third century AD.
3. Fragment numbers 1 and 2 of Heraclitus' sayings (after Laertius). Logus is also the Christian "word," as "In the beginning was the word."
4. Fragment number 4 of Heraclitus' sayings.
5. A portion of number 5 of Heraclitus' sayings. (In "The Republic," Plato speaks of ". . . they see only their own shadows, or the shadows of one another, which the fire throws on the . . . wall of the cave.")
6. Fragment number 13 of Heraclitus' sayings.
7. Fragment number 15 of Heraclitus' sayings.
8. A portion of fragment 15 of Heraclitus' sayings.
9. Fragment number 48 of Heraclitus' sayings.
10. Heraclitus refers to God or gods in 14 fragments. God is his mother's Jewish God, the essence of fire.
11. A portion of fragment 20 of Heraclitus' sayings.
12. Fragment 57 of Heraclitus' sayings.
13. Fragment 61 of Heraclitus' sayings.
14. Fragment 14 of Heraclitus' sayings.
15. Fragment 35 of Heraclitus' sayings.
16. Fragment 119 of Heraclitus' sayings.
17. Fragment 32 of Heraclitus' sayings.
18. Fragment 121 of Heraclitus' sayings.
19. Fragment 20 of Heraclitus' sayings.
20. Fragment 20 of Heraclitus' sayings. The concept of divine fire is a central belief of the early Stoics centuries after Heraclitus and passed through them to early Christianity. The teachings of Jesus are essentially Stoic in character.
21. Fragment 21 of Heraclitus' sayings.
22. Fragment 22 of Heraclitus' sayings.
23. Fragment 125 of Heraclitus' sayings.
24. Fragment 127 of Heraclitus' sayings.
25. Fragment 130 of Heraclitus' sayings.
26. Fragment 51 of Heraclitus' sayings.
27. Fragment 117 of Heraclitus' sayings.

28. A measure that varied between 157.5 and 178.3 meters.
29. Fragment 112 of Heraclitus' sayings.
30. Fragment 17 of Heraclitus' sayings.
31. The word "soul" occurs nine times in the fragments.
32. Plato said much the same thing a century later.
33. Fragment 16 of Heraclitus' sayings.
34. Fragment 114 of Heraclitus' sayings.
35. Fragment 113 of Heraclitus' sayings.
36. Fragment 10 of Heraclitus' sayings.
37. Fragment 8 of Heraclitus' sayings.
38. Fragment 82 of Heraclitus' sayings.
39. Again we refer to Plato's cave. There men saw only the shadows of substance as dreamers do. In our waking state we can never know if the natural laws we find are really true.
40. Fragment 7 of Heraclitus' sayings. And see Mathew: Chapter 7, Verse 7 ". . . Seek and ye shall find."
41. Fragment 24 of Heraclitus' sayings.
42. Fragments 41 and 42 of Heraclitus' sayings. The saying "All is flux" is universally attributed to Heraclitus in the Middle Ages, but there is no preserved fragment.
43. Fragment 55 of Heraclitus' sayings.
44. Fragment 36 of Heraclitus' sayings.
45. Fragment 18 of Heraclitus' sayings.
46. Fragment 19 of Heraclitus' sayings.
47. Fragment 9 of Heraclitus' sayings.
48. Machiavelli would agree.
49. Fragment 104 of Heraclitus' sayings.
50. Fragment 36 of Heraclitus' sayings.
51. Darwin must have read Heraclitus.
52. Fragment 45 of Heraclitus' sayings.
53. Fragment 58 of Heraclitus' sayings.
54. Fragment 100 of Heraclitus' sayings.
55. Fragment 59 of Heraclitus' sayings.
56. Fragment 60 of Heraclitus' sayings.
57. Fragment 91 of Heraclitus' sayings.
58. Fragment 103 of Heraclitus' sayings.
59. Fragment 118 of Heraclitus' sayings.
60. Fragment 19 of Heraclitus' sayings.
61. Fragment 108 of Heraclitus' sayings.
62. Fragment 109 of Heraclitus' sayings.
63. Fragment 108 of Heraclitus' sayings.
64. Fragment 73 of Heraclitus' sayings.
65. Fragment 105 of Heraclitus' sayings.
66. Fragment 85 of Heraclitus' sayings.
67. Fragment 122 of Heraclitus' sayings.
68. Fragment 77 of Heraclitus' sayings.
69. Fragment 71 of Heraclitus' sayings.